MW01088903

The DIVA Poaches
a Bad Egg

The DIVA Poaches a Bad Egg

KRISTA DAVIS

KENSINGTON PUBLISHING CORP.

kensingtonbooks.com

KENSINGTON BOOKS are published by

Kensington Publishing Corp.
900 Third Avenue
New York, NY 10022

Library of Congress Control Number: 2025930757

ISBN-13: 978-1-4967-4345-9

First Kensington Hardcover Edition: June 2025

ISBN-13: 978-1-4967-4347-3 (e-book)

10 9 8 7 6 5 4 3 2 1

Printed in the United States of America

The authorized representative in the EU for product safety and compliance is eucomply OU, Parnu mnt 139b-14, Apt 123
Tallinn, Berlin 11317, hello@eucompliancepartner.com

Dedicated to my wonderful readers.

Acknowledgments

I have had the opportunity recently to attend some Kensington Mini-Cons and meet readers. They talk about Sophie and her friends as though they are certain she exists, and nothing makes me happier. There is always some discussion about who Sophie might end up with. Mars, Wolf, or Bernie? I'm amazed by how often Aunt Faye is mentioned even though she is merely a spirit and a portrait on the wall in Sophie's kitchen. So it is with great pleasure that I give you a peek at Aunt Faye's life in this book. I hope you will love her as much as I do.

As always, I am grateful to my author friends for their friendship and input. We are far apart in miles, but it's as though they are in the next room, ready to share a laugh or a problem. Thank you, Ginger Bolton, Allison Brook, Laurie Cass, Peg Cochran, Kaye George, and Daryl Wood Gerber.

Thanks also go to Susan Smith Erba, Betsy Strickland, and Amy Wheeler, who are never afraid to tell me exactly what they think and keep me grounded.

My editors, Wendy McCurdy and Sarah Selim, and publicist, Larissa Ackerman, are behind the scenes, but they stay on top of everything and don't get enough credit for the hard work they put into bringing my books to you.

And none of this would happen at all without my agent, Jessica Faust. In the ever-changing world of publishing, Jessica is my rock.

Cast of Characters

Sophie Winston
Mars Winston—Sophie's ex-husband
    Aunt Faye—Mars's deceased aunt
Nina Reid Norwood—Sophie's best friend and neighbor
Bernie Frei—Sophie's friend
Natasha—Sophie's friend
Mitzi Lawson—Interior designer
Helena Inger Nofsinger—Real Estate Executive
    Thurman Nofsinger—Helena's husband
      Robbie Inger Nofsinger—Helena and Thurman's son
      Mary Nofsinger—Robbie's wife
        Mike Inger Nofsinger—Robbie and Mary's son
        Denise Nofsinger—Mike's wife, an interior designer
Jacky Inger Finch—Helena's sister
    Stu Finch—Jacky's husband
Annie Griggs—Nanny
Matt Stewart—Etiquette authority
Lillith Rollins—Interior decorator
Rachel Powers—Interior decorator

Chapter 1

"**D**on't look at me."
The woman's voice came from behind me. We were in the convention hall of an enormous Washington, DC, hotel. The hall had been turned into a gallery of home furnishings and clever household ideas for the House and Home Expo geared to interior designers and decorators.

Pillows and fabrics in every imaginable color had me thinking about redecorating my home. At least updating things a little bit. I had seen a lot of local interior decorators whom I knew, but the last thing I expected was a spy-style covert communication. Did this woman have the wrong person? It took every ounce of determination I had not to turn around and face her.

Her voice was familiar to me. I picked up a rococo mirror and, pretending to admire it, aimed it behind me.

I should have known. Mitzi Lawson, a well-known interior designer, was doing her best to feign interest in a turquoise and yellow fabric. Mitzi and Denise Nofsinger owned one of the best interior design companies in Old Town Alexandria, where I lived, just across the Potomac River.

"Hi, Mitzi."

"Shh!"

"Why the subterfuge?" I asked in a whisper.

"Meet me tomorrow morning at the Inger House at eleven. Come in through the alley and the back gate."

"Mitzi, what's going on?"

She didn't respond. I raised the mirror again. "Mitzi?"

She was gone. I tried to act natural when I turned around. There was no sign of the woman with short curly brunette hair and big brown eyes. But on an order pad, someone had left a big checkmark.

Mitzi remained on my mind all day while I handled minor problems and made sure the convention went smoothly. It was ending that evening, which meant my involvement was coming to a rapid end. By six o'clock in the evening, vendors were hard at work packing up their exhibits. The convention participants began to wander through the hotel in evening attire as they headed for the cocktail reception before a gala dinner. At eleven o'clock, I swept through the convention display hall again. It was a bit of a mess, but the hotel cleaning crew was already on top of it. All that remained of the convention were the attendees, who would be checking out in the morning. After quick consultations with my client and the convention services manager of the hotel, I headed for home. It was nearly one in the morning when I drove across the Potomac River and into historic Old Town, Alexandria, Virginia, where the streets were lined with Federal-style houses built in the 1800s. Saturday night traffic slowed my progress. I was pleased when I could turn onto my blissfully quiet street.

My classic Ocicat, Mochie, met me at the door, mewing complaints about having been home alone. He was supposed to have exotic spots but had been born with bracelets on his legs and bull's eyes on his sides. I swung him up into my arms and held him tight. "I missed you, too. Or are you just hungry?" Probably the latter, I thought. He might have missed Daisy, my hound mix, though. She had spent the week with my ex-husband.

In the kitchen, I pulled a can of kitty salmon out of a cabinet and served it to Mochie, who ate as if he hadn't seen food in days. "Really, Mochie? I was here this morning."

I collected the mail, browsed through boring advertisements, tossed them in the trash, and headed upstairs to bed.

SUNDAY

Not surprisingly, I slept late the next day. After a big convention, I tried to keep my calendar light so I could catch up on other things. After a relaxing shower, I pulled on stretch-every-which-way jeans, resenting that they felt snug on my waistline, and an oversize V-neck cotton sweater in burgundy. Not the sort of attire I usually wore for business. But I had a hunch that Mitzi hadn't asked to meet me about a convention or major event. October had swung in a little cooler than usual and my only major plans for the day were to pick up Daisy and meet with Mitzi.

Mochie's persistent mews let me know he thought he was starving again. I fed him first, then fried a couple of eggs sunny side up for my breakfast. I ate them with a slice of utterly delicious pumpkin bread loaded with just the right combination of cinnamon, nutmeg, and cloves. Good enough to offer to company if anyone dropped by. I cleaned up the kitchen and prepared to head over to the Inger House.

Mochie jumped up in the bay window, probably watching for Daisy to come home.

I grabbed my purse and said goodbye to Mochie, who lounged in the sunshine. I hurried out, pausing to lock the door behind me. The Inger House was only five blocks away. The sun had warmed the day, but a brisk cool wind blew. The beautiful golds and oranges of harvest mums and pumpkins decorated doors and stoops.

I wasn't much of a runner, but I did my best to hurry at a half jog, half rapid walk. Mitzi evidently didn't want anyone to see me entering the building. That was odd. I told myself there could be half a dozen reasons she might want me to come in through the back door. Maybe the front door wasn't working properly. Maybe a construction change had blocked the front door. Maybe it had been painted recently and she didn't want anyone touching it and marring the finish.

I was twenty minutes early when I reached the address Mitzi had given me. I sauntered to the end of the street and turned left in search of the alley behind the house. An old wisteria plant grew up a crumbling brick fence. Surprisingly, on the other side of the gate, the fence looked new. Had someone insisted on saving the plant and refused to tear out the old brick? An arch curved over the gate, which looked as if it had come from the Middle Ages. Vertical black planks were held together by horizontal black planks that had been bolted on with large square screw heads. The gate had been painted some time ago, but someone had stopped painting too soon and left the very bottom portion a dingy, worn gray. I pushed the gate open and dodged through an overgrown garden with red brick paths.

I knocked on the door on the side of the house.

No one answered.

Hoping that Mitzi had unlocked the door, I grasped the weathered doorknob and turned it. Something stopped the door from swinging inward. I peered through the glass window in the door.

Denise Nofsinger lay on the red brick floor of the kitchen. Her right hand stretched out as if she had fallen when she was reaching for the doorknob.

"Denise!" I called. She didn't react.

I paused long enough to call 911. When I was certain an ambulance was on the way, I slipped the phone into my pocket. Kneeling, I reached inside and tried to move her so I wouldn't injure her by pushing the door open. "Denise! Denise, can you hear me?"

She didn't move, but I was able to gently open the door wide enough to wedge inside.

I kneeled beside her. "Denise?" I said softly. I placed two fingers on her wrist, but found no pulse. Oh no!

"Denise?" I gently moved her hair out of her face and tapped her cheek, but she still didn't respond. I didn't see any wounds on her skin or head. I gazed around the kitchen. There was no blood anywhere. Could she have had a heart attack or a stroke? Denise was young for that sort of thing, but sometimes it happened.

I rolled her over onto her back and cleared her mouth. I started CPR and chest compressions, muttering, "five compressions, three breaths," the whole time.

I gazed around the small kitchen floor. Nothing had fallen on her.

Sirens wailed close by. I had to open the front door. Could someone have hit Denise? Pushed her and then she banged her head? Where was Mitzi? Injured in another room? Was the attacker still in the house? If so, wouldn't the sound of the sirens spook him? Would he be in a rush to get out? After one last attempt at chest compressions, I stood up.

In haste, I plucked a cast-iron frying pan from a hook on the wall and ventured toward the front door. There was no door from the kitchen to the rest of the house, simply a doorway that led to an old-fashioned butler's pantry. With upper and lower china cabinets on both sides, there was no place to hide. My phone rang. I ignored it and let it roll over to voice mail.

I could hear boots outside, and someone knocked on the door.

The butler's pantry led to a formal dining room that appeared to be undergoing a refresh. A beautiful mahogany table gleamed, but there were no chairs. I hustled to the foyer and unlocked the door.

"She's through there," I blurted to the emergency medical responders. "I've been trying chest compressions, but I can't revive her."

They strode through the house, calm and steady. I guessed their hearts weren't pounding like mine. My phone rang. Out of habit, I pulled it from my pocket. It was just my friend Natasha. I let it roll over to voice mail.

Happily, Wong walked in right behind them. I relaxed because Wong was one of the best cops I knew. Sharp and clever, she had the ability to see through a lot of baloney. We shared a fondness for food, especially of the cupcake variety. Her straining uniform was a testament to that. Unfortunately for Wong, she had married the wrong man by a mile. She'd been married to him when she joined the police force and continued to use the name Wong even though they'd divorced years ago. "Am I glad to see you!"

"What's going on here?" she asked, following the EMTs. We watched them from the butler's pantry.

"I was supposed to meet Mitzi Lawson, but when I arrived, I found Denise Nofsinger sprawled on the floor in the kitchen. I saw Mitzi yesterday. She was afraid of something or someone. I think Mitzi was working on this house with Denise."

The EMTs asked me several questions, but I didn't know Denise's date of birth or medicines that she might be taking. "She's married to Mike Nofsinger, if that helps."

Wong and I returned to the foyer.

"Stay here," she said. "I'm going to have a look around."

The front door flew open, and Mitzi rushed inside. "Why is there an ambulance?"

Wong spoke calmly. "The paramedics are with Denise. Does she have any medical conditions?"

"Is she all right?"

"Mitzi!" said Wong. "Does she have any medical conditions? They need to know."

"She's diabetic."

Wong relayed that information, and moments later, the EMTs walked through with Denise on a stretcher.

"Denise!" Mitzi ran toward them.

Wong spoke gently. "Mitzi, don't block them. They need to rush her to the hospital."

Mitzi backed away and shouted, "I'm coming, Denise! I'll be right behind them."

As they loaded Denise into the ambulance, Mitzi turned to Wong. "What happened? Was she attacked?"

"We don't know."

I told Mitzi that I had found Denise on the floor of the kitchen, but thought I should limit the part about not being able to revive her. After all, I wasn't a medical professional.

"Was she bleeding?" asked Mitzi.

"I didn't see any blood," I said.

Mitzi scrounged in her purse. "Here's the key to the back door. Lock up before you leave? I need to get to the hospital. Has anyone called her husband?"

"If you have his number, you should do that," said Wong. "Right now. What is his number?" She pulled out a notepad and jotted Mike's number on it.

Mitzi made the call. "Mike? Something has happened to Denise. She was found on the floor of your kitchen." There was a silence. "I don't know. No one knows. I'm on my way to the hospital. . . ." Mitzi left the house with the phone to her ear.

"I'm going to have a quick look around," said Wong.

"Is that cop speak for *you're making sure the person who attacked Denise isn't still in the house?*"

"Yeah, pretty much."

I followed her into the massive living room. Just in case someone was still lurking in the house, I didn't want to be alone.

"This must have been quite the home once."

Wong was right. The rooms were unconventionally large for Old Town, with impressive crown moldings. But some of the furniture needed updating. Chair cushions sagged from decades of use. The almond wallpaper with a pattern of delicate blooms on it was actually back in vogue again, but had faded and now appeared shabby. Much of the furniture looked to be inlaid mahogany and would probably fetch a pretty price in an antiques store. In true Old Town style, the floors were old and creaked as we walked, but were probably a point of pride. With a little updating, it would be a showplace again.

"Who owns this house?" she asked.

"It's commonly known as the old Inger House. I understand it has been in their family for generations. You probably know them as the Nofsingers. I think Helena Nofsinger and Jacky Finch were Ingers before they married."

Wong kept going. We entered a sunroom that made me swoon. It was a conservatory of the sort often seen in grand British homes. Vertical green panels held glass from floor to ceiling in an art deco style. At the ceiling level, the glass and the motif continued up to a peak. A practical brick floor probably absorbed the heat from the sun during the day. Massive vines had been trained up the walls. Furniture was scarce and bleached from years of sun exposure.

"Can't hide in here," said Wong.

We exited through a different door into a family room with a formal fireplace. It looked to me like the sort of room where the family had gathered at the end of the day to relax together or watch television. Giant squarish brown leather chairs were weathered and softened from wear. A long camel-colored sofa showed dents where people had occupied it over the years. The artwork was mostly of hunting dogs and horses in gilded frames. Family mementos crowded the mantel in no particular order. It had been a much-loved room. In the far corner, one door led to a bedroom and another to the foyer. The bedroom probably hadn't been used in years. The wallpaper featuring roses had faded, but must have been very beautiful in its day. All manner of clutter from newspapers to magazines and stacks of clothing had been loaded on top of the bed. Ancient luggage lay in piles on the floor. A large, elegant armoire stood against a wall close to a window.

Wong opened the armoire. "Hmmpf. Big enough to hide in."

Luckily no one hid inside among the clothes on hangers.

Wong opened a closet door. To our surprise, it turned out to be a tiny bathroom that had probably been added in the fifties from the looks of the plumbing fixtures and pink tile. Inside the bathroom was another very narrow door, probably a closet for towels and such.

"That's curious," said Wong. "No wonder they needed the armoire. There's no place to hang clothes."

I followed her through the foyer and up the stairs. There were no less than five bedrooms. And every single one of them was clad in a different discolored wallpaper. A door at the end of the hall opened to stairs that led to the attic.

"At least it's not summer. Attics get so hot," said Wong.

I followed her to a veritable treasure trove. A sea of antiques spread from one end to the other. Tables, chairs, dolls, porcelain dogs, vases, trunks, lamps—it went on and on. There was so much that I forgot all about a possible intruder until Wong said, "Well, he's clearly not here."

We clambered down the stairs, closed the door, and walked down the main staircase to the foyer, which offered two more doors. One turned out to be a closet, and the other led downstairs to a basement.

Wong didn't even pause before loping down the stairs. I, on the other hand, had seen enough movies to know that the upstairs door would slam shut behind us, imprisoning us in a nightmarish basement.

I waited for her. Wong didn't spend much time there. She returned, looking just fine.

"Was it spooky?"

"Just a typical Old Town basement, except bigger. People try to make the best of them, but there's not much you can do with low ceilings and old pipes running every which way. If anyone attacked Denise, he's definitely gone. You didn't happen to see anyone running out of the house, did you?"

Chapter 2

Dear Sophie,
My husband and I found a wonderful old house
that we would like to buy. He's all for it, but I'm
worried because there's wallpaper in every room. I
know wallpaper is back in fashion, but this is faded
and screams 1960s mod. I expect Twiggy to show
up any minute. How hard is it to remove wall-
paper?

No Wallflower in Wall, Pennsylvania

Dear No Wallflower,
Removing wallpaper is a universally loathed job.
At a minimum you will need wallpaper stripper,
sponges, and a paint scraper. You may find a steamer
helpful. Most of all, you will need a lot of determi-
nation.

Sophie

"Do you really think I would have let you search the whole house if I had seen someone running from the scene of the crime?"

Wong nodded. "There could always be a second person. Why exactly were you meeting Mitzi here? You have to admit that the timing is odd."

I hadn't thought about it that way. "Are you suggesting that Mitzi wanted me to find Denise?"

Wong shot me a look. "It's curious that she was running

late to meet you. I have a bad feeling there's more to this than you're telling me."

"Yesterday I saw Mitzi at the decorating event in DC and she was acting very odd. As if she didn't want to be seen with me. She asked me to meet her here today. But when I arrived, I found Denise in the kitchen splayed out on the floor."

"You don't know why? Were they consulting with you on decorating?"

"No. I haven't been in touch with either of them in a while."

Wong frowned. "Let's lock up."

We returned to the kitchen. I picked up a few bits of paper that must have wrapped medical equipment. I found a basic plastic trash can under the sink and tossed them inside.

Wong waited for me in the dining room. "What an elegant home. I wouldn't mind living here."

"I hope they won't be ditching all the furniture," I said, admiring the mahogany table and china cabinet. As I gazed at them, I thought I saw a tiny bright yellow something under the china cabinet. I walked over and dropped to my knees to look underneath it. A pin lay on the floor. I picked it up and showed Wong. Letters formed the peak of a little triangle at the top. "Synergy," I read aloud.

"Oh yeah. That's the gym. Well, it was a gym, very popular with weight lifters, but I hear they have all kinds of health programs now. I've been meaning to get a massage there. I hear they're pretty good."

I left the pin on the dining table.

We locked the front door, left through the back door, and walked through the yard and the alley.

Wong kept the key. "I'll take this over to the hospital and give it to Mitzi."

We had reached the front of the house. "Are you going to question her?"

"You bet I am." Wong waved and hustled down the street.

Would Mitzi try to pull some kind of con? Did Mitzi and Denise have a falling out? Were they splitting up their company? Could Mitzi have set me up? I looked forward to hearing what Wong would find out

I turned to look at the house. The three-story home was gorgeous. The kind of house people admired as they drove by, but few of us had the opportunity to live in. The brick had been painted beige and all the trim work was a pristine white. There was almost no garden at all in the front, but a matching brick wall extended to the right. A black iron gate permitted passersby a peek at the lush garden outside the sunroom.

It would be easy to hide in a house that large. I would check up on Mitzi tomorrow. She must have some clue what was going on with Denise. It was entirely possible that the house had nothing to do with whatever happened to Denise. Maybe someone had followed her inside because of some animus toward her. But she had locked the front door. I had to unlock it for the first responders. The conservatory! I bet it had a door. Someone had managed to get inside somehow.

I was still thinking about that as I turned toward my block. I groaned inwardly at the sight of Natasha at my front door checking the time on her watch.

"Sophie!" She waved at me. "Where have you been?"

It was a rhetorical question because she babbled on as I approached her and unlocked my front door.

"Don't say no. You simply must do this. If not for yourself, then for me. Plus, you'll have to talk Nina into it. I would have used members of my own family, but they're all so difficult, and you know how my mother is. I love her, of course, but she doesn't have the right presence for TV. You know what I mean." She paused for a moment. "You can't wear that. Run up and change into something trendy. Never mind, I'll come with you and go through your closet. You have no taste when it comes to your clothing."

I positioned myself at the bottom of the stairs and placed one hand on the newel post to stop her cold. "Maybe you should tell me what you're talking about first."

Natasha and I had grown up together in a small town where everyone knew everyone. The two of us competed constantly, which she enjoyed and I despised. I wasn't a competitor by nature. But when Natasha's father abandoned her at the age of seven, Natasha compensated by trying to be the best at everything. If it was a contest, she *had* to win.

I drew the line at the beauty pageants she loved so much. Unlike me, she was tall and willowy with dark hair that was always perfectly coiffed. At that very moment, she wore an elegant, black, V-neck dress that followed her curves and was cinched in at the waist. I wondered if she could sit in it. Her four-inch heels matched the beige satchel that hung from her arm. A far cry from my jeans and bulky sweater.

I tried to focus on what she was saying.

"He wants three friends to throw a brunch! Isn't that great? Of course, it has to have an autumn theme. Nothing corny. No Halloween schtick. Just rich fall colors. I thought of you immediately."

"Your half-sister cooks for a living. Why wouldn't you involve her?"

"She's obnoxiously opinionated. I really don't know where that came from. You're so much easier to work with."

And then she gave herself away by looking into my dining room. My former husband, Mars, inherited the house from his Aunt Faye and I bought him out in our divorce. Aunt Faye's portrait still hung over the ancient fireplace in my kitchen. She loved to entertain and expanded the house considerably in the 60s. Consequently, I had a ridiculously large dining room, which opened onto a living room built to accommodate huge parties.

"I thought we could shoot it here. We'll decorate for a fall gathering and, best of all, we'll be showing off our favorite brunch recipes as we make them! It will be fabulous. We'll invite Mars and some of his friends."

Aha. Now she was revealing her true intentions. Natasha had chased Mars and lived with him until he'd had enough and broke off their relationship. I still thought she had probably been responsible for hastening the demise of my marriage to him, but it was well in the past and I knew deep in my heart that Mars and I had split for other reasons. It would have happened anyway. But Natasha had trouble letting go of him even though Mars had made it abundantly clear that they were through.

She glanced at her watch. "You have to get dressed. We're meeting him in an hour at The Laughing Hound."

Someone rapped on my kitchen door. Thinking it might be Wong, I hurried into the kitchen. Nina peered in through the window in the door. I let her in.

Nina had been my across-the-street neighbor and best friend for years. Married to a forensic pathologist who spent most of his time traveling, Nina had plenty of time to volunteer at the shelter and rescue animals.

Natasha eyed her with one eyebrow raised. "Red? You'll upstage me in that dress."

Nina smiled as if she had planned exactly that. "I don't know why you're upset. At least I'm here and ready to go."

"I didn't know anything about this appointment," I grumbled.

"I called you, but you didn't answer your phone," Natasha complained.

I had had about enough of her. "Did it occur to you that I might have been busy at the time? We think someone attacked Denise Nofsinger. I was calling an ambulance."

They both gasped.

"Is Denise all right?" Nina leaned over to pet Mochie.

"I'm not sure. I should call and find out."

In an irritated tone, Natasha said, "Hurry up and change clothes first."

"Natasha, just reschedule the meeting."

She recoiled as if I had thrown hot coffee on her. "We're only getting this opportunity because something else fell through. If we don't jump on it now, they'll move on to someone else who can pull it off and won't let them down. Have you seen all the social media postings about fall brunches? They're the hottest trend! We are not turning down an opportunity to host one on television!"

"Don't *ever* do this to me again." I hoped I sounded harsh.

"The two of us could go, Natasha." Nina placed her hand on the door lever as if she were going to open it.

Natasha took a deep breath and froze momentarily. Reluctantly she whispered, "They want Sophie. They won't do it without her."

"What?" I peered at her. "Who are these people? Someone I know?"

"Ellerbe Halberman. Apparently, it was his wife's idea." Natasha's voice grew soft, almost a whisper again, and she rolled her eyes. "His wife likes Sophie's advice column."

I tried to hide a smile. Natasha had a similar advice column of her own. That information must have irritated her to no end! "Is there anything else you haven't told me about this?"

"No."

I wasn't buying Natasha's innocent expression.

She followed me to the staircase.

"I can dress myself. I've been doing it for years."

"Not very well," she muttered.

"I heard that," I said, hurrying up the stairs. I returned in no time wearing a cream-colored suit that I liked. The gold buttons on the jacket dressed it up a little. I braced myself for complaints, but they were so eager to go that Natasha must have forgotten to criticize my outfit.

Our friend, Bernie Frei, owned The Laughing Hound, so we knew the restaurant very well. The hostess led us to the elegant dining room.

Ellerbe Halberman turned out to be a small fellow whose round wire-rimmed glasses rested on prominent cheeks. He clutched my hand in both of his. "Sophie Winston! If only my wife could be here now. My goodness, but I have heard a lot about you."

"Thank you." Was that the right thing to say? "I hope your wife will be able to join us for our televised brunch."

"Could she? Really? It would mean the world to her."

"I don't see why not. We will need guests, won't we? You should both be on our guest list."

"You're just wonderful!" I knew his gushing was silly. I wasn't anything special. But I did notice Natasha's ire.

The lunch meeting went well. Except for the filming part, which wasn't my responsibility, all we had to do was cook some lovely dishes and then host a brunch in my house. Except for a few casual floral arrangements and some extra fall touches in my home, I didn't have to do much to prepare. The whole project seemed doable. The complicated part of film crews, filming, and timing fell to Ellerbe and Natasha.

On my way home, I stopped by the house catty-corner from mine. It was a huge old place, big enough for my ex-husband, Mars Winston, to have an office where he worked from home. Our friend, Bernie, owned the property, and Mars had moved in when he broke off his relationship with Natasha. I felt certain that he hadn't intended to stay there long, but their arrangement proved convenient for them and sometimes it was just easier to go with the status quo.

I could hear Daisy whining on the other side of the door. She must have recognized my footsteps or maybe she could already smell my scent. "Hi, Daisy! Are you ready to come home?"

A falsetto voice answered. "No! I like it here. Go away."

I laughed at Mars's attempt to keep her.

He opened the door and Daisy shot out, winding around my legs and wagging her tail as fast as it could go. "Hi, Sweetie Pie," I cooed, trying to pat my whirling hound mix. "Thanks for keeping her while I was tied up."

Daisy belonged to both of us. When we divorced, neither one of us wanted to give her up, so we shared custody, which had turned out to be helpful when one of us was exceptionally busy with work or went out of town.

"Are you sure you don't want to leave her with me a little longer?" Mars had the good fortune to be almost as handsome as his political clients. Confident, funny, and amazingly comfortable everywhere he went, from Senate offices to my uncle's country farm. He had a manner that put people at ease.

"Good try. It's lonely in my house without her. At least you have Bernie and his cats. By the way, Natasha, Nina, and I are hosting a brunch in a couple of weeks. You and Bernie are invited. It will be filmed for a streaming channel, so don't wear something sloppy."

"Sounds like fun. Who else is coming?"

"I'm not sure yet. Probably Wong, Humphrey, and Francie."

"Count me in."

I left with a very happy Daisy, who ran into my backyard as soon as we were home. I presumed she wanted to check out which squirrels had visited while she was away. I joined Daisy for a few minutes. My landline phone was ringing inside the house. I let it go to voice mail. The afternoon sun warmed the fall day and shone on red and gold leaves, enhancing their colors. The phone rang again inside my house. Someone was being persistent, and my instinct to run to the phone and answer it was hard to resist. I knew perfectly well that it would stop ringing by the time I reached my kitchen. Maybe the person had left a message.

The third time it happened, I couldn't help myself. I ran around the corner of the house to the kitchen door. Daisy passed me and waited patiently. We entered the pleasantly cool kitchen, and the phone stopped ringing.

I walked down the hallway to my home office, and the phone rang again. I grabbed for the receiver. "Hello?"

A soft voice whispered, "Sophie, I'm so glad you finally picked up. I can't call on my cell phone. I think someone's tracking it. I'm going to buy a new one and I'll swing by your house to give you the number."

"Mitzi? Is that you?"

The line went dead. That was odd. She hadn't mentioned Denise. Maybe she was out of the hospital. I tried calling Mitzi. But it just rolled over to voice mail. Troubled by this new development, I went upstairs and changed into jeans and a sweater again. Mitzi said she would drop by. I hoped she was all right.

I made a mug of hot tea and settled in my office to write my column in which I answered questions about the domestic life. But Mitzi worried me and was never far from my thoughts.

As night fell on Old Town, I fed Mochie and Daisy. My dinner consisted of leftovers and frozen soup I had made months earlier.

I continually looked out the window, but there had been no sign of Mitzi. Should I call someone official like Wong? What would I say? I didn't know where Mitzi was. I tried calling her cell number again. As before, it rolled over to voice mail.

Just after eight o'clock that evening, Daisy ran to the door in the sunroom and whined. I followed her and peered into the darkness. A woman gazed over the lawn with her back to me, but I recognized the curly hair and opened the door. "Mitzi?"

She skittered inside fast. "Oh! You have a dog. That's wonderful."

"This is Daisy."

"Is she a good guard dog?" asked Mitzi.

"Not particularly. As you can see, she's not barking at you."

"Pity." She gazed around the glass sunroom. "Can we go somewhere more private?"

"Sure." I led the way to my living room, where I drew all the curtains closed, including those of the dining room that faced the street. "Have you eaten? I have soup."

"I'm fine, thanks." She released the handle on a carry-on piece of luggage.

"How about a cup of tea?"

"Good. That would be very good. I need to stay up and alert."

I hurried into the kitchen and drew the curtains there before putting on the kettle and pre-heating the oven. "Are you going somewhere?" I called to her.

Mitzi stood near my front door, looking around anxiously. "Yes. I don't know where, though. I have clients and I can't let them down. I don't want to be an imposition, Sophie, but you saw what happened today. I need to go into hiding while I figure out what's going on."

I took chocolate chip cookies out of the freezer and slid them into the oven. She watched carefully as I placed tea bags in the mugs.

"Relax, Mitzi." I couldn't help thinking of Wong's suspicion that Mitzi might have set me up to discover Denise. She looked terrified. I didn't know if she was a good enough actress to pull that off.

"I'm not out to get you," I said.

Tears rolled down her face. "Someone is. Denise is dead! And I'm next."

Chapter 3

Dear Sophie,
I keep hearing about coastal grandmother style.
What is it exactly? Does it require living near a
beach?
                              Nana Sue in Tucson, Arizona

Dear Nana Sue,
You can have a coastal grandmother style décor no
matter where you live. It's a mix of soft white
walls, with airy light blues and sandy tans as ac-
cents. It's a very comforting aesthetic. Think re-
laxed furniture and casual entertaining with wine
and cheeses.
                                                Sophie

"Dead?" I nearly spilled the tea.

"They weren't able to revive her." Mitzi's voice broke as she spoke. She covered her face with both hands. "I can't believe it. She can't be gone. She just can't!" Mitzi wiped her eyes and I handed her a box of tissues.

The oven buzzer went off. I removed the cookies by rote,

still coping with the shocking news. "Do they know how she died?"

Mitzi's curls wobbled as she shook her head. "There weren't any obvious signs. They're saying heart failure, but that could be just about anything. Right?"

"Did Denise have heart problems?"

"No! If she did, she never mentioned it. I think she would have told me. We were very close."

I placed the cookies on a platter and handed it to her. I filled a tray with mugs of tea, cream, sugar, napkins, and spoons, and carried it into the living room. Mitzi, Daisy, and Mochie followed me. I set the tray on the coffee table and sat down.

"I can't believe it," I said. "I thought for sure she would be going home last night." Of course, I hadn't been able to find a pulse. And the EMTs hadn't been able to resuscitate her. I should have realized it wouldn't end well. The little spark of hope in the back of my mind that the emergency room would be able to bring her back had been nothing but wishful thinking on my part. "I'm so sorry, Mitzi."

She nibbled on a chocolate chip cookie. "I'm scared out of my wits."

"You didn't want to be seen with me at the design show. What was that about?"

"Everyone knows what a sleuth you are." She snarfed the rest of the cookie and took a sip of her tea. "Sophie, someone has been following me. I'm almost sure of it. No! I *am* sure of it. And now Denise is dead for no apparent reason."

I needed to soothe her a little bit. After all, while Denise's death wasn't expected, there were some other possibilities. "Mitzi, there's always the chance that Denise had a condition that she didn't tell you about. Some people are very private about their health. Or maybe she didn't know she had it! And even though you think you're being followed, there's no reason to imagine that there's a connection between her death and your stalker. Is there?"

Mitzi looked me straight in the eyes. "I don't have a reason to believe there's *not* a connection."

"Why do you think you're being stalked?"

Mitzi nibbled at another cookie. "It began a little over a week ago. I was walking home after dinner and felt like someone was following me. I kept turning around to check but never could pinpoint anyone. When I was home, I was fine and forgot all about it. But I have windows on both sides, toward my little garden and toward the street. Later that night, when I was going to bed, I turned off the lights and remembered that I forgot to leave dry food out for my cat, Poppy. I went to the kitchen and set out some food for her, so she wouldn't wake me at two in the morning. When I returned to my bedroom, I glanced out the window and thought I saw someone hanging around under a tree near the sidewalk across the street."

She held up her hand, as if to stop me from pointing out the obvious. "It was only a shadow. It could have been some guy with a crush on my neighbor. Or someone I don't know waiting for someone else. Or a person waiting for a dog to poo."

"That's understandable. So you may not have a stalker."

"But then, Denise and I were looking over the Inger House. You know, tossing around ideas about what she could do and at what point she and her husband might move in."

"Wait a minute. Denise was moving into the Inger House?"

"Yes. Jacky and her husband moved out. Denise's husband is next in line for it because his father turned it down. They keep it in the family."

Mitzi sipped her tea. "Anyway, I saw part of a face spying on us through a window. I screamed and it disappeared. When I told Denise, she ran to the window to look outside, but she didn't see anyone. After that, I was on alert. I'm careful about where I put things in my house. I'm scared to death that one day I'll come home and find things rearranged. I practically walk along streets like a crab with my back to buildings because I need to know who is around, especially behind me."

"Did you report this to the police?"

"I tried. Basically, the cop said there wasn't anything to go on. I should make sure my doors were locked, yada, yada, as if I wasn't already doing everything I could. I had nothing. No ugly phone messages, no letters, nothing in my home that was disrupted. There wasn't any proof that I was being stalked, much less who it might be. He said to call nine-one-one if anything else happened. Look at me now. Denise is dead and I'm creeping around in the dark, scared to death, not knowing where I can go to be safe."

"You can stay here if you like."

"Thank you. But I think I'm better off in a place where no one would think to look. I considered a hotel. But people can be bribed. You know?"

Her hands curled into fists, she crossed her arms in front of her, clearly afraid.

"Mitzi!"

"I don't know what to do. I don't want to die!"

"Of course you don't." I should have made chamomile tea to help her relax.

"Someone wants to kill me, Sophie. They already got to Denise." Her voice squeaked.

"You're safe here." I tried to sound calm and soothing.

"I know *you* wouldn't poison me. But someone killed Denise. I can't be too careful."

She wouldn't like hearing it, but I had to say it. "We don't know that someone killed Denise. She might have died of natural causes. It's rare in someone your age, but it happens."

Mitzi shot me a doubting look.

"Is that why you're not answering your phone?"

"I think they're tracking me. It has to be through my phone, don't you think?"

"That's possible."

"I threw it into the Potomac River."

"That would account for your failure to answer my call."

Mitzi pulled a phone out of her purse. "I just bought this. It's a throwaway phone. Here's the number." She handed me a slip of paper. "Put it in your phone under a fake name, okay?"

"All right." I gazed at her. Poor thing. I would be every bit as frightened as she was. "You keep saying *they*. Do you think it's more than one person?"

"I have no idea. Even worse, I don't know what Denise and I did! We're interior designers for pity's sake. Did we install a wallpaper that they hate? Paint a room the wrong shade? I run into tough clients sometimes. There are plenty of people who are difficult to please. Usually over the cost of something, but I am very upfront about money. I don't want that kind of squabble, so I do my very best to avoid it by laying out all the costs up front. But this! It's too drastic."

"Maybe you saw something in someone's home that they don't want to become common knowledge."

"That's possible." She brightened up. "I'll make a list of my most recent jobs. Sophie, if you were me, where would you go?"

"I have an idea. You try to relax. I'll be right back."

I hurried into my little office located between the living room and the sunroom. I picked up the phone and called Mars.

He answered the phone with, "Does Daisy miss me?"

"Terribly," I responded. "Is your rental unit occupied right now?"

"Nope."

"Wonderful. What do you charge and how long can I have it?"

"Is everything all right?" asked Mars.

"Yes, fine."

"You have plenty of room for guests," he pointed out.

"I know that."

He gave me the price and dates.

"That's a little steep, don't you think?"

"It's the going rate," he said.

"I'll come over for the key in a bit."

"See you then." He ended the call.

I returned to the living room. Mochie had snuggled on Mitzie's lap as if he knew she needed comfort. She stroked him, which elicited soothing purrs.

"Good news. I have a place for you to hide out. Let me know what you want to eat, and I'll be happy to pick it up and drop it off."

"How did you do that?"

"I have a friend with a rental unit."

I went over the price with her but knew she would agree because she was in a panic. "If anything happens and you're afraid, just come over to my house. It's only a few blocks away."

She reached out and hugged me. "Thank you for helping me, Sophie. I don't know who else to turn to."

"May I see your purse?"

Mitzi frowned but readily handed it over. It was a huge tote kind of bag, and it was packed. One by one, I removed items and placed them on the table. Wallet, a combination calendar and notebook, tissues, two key fobs with keys, aspirin, a little bandage container, a coin purse, brush, comb, contact lens solution, extra contact lenses, reading glasses, ten small fabric samples, business cards from the decorating convention, a measuring tape, and no less than five tiny measuring tapes with company insignia that were given away at the convention. I was beginning to think I would never reach the bottom. At long last, it was almost empty. I reached into an interior side pocket and pulled out a small round item.

"What's that?" she asked.

"This isn't yours?"

"I don't even know what it is. Something I picked up at the convention?" She turned it over and examined it.

"Do you have anything in your purse so you can track it in the event it's stolen or lost?"

"I never even thought of that. What a good idea. Do you know what this is?"

"It's proof that you're being stalked. It's a tracking device."

She threw it on the floor as if it were hot to the touch.

I picked it up. "They can't see or hear us. But the person who slid it into your purse knows where you are."

"I can't leave it here. They'll start watching your house."

I appreciated her concern, especially because that option didn't sound very appealing to me.

"Let's go get the key to your temporary digs. Daisy and I will walk you over there and make sure you get inside safely."

I packed a tote bag with coffee, tea, milk, cookies, fresh eggs, bread, butter, local apple butter, and fruit for her so she wouldn't have to go out right away for food. I called to let Mars know we were coming to his back door and asked him to turn off his porch lights.

When Daisy was suited up in her harness, the three of us walked over to get the key from Mars.

On the way, I told her who owned the house where she

would be staying. "Mars is reliable. He'll keep quiet about you being there. But if you don't want Mars to know that you're the one renting it, you can stay in the shadows, and I'll just get the key from him."

"He seems like a pretty decent guy."

Mars answered the door and invited us inside. "Mitzi! I didn't know it would be you renting the house. We don't have anyone staying there right now anyway, so how about you just pay the cleaning fee when you leave?"

Mitzi thanked him profusely. "That would be great! It's wonderful that you're willing to let me stay there. I think someone is following me. I'm afraid to stay at my place."

Mars's mouth twitched to the side. "So that's why you didn't want the lights on."

I held out the tracking device to him. "I found this in her purse. The stalker must have slipped it in there when she wasn't looking."

"So he knows that I'm here right now," Mitzi said, glaring at the tracker. "I have to get rid of it."

"How about this?" said Mars. "I'll take the tracker and plant it at a hotel overnight. Tomorrow, Sophie can pick it up and turn it over to Wolf."

"Wolf?" Mitzi looked at me. "Who's that?"

"A police detective," I said. "You can trust him. The worst that will happen is your stalker might turn up looking for you and find Wolf instead."

"That's brilliant! He'll think I'm staying at a hotel." Mitzi threw her arms around Mars. "Thank you so much!"

Mitzi, Mars, Daisy, and I left his house at the same time, hoping the stalker was watching the tracking device. Mars left by the front door, while Mitzi and I sneaked out the back and down the alley. We saw Mars turn and walk by us at the very next corner. But Mitzi, Daisy, and I kept walking to the rental unit. Daisy and I went inside with her and checked it out. It was small but charming. Perfect for a vacation in Old Town.

"Are you certain you wouldn't rather stay with me?" I asked. "Safety in numbers and all."

"Now that the stalker probably knows that I went to your house and Mars's, I think this is safer. He can't possibly know that I'm here unless he followed us in person." She pulled a curtain aside just a bit and peered out at the street. "This is great."

One thing was bothering me, though.

"Mitzi, why did you tell me to enter Mike's house through the back?"

"Because of the stalker."

"But you came in through the front door when you arrived."

"I was running late. A client held me up. We're freshening up her very formal living room. She wants it changed to coastal grandmother style. I love clients who know exactly what they want. But it was my first time seeing it and she wanted to keep talking about it. I hurried over to the Inger House and when I saw the ambulance in front of it, I headed straight for the front door instead of going around back like I had planned."

I supposed that made sense. If the ambulance was in front of the house, then the front door would most likely be unlocked. Otherwise, they would have parked in the alley.

"Is there anything else you need?"

"Just a good night's rest."

"Daisy and I will go out the back way. If anything happens, don't be afraid to call nine-one-one."

"Sophie, I can't thank you enough."

"Stay safe." Daisy and I walked out into the dark night and through a tiny courtyard behind the house. I opened the gate and made sure it was securely fastened behind me.

It was late but lights still shone in some homes as we walked through the alley and out to the quiet street. Everyone was getting rest to gear up for another busy day. I shivered when a fall wind blew and dry leaves rattled down the street.

I would be as frightened as Mitzi if I knew someone had been tracking my movements. Part of me wished that Wong hadn't been suspicious of Mitzi. I wanted to believe her. She could have placed the tracker in her purse herself, and then conveniently tossed her phone into the Potomac so it couldn't be verified that she was tracking her own purse. But her surprise and confusion seemed genuine to me. And what would she gain by faking it? Did she think she would draw suspicion away from herself in the death of her business partner? I hated that I even considered that possibility.

Chapter 4

Dear Sophie,
I love having people drop by my house. It makes me feel like I'm special. But what am I supposed to serve on a moment's notice? I'm always at a loss and instead of enjoying my company, I'm a wreck trying to figure out what I can do with one green pepper, a loaf of sandwich bread, and pickles.
Clueless in St. Charles, Illinois, Pickle Capitol of the World

Dear Clueless,
It's not that bad. The next time you're shopping for groceries, pick up a box or two of crackers. Most of us have some leftover cheese in the fridge, don't we? It doesn't have to be fancy, though I love choosing something new or seasonal to try. When people drop by, it takes less than five minutes to put out a cheese board with crackers. Want to dress it up? Add a cluster of grapes or some apple slices or a few chocolates!
Sophie

TUESDAY

In the morning, I walked Daisy before breakfast. The brisk air of fall required a jacket, but it was a clear sunny day, perfect for walking. We strolled by the house where Mitzi had spent the night. I tried very hard not to stare at it lest I draw attention to the place. The curtains were still drawn. That could mean Mitzi was being cautious or that she still slept. Either way, it was probably a good thing.

I stopped at my favorite coffee shop and indulged myself by buying a pumpkin latte for me and a pup cup for Daisy. We settled at a bench overlooking the Potomac River where ripples of water sparkled in the sunshine.

I phoned Wolf, hoping to speak to him about Mitzi. I heard a phone ring nearby. But my call to Wolf rolled over to voice mail. I was beginning to loathe voice mail. What was the point in carrying phones around if no one answered them?

Not a minute later, Daisy wagged her tail wildly, and Wolf slid onto the bench beside me and set his latte down. "Good morning, Daisy! How's my favorite doggy?"

I had dated Wolf Fleishman for a while. Things had been a little awkward for us after that, but we had managed to work out our relationship in a mostly unspoken friendship. He had slimmed down a little bit, which I knew was as hard for him as it was for me. We were both very fond of food. The sun gleamed on the silver hair around his temples.

"Good morning. So that *was* your phone I heard ringing."

He smiled. "I haven't had any reports of a murder this morning, so I'm hoping that's not why you called me."

Oh dear! I didn't want him thinking I never called for any other reason. "We're having a brunch next weekend that will be televised. Want to come?"

"Televised? I don't know. I'm not much for that kind of thing. TV? Really? Who's we?"

"Natasha, Nina, and I. You could bring your wife if you like."

He shot me a side-eye. "That's not going to happen. But she'll be out of town for a few weeks, so maybe I will come. But only if you promise to tell me which foods were prepared by Natasha."

I laughed aloud. "Deal. On a different subject, what do you know about the death of Denise Nofsinger?"

Wolf shook his head. "Not much. I heard about it from someone. It hasn't come to my department." His tone grew deeper and serious. "You wouldn't be asking if you didn't suspect something. What's up?"

"Maybe nothing." I told him about Mitzi and what had happened to her. "She's convinced that Denise was murdered and now the killer is after her. Wong responded to the nine-one-one call. There's probably a report on it."

"Where is Mitzi now?"

"In a secret location. I found a tracking device in her purse."

Wolf grinned at me. "Is the secret location your house?"

"No, it is not. Mars hid the tracker at a local hotel."

"What a great setup for a sting. We could arrange for a team to be ready. An undercover officer could pick the tracker up and bring it to us at a select location, and the perpetrator might walk right into our hands."

"I was hoping you would see it that way."

"Have Mitzi sit tight, and I'll see what I can do. Why didn't she come to the police on her own?"

"She says she did. But Denise only died yesterday. Prior to that, there wasn't much to back up her fears. Mars told her we would get in touch with you today."

"Are you finished with that?" He pointed to my latte.

"Yes."

He took it as well as Daisy's empty pup cup. "I'll give you a call about this."

"Thanks, Wolf."

He ambled off to throw away our trash.

I rose and started for home. There wasn't anything more that I could do for Mitzi. Her problem was in the proper hands now.

I hadn't been home for ten minutes when there was a commotion at my kitchen door. Nina opened it and marched into the kitchen with Natasha at her heels. Natasha carried a fancy legal pad with flowers printed along the borders.

Nina's little white fluffball, Muppet, had come with them and already played with Daisy.

Natasha and Nina both spoke at once.

"Hush!" I waved my hands at them. "One at a time, please. Natasha, you go first."

"We have to come up with a plan of what we're going to serve for brunch. We don't all want to cook the same dish. I am the best cook among us"—she flicked a glance at Nina—"and I don't think I need to point out that some of us don't cook at all. Obviously, I should make the main breakfast dish."

She had a point about Nina. She loved to eat but had been known to order dinner from a restaurant and transfer everything to pots and pans so her mother-in-law would think she had cooked.

"Nina?" I asked.

"Natasha wants to bake a brunch casserole." She glared at Natasha. "With hot peppers and black squid ink pasta?" She shot me a horrified look.

I put on the kettle for tea and reached into the fridge for a deliciously soft and crumbly Roquefort cheese as well as a cranberry cheddar cheese. I placed them on a small wooden board along with an assortment of crackers, a sliced apple, and a few serving knives. I brought it to the kitchen table with paper napkins in the bright fall colors of leaves. I could throw them away for almost instant cleanup.

I placed tea mugs on the table along with cream and sugar. As I sat down, I said, "Natasha, you have the legal pad, so you can write down what we decide to serve. As for the casserole, I think that people have different tastes. For instance, I know that you won't touch the crackers that I set out. But you might partake of an apple slice."

Natasha frowned at me and immediately snatched a cracker.

"What I'm getting at," Nina said, "is that we should offer three different main course recipes, and three different brunch cocktails and three different brunch desserts."

"But I planned on making more dishes," Natasha protested.

"That's fine," I said. I think we'll have quite a crowd. But let's make a list so we're not duplicating anything."

An hour later, the cheese, crackers, and apple slices were gone. We had a menu and Natasha would be responsible for sending out invitations. Nina and I were to text her if we added someone to the guest list.

Natasha gazed around my kitchen. "Now all we have to do is decorate your house."

Nina giggled. It wasn't a big secret that Natasha and I had very different tastes in décor. To be honest, I was glad about that. Life would be boring if we all loved the same things. Nevertheless, I wasn't eager to have her alter my home to suit *her* preferences.

Before that line of conversation could get much farther, I hurried to say, "Natasha, you create such beautiful flower arrangements. Why don't you make a couple for the living room? Nina and I will take care of the rest."

That appeared to soothe her. Natasha departed much happier than she had been on arrival.

"I do not know how you manage to handle her!" said Nina.

"She wants to be the star of everything. If you make her feel like she's in charge of something, then she's happy."

"She drives me bananas. I can tell you I will not be eating anything containing hot peppers or squid ink."

"Yes, you will. You won't be able to resist trying it."

Nina burst into laughter. "You know me so well! But seriously, who serves pasta for brunch anyway?"

"Dinner tonight?" I asked. "I need to try out my recipe."

"Absolutely. I'll bring one of mine with me."

We agreed to eat at six and Nina took off with Muppet.

I made a quick grocery list and headed to the store for ingredients. I hadn't been a fan of butternut squash until I tried roasting it. That changed everything. To me, the flavor was pure fall. And it meshed nicely with maple syrup, which was perfect for brunch. I browsed through the store and chose a lovely butternut squash. I was checking the eggs to be sure none were broken when a soft voice said, "Hello, Sophie."

I looked up to find Helena Nofsinger, the matriarch of the Nofsinger family. Her hair had gone a stunning silvery white that brought out the blue in her eyes. She wore no makeup other than a slash of lipstick. Helena's family had been in real estate in Old Town for decades.

"Helena! How are you holding up? I'm so very sorry about Denise."

She closed her eyes briefly and sighed. "We will all miss her terribly. Such a lovely young woman. It's going to take Mike a long time to recover. He's simply broken. She was far too young to have something like this happen."

"Have they determined the cause of death?"

"Not yet. They tell me you found her. Thank you so much for being kind to her at the last moments of her life."

"I wish I could have saved her. I apologize for holding you up. You must have so much to do. You're buying food. Aren't friends bringing you casseroles?"

Helena gazed at me for a long moment and mustered a wan smile. "Thank you for asking. Every time I see you, I think of Faye Winston. She would be so pleased that you're the one living in her home. She loved Mars, of course, but you have her spirit and the same panache for entertaining."

I was taken aback. I had always felt a little bit guilty for buying out Mars's share of the house. It had belonged to *his* aunt, not mine. By all rights it should be in his family. "You knew Faye?"

"Oh my, yes. She was a big influence on my life. And my sister's, too. She was like a fairy godmother to us, taking us under her wing and teaching us how to be ladies. Each season, she had a tea party for us and invited other girls in town. My father was outraged." Helena threw her shoulders back and held her head high. "Faye told him 'It's what proper young ladies do!' She was the only person I ever knew who could stand up to him. I don't think we would have gone to college if it hadn't been for Faye. She was a remarkable woman. I loved her dearly."

"Then you and Thurman must come to a brunch we're having." I told her about the brunch show we were planning. "I have a portrait of Faye in my kitchen. I would love for you to see it."

"Thurman and I would enjoy that. In answer to your question about people bringing food, most of them are thinking of my grandson, Mike, at this time, of course. Can you even imagine being a widower at his age? It breaks my heart. He has been the recipient of many a casserole. Denise's parents will be arriving tomorrow, and we'll be receiving friends at our house. That will be catered, but I thought I'd better have something to serve her parents when it's just family. Besides, I desperately needed to get out, away from the ringing telephone. This was my excuse to escape for a short time."

"If there's anything I can do for you, please don't hesitate to call."

"Thank you, Sophie. It was lovely chatting with you. I look forward to the brunch!" Helena went on her way.

But I couldn't help wondering if Denise's death was from natural causes. Would Mike still want to live there now that his wife had died in the house, or would they finally sell because the memories would be unbearable for him?

After unloading the groceries, I settled at my desk and concentrated on my event-planning business. Wolf called while I was eating a roast beef sandwich with a little spicy wasabi mayonnaise for lunch.

"Hi, Soph. The autopsy report on Denise Nofsinger just came in. It appears she was severely hypoglycemic, meaning very low blood sugar, which caused cardio-respiratory arrest. The pathologist located two injection sites on the back of her upper right arm."

"So, it could be self-injection, or someone might have killed her with an overdose?"

"Exactly. Most likely an accidental overdose. Because there's no murder, I'm off the case. But stalking is certainly a crime, so I'm passing it along to Sergeant Baxter. He'll need to interview Mitzi." He gave me a phone number for her to call to arrange the interview.

"Thanks, Wolf. Having a stalker is creepy enough, but I'm sure she'll be glad to know that it's not related to Denise's death."

As soon as I hung up, I called Mitzi to relay the information.

"He's wrong," she said.

"Denise wasn't diabetic?"

"Sophie, haven't you ever had a gut feeling about something? I'm not a pathologist, but Denise was smart. She wouldn't have been that careless. And why would she have jabbed herself twice?"

I didn't know if Mitzi was correct or agitated and scared. But I knew what she meant about that gut feeling. Especially when it came to friends. "Tell Sergeant Baxter that when you meet with him." I gave her the number to call. She promised to phone him immediately.

Chapter 5

Dear Sophie,
My powder room is tiny. Another person is recommending wallpaper that goes floor to ceiling, but that will overwhelm our tiny space. I would hate anything loud, but I like the idea of wallpaper. Do you have any suggestions?

Quiet in Wall, Pennsylvania

Dear Quiet,
One of the loveliest wallpapers I have seen is a pattern of birds on a soft, muted gold and peach background. It won't take over if you install a chair rail on the bottom half of the walls. The combination is lovely and works in colonial, formal, and farmhouse style décor.

Sophie

Two hours later, Wolf called and asked if I could come to the Inger House for a few minutes. I agreed. Nina spied me leaving and waved me down.

"I thought we were having dinner."

"Wolf called and asked me to come over to the Inger House."

"I've always wanted to see the inside. Think he'd mind if I come?"

"If he doesn't want you there, I expect he'll say so."

In a matter of minutes, we arrived at the house. It was the first time that I noticed the door knocker, which was obviously antique. A bald eagle looked to the right, his wings spread up above his head. Feathers enhanced his body, and he wore a shield over his chest. A line of leaves arched over his head and reappeared below as the knocker. I rapped it.

Wong opened the door. "Hi, Sophie. Nina."

"Hi! What's going on?"

Wolf walked out of the dining room into the foyer. "Thanks for coming, Soph. I would like you to have a look around."

"I thought you were off the case."

He cocked his head. "Something came up."

"Okay, what am I looking for?" This made no sense. I didn't have any investigative training.

"Is anything different than it looked yesterday? Any changes? Anything missing or out of place?" asked Wolf.

I gazed around the foyer, which hadn't had much in it and appeared the same to me. I wandered into the dining room with Nina right behind me. Same beautiful table, same antique rug. I shrugged. "The cast-iron frying pan is where I left it on the table. I found a small yellow button with the word Synergy on it under the buffet. I left that on the table, too, but it's gone now. Is that what you mean?"

"Keep going," said Wolf.

I entered the kitchen. It looked just as it had the day Denise died. "Everything appears the same. The counters are empty. The tiny table in the back looks the same."

"Nina, were you with Sophie yesterday when she found Denise?" asked Wolf.

"No."

"Pity. More eyes would have been helpful. Sophie, did you touch anything, clean anything up? Throw something away?"

"No. There was no time for that. I was focused on Denise. Oh wait! After the EMTs left, I picked up a few pieces of paper that were on the floor." I walked over to the kitchen sink and opened the cabinet. The trash had been emptied. "I put them in here, but they're gone."

Wolf nodded. "Tell me what else you saw."

I thought back to the kitchen. "I remember having the impression that no one lived here. You know, there aren't any knickknacks or the kinds of things we use every day."

"Did you see anything on the countertops?" he asked.

"No. I think that's probably why it felt so empty and unoccupied. There wasn't a sugar bowl, or salt and pepper shakers, or a dish towel. You know how a house looks when someone moves out."

"Yet they left a cast-iron skillet?" asked Nina.

I shrugged. "Maybe Jacky and her husband don't like them. Or didn't think they would use it anymore. They're heavy. Not everyone can handle that. They left a lot of furniture, some of which must be antiques that would fetch a good price."

"Did you see a purse?" Wolf watched me carefully.

"Mitzi had one when she arrived. She had a key to the back door, which we used to lock up after everyone left and Wong searched the premises."

"Any other purses?" asked Wolf.

"Not that I recall. You were there, Wong. You're probably much more observant than I am. Did you see one?"

Wong glanced at Wolf. He nodded.

"I didn't see one, either. We were hoping you had noticed one."

All of a sudden, I realized why they were asking. Most women carried a purse when they left their homes. Where were Denise's phone and wallet? "Someone took her purse. Someone must have been there with her before I arrived!"

"Wait, wait, wait. Hold everything," said Nina. "I know I'm not supposed to do this, but I leave my purse in my car all the time. Maybe she drove over, and her handbag is in her car."

"Good thinking, Nina." Wolf nodded his approval.

Nina squared her shoulders and beamed with pride.

"Except her car was in the garage of their condo. There are cameras. It never left that day."

"She took her husband's car, then?" Nina suggested.

"Another good thought. Mike's car was parked at their condo as well. He was on foot, having a look at a building the company wants to acquire."

"The point of all this, then," I said, "is that someone must have been here with Denise. That person did not call for help, which would suggest that said person wanted her to die."

"Or he outright killed her," said Nina.

Wolf didn't correct her.

"You now think she was murdered?" I asked.

Wolf took a deep breath. "It's possible. The coroner can't rule out homicide."

"Then the killer took her purse because he used insulin she might have carried with her?" asked Nina.

"Good point. Most of my diabetic friends carry sweets in case their blood sugar gets too low. And a glucometer to test blood sugar, not to mention emergency insulin," I said. "Maybe that's why she was sprawled with her head and outstretched arm toward the door. From the beginning I thought she was trying to get outside or away from someone."

"I hate to think that." Nina shuddered.

"Me too. Whoever it was must have placed her purse where she couldn't reach it. Poor Denise. I bet she was trying to get outside to yell for help, but then she was too weak to make it that far."

"It was someone she knew," said Wong. "Most people probably didn't even know she was diabetic."

"You might check with Mitzi about the purse," I suggested. "I don't remember her saying anything about one, but she might have grabbed it to give to Denise at the hospital."

"Will do." Wolf thanked us for coming.

"I'm trying out a brunch recipe for dinner. Would either of you like to join us?"

They both declined, citing work as an excuse. But I made sure to invite Wong to the brunch gathering.

When we returned to my house, Nina and I chatted while I prepared the recipe I had in mind. I peeled the butternut squash, cut it into little squares, and slid all the pieces onto a tray. I added small chunks of shallots. I poured a little bit of oil over everything, sprinkled them with salt, and then tossed them with my hands to spread the oil and salt around among them. After shaking the tray to spread them out into a single layer, I slid the tray into a preheated 400-degree oven.

"How well do you know Denise's husband?" Nina poured each of us a glass of white wine.

"Mike? Not very well. I've seen him with Denise at local events." I took eggs out of the fridge. I wasn't sure how my dish would turn out, but sometimes winging a recipe yielded tasty results. "You're thinking that the police always look at the husband first?"

I turned my attention to dessert and whipped up a pumpkin mousse with spices that smelled like fall. Cinnamon, nutmeg, and just a touch of cloves.

Nina looked out the bay window and stroked Mochie. "There's that. But I was wondering what would motivate someone to take her purse. Of course, there's the odd chance that the person might not have known her at all, happened upon her, and took the purse for whatever cash she might have been carrying."

"Absolutely true. But that person probably would have bopped her over the head. Murdering someone with insulin suggests a meticulously planned murder. After all, the killer had to procure the insulin."

"Which leads straight back to her husband, who had access to Denise's insulin," said Nina.

"I imagine he'll be getting a visit from Wolf tonight or tomorrow at the latest."

"Don't you wish we could be there? Like little flies listening in."

Not particularly fond of flies, I grimaced at the thought. "Maybe bees. I don't like the ones that sting, but they seem cleaner than flies."

Nina laughed at me as I took the butternut mixture out of the oven, cracked eggs over it and returned it to the oven.

The two of us enjoyed dinner, but decided my recipe needed a little more punch in the way of thyme. For dessert, we tried the pumpkin mousse, which was deliciously creamy.

That night when I went to bed, I couldn't help thinking of poor Denise. Had she opened the door to the person who killed her? Was it someone she knew and didn't fear? Her husband? Another man she was secretly seeing or one who had eyes for her and felt spurned? Someone whose house she was working on? The possibilities were endless.

But in my mind, I could feel her horror when she realized why that person was there and that she had been injected. She turned and ran, stumbling in her low blood sugar state of confusion, trying desperately to leave the house. Wanting to be outside in the hope someone might hear her call for help. But it was too late.

I should have tried to get Denise out of my mind, but I couldn't help thinking about Denise and Mitzi. I reached for a notepad on my bedstand and jotted connections between them. They worked together. They had both attended the decorating convention. They were about the same age. One was attacked and the other was being stalked.

The list didn't help as much as I had hoped. It was possible that the two of them had upset a client. Murder seemed like a ridiculously strong revenge for the wrong color of drapes, but I didn't dismiss that notion. Along the same lines, maybe they had ticked off another decorator.

WEDNESDAY

In the morning, after letting Daisy out and back in, I lingered over my tea, pondering what to bring Helena. A pumpkin Bundt cake perhaps. It would serve a lot of people and could be offered for breakfast, at teatime, or as dessert. In fact, it might even be a choice item for the brunch we would be having.

I spent the next couple of hours baking the cake. While it cooled, I retreated to my office to return calls and take care of business. After drizzling a sweet white glaze over the cake, I called Helena to see if it was a good time to bring it over. Her husband Thurman answered the phone and said it was great timing. I could hear a lot of voices in the background. I checked with Nina to see if she wanted to join me. She promised to be ready in twenty minutes.

I hurried upstairs and changed into appropriately somber clothes. Black trousers, a white blouse, and a black knit jacket in the style of Chanel would do. After I packaged the cake in a disposable paper Bundt cake box so Helena wouldn't have to worry about returning a cake platter, I met Nina out on the sidewalk.

We stopped at the florist on the way so Nina could pick up a bouquet of white lilies to bring Helena. Cars lined the street as we approached her house. Situated at the end of the street, the red brick house was slightly set back off the sidewalk. Bushes almost hid a small patio to the side of the house. Stately black shutters flanked tall windows and matched a black front door. It appeared to be two stories tall, not a particularly large house. A couple was leaving as we arrived, so we simply walked inside.

"Nina, darling," Thurman Nofsinger bellowed in a deep, rich voice. He held out his arms to her for a hug. I knew him socially, but not terribly well. Helena and Thurman were regulars at the charity events I often organized. He had always struck me as boisterous but kind. Often the life of the party, Thurman had a knack for making everyone feel welcome, as if he was delighted to engage each person. I wasn't sure I had ever seen him without a drink in his hand. I'd heard he golfed a lot, but his figure suggested he ate well and used a golf cart.

"And Sophie, too!" I received a half hug because I still carried the cake.

"Oh, cake! Thank you for coming. We are so grateful to all our friends for supporting us at this terrible time."

I didn't dislike Thurman, but as I listened to him, it dawned on me that what I had always chalked up to being comfortable with himself and his life was actually kind of slick. His friendliness was certainly welcoming, but so over the top that it struck me as more of an act. I wondered what he was like in private. I excused myself and headed for the kitchen to set down the heavy cake. I placed it on the island.

Helena's kitchen had been renovated since I last saw it. Beautiful cream-colored cabinets were accented with brushed gold handles. She had installed the kind of oven most of us only dreamed of. The giant eight-burner cooktop with two small ovens and one large one underneath gleamed in off-white enamel. Brushed gold handles complemented it like tasteful jewelry. They must have extended the wall to enlarge the kitchen, because they now had a breakfast nook that overlooked the garden in the rear.

Helena's sister, Jacky, bustled into the kitchen. "Sophie! It's so good to see you." Jacky bore a remarkable resemblance to Helena. She wore her silvery hair shorter in a tousled pixie style. While Helena's skin remained quite pale, Jacky had a robust tan. She was plumper than her sister, and not as demure. "Do you need a cake plate for that?" She pulled one out of a cabinet and handed it to me.

"Thank you. I'm so very sorry about Denise."

Jacky slapped a hand against her chest. "We are simply rocked by this. No one ever imagined anything so horrible. She and Mike were just starting their lives together. I keep expecting her to walk in!"

The cake box came with a white base that could stay underneath the cake, but it needed a platter to catch crumbs. I lifted the cake with the base and slid it onto the white plate.

"Cake! It looks delicious," said a male voice.

"Stu, you have to limit yourself," cautioned Jacky.

The cake in place, I looked over at Jacky's husband, Stu Finch, who patted his stomach.

"This is an exception. No one can diet through a funeral."

Jacky whispered, "It's a good thing Denise's parents are taking her home to their family plot to bury her. The influx of tempting food will stop for us."

Stu sighed. "It's all so sad. We're flying out tonight."

"That's soon! Is there anything I can do to help you?" I asked.

"I don't think so. We're packed and ready to go. Helena has someone coming in to clean up after everyone leaves. But thank you for offering."

"If anything comes to mind, just let me know. I would be happy to help."

They thanked me again and hurried back to the rest of the crowd. I gazed around the kitchen. All I needed was a knife to cut the cake. I opened drawers until I found one.

"I'll go back to your place with you." It was a woman's voice. She spoke softly.

I didn't see anyone. Maybe she was standing near one of the entrances.

"Look, I want to be alone." A man. He sounded firm.

"I know how tough this has been for you. Let me help you through this. I could start boxing some of her things."

Oh! That was awful. Denise had only died a couple of days ago. The nerve!

Chapter 6

Dear Natasha,
My father's second wife has passed away. She has
two sons from another marriage. Neither of them
lives in our town. Everyone seems to expect me to
go through her belongings and dispose of them.
That doesn't seem right. I hardly knew the woman.
Who should be doing that job?
                    Not Me! In Deadwood, South Dakota

Dear Not Me,
You have every right to decline such an unsavory
task. One of her relatives should undertake that
job with the assistance of her husband.
                                        Natasha

"I don't want you touching anything that belonged to
her." Now the male voice sounded angry. I couldn't
blame him. It had to be Mike, the young widower.

I wondered whether I should rescue him by interrupting.

"Let me do it, Mike." She spoke as if she were soothing
him. "You can't recover if you see her everywhere in your

condo. You'll be miserable. You need to start fresh. I can assist you with that."

I had no idea who she was, but I didn't like her! Instead of butting in, I coughed so they would know I was there.

Silence followed.

I set the cake on the dining table. I cut the first two slices, slid them onto plates, and placed forks beside them. In my experience, people would pass by a dish that hadn't been cut or sampled yet. No one wanted to be the first.

Matt Stewart, a local event planner, had inherited the title of etiquette expert from his mother. He had a great sense of humor and privately poo-pooed the designation, but had been clever enough to make money off it by compiling her etiquette advice into a book and appearing on television shows as an authority on the subject. "How clever of you to cut the first slices of cake. It annoys me when everyone stands around talking about a cake, but no one bothers to cut it."

"Hello, Matt. Are you working or a friend of the family?"

"I go way back with Helena and Jacky. All the way back to grade school, actually."

"May I offer you a slice?"

"No, thank you." He appeared to be assessing someone, and muttered, "Pity that people don't wear hats much anymore. They hide so many sins."

I looked to see whom he was talking about. "Do you mean Jacky?"

"Mmm. Her hair looks like she came here through a wind tunnel."

"I believe it's supposed to look like that."

"Good heavens! She was always so beautiful. Why would she wear it that way?"

I wanted to find fault with Matt. After all, no one was perfect. But his mother's strict rules had worn off on him.

His black suit fit perfectly. I felt certain his gray tie with a simple small blue diagonal stripe and white shirt had been carefully selected.

"Poor Robbie," he murmured. "First his mother-in-law, and now this."

"What happened to his mother-in-law?" I asked.

"You didn't hear? His wife, Mary, has been flying back and forth to take care of her mother. They're planning to move her here. That's the reason they decided to give the Inger House to Mike and Denise. By all rights, it was Robbie and Mary's turn to live in that mansion. It was either renovate the Inger House to accommodate her parents or move them to their house. They chose the latter. Just between the two of us, I think Mary prefers living out in Great Falls. She says it's because of her horses, but I have always thought the real reason was to obtain some separation from Robbie's family. Some families can be overwhelming."

For an etiquette specialist, Matt certainly was prone to gossip. "I had no idea." I looked over at Robbie. Unlike his mother, Helena, he still had dark hair. My heart went out to him. Bags hung under his eyes as if he hadn't slept. There were too many things happening in his life right now.

"Stu is a lucky man," said Matt. "It must have been a big decision to move out of the house. Jacky has lived there almost her entire life. But the stairs probably pose a problem for them now."

"Were you close to Denise?" I asked.

"Not until recently. When I saw Helena's kitchen, I hired her on the spot. I must say that she had impeccable taste and a good eye for color."

"That's high praise."

"Duly deserved. I asked her to change my dining room into a music room. It solved two problems for me. I was sorely in need of a sound-proofed room. You know how these old buildings are. My poor neighbors have been tolerant of me playing my violin, but I'm restrained in an effort to be considerate. And frankly, I am not in the least bit interested in having dinner parties. The dining room is beautiful, but it's rarely used. It's a win-win situation for me."

Probably for the neighbors as well, but I didn't say that out loud.

"Yes, I have been a longtime friend of the Nofsingers. Mike did quite well in his choice of a bride. Poor fellow. I hear he is bereft. Oh, there he is. Would you excuse me? I must express my sympathies to Mike."

When I turned around, I saw Mike. He wore his light brown hair cut short in the latest style. His eyes were bloodshot, and he nodded blankly at the people who shared their condolences.

Rachel Powers, a blonde with roots that gave away her natural dark hair color, had her arm wrapped around him. She was pretty and had taken care with her appearance. Her dress showed off her lovely figure, and she had a knack for applying becoming makeup. An up-and-coming interior designer, I knew her from the League of Women Designers, for whom I had arranged several events. I thought she had been friends with Denise.

An elderly woman sat nearby, scowling at her. Her gray hair had been pulled smoothly back off her face, which was amazingly unwrinkled for an older woman. I had trouble assessing her age, but the bony hand that gripped the top of her cane led me to believe she was quite elderly. The soft peach shade of her shiny nail polish matched the dress she wore.

A young woman with the same shrewd eyes as the elderly woman looked to be about Mike's age. She stood beside the elderly woman's chair, watching Mike and Rachel. Her lips pulled into a disapproving line.

The old woman's eyes met mine. "Who are you?"

Helena heard her question and rushed over. "This is Sophie Winston, Aunt Annie. She lives in Faye's house."

A beautiful smile crossed Aunt Annie's face. "Are you related to Faye?"

"My ex-husband was her nephew."

One of her eyes squeezed into a squint. "That would be little Marshall."

There was nothing wrong with her memory. "Yes!"

"You divorced him? He didn't treat you right?"

I didn't want to get into details in front of all these people. "He's a fine man. Our lives just took us in different directions."

"Uh huh." Her tone indicated that she didn't believe a word of what I had said. "You brought that beautiful Bundt cake over there. What kind is it?"

She wasn't missing a thing! "Pumpkin."

She appraised me unabashedly. "Good choice. Not too sweet, I hope? People use too much sugar these days. We didn't do that back when I was baking."

"I hope you'll like it."

Helena bent and whispered something to the old woman, who nodded her head and gazed at me with new interest.

Helena turned to me. "Could we speak with you for a moment, please? Right this way to our den."

I followed her along the hallway into a room decorated in a golden peach shade from the walls to the furniture. Several comfy chairs and a couple of sofas suggested that this room was often used when the entire family gathered. A large screen TV hung over a fireplace that looked like it was often used. Bookshelves lined two walls end to end. But instead of being set up in pretty arrangements to showcase the shelves, they were packed with books.

We were joined by her husband, Thurman, her sister, Jacky, and husband, Stu, and Mike's parents, Mary and

Robbie. The elderly woman called Aunt Annie walked in, leaning on her cane.

"I hope you won't think us rude," said Helena. "It's just that it's so urgent."

"Drinks, anyone?" asked Thurman, heading for what appeared to be a liquor cabinet.

"Thurman!" Helena scolded. "Would you please sit down? Sophie, we need your help."

Mary, who appeared uncomfortable in a black dress, began to weep. "This can't be happening."

Helena drew a sharp breath. "Robert, perhaps you could escort your wife outside while she composes herself."

"No!" Mary glared at her mother-in-law before shifting her focus to me. "The police think Mike killed his wife!"

"Do they have some kind of evidence that implicates Mike?" I asked.

"No! He loved Denise," wailed Mary.

Helena sat primly. "Detective Fleischman took him in for questioning."

"I see. I'm sure you can understand that the police always look to the spouse first. It's sad but true that there are many incidences of married couples having disagreements that culminate in murder."

"Murder?" Mary shrieked. "My son did not murder his wife."

"In that case, they will look to other people as suspects. In any event, I would recommend that Mike obtain legal representation."

Helena flicked her hand impatiently. "Thurman called Alex German."

"They say he's an excellent attorney," Thurman said. "If he's half the lawyer that he is a golfer, then our Mikey is in good hands."

I wasn't thrilled by that news, but it didn't really involve me. I had dated Alex for a time. While I was the one who broke off the relationship, I hadn't handled the breakup as smoothly as I probably should have. We had reached the point where it was no longer awkward to run into each other on the street, but I didn't relish those encounters. "He's a good choice."

Jacky leaned forward toward me. "Please take our case. We have to help little Mikey. I can't bear to think of him in a jail cell."

"Ohhh." Now I understood what they wanted from me. "I'm not a lawyer or a private investigator. The police will be making an in-depth inquiry, and they have access to a lot of technology that I don't have."

"We have great respect for the police." Thurman tapped his knee nervously. "But they have many crimes to look into. We need someone who can establish that our Mikey did not do this heinous act."

"Mrs. Winston," said Robbie.

"Ms. I believe?" corrected Jacky's husband, Stu, with a smile. He didn't have Thurman's polish, but the way he assured his wife by taking her hand into his was very sweet.

"Sophie will do just fine."

"Sophie," began Robbie again, "Mike would never kill anyone. Certainly not his own wife. He loved Denise. They were the perfect couple."

I observed Mike's parents, Robbie and Mary. She seemed understandably distraught. Her dark blond hair frizzed out a bit around her shoulders. Her belted black shirtwaist dress with flat shoes wasn't quite as formal as Helena's or Jacky's attire.

Robbie had the same straight nose as Helena and Jacky. The resemblance between him and Mike was uncanny.

"Can you help us?" Helena's lips grew taut.

"We can pay you. Money is no object when it comes to Mike." Jacky's eyes welled with tears. "We need your help finding the real murderer so Mike will be absolved of any wrongdoing."

I could understand that their main concern was Mike. His family obviously loved him and wanted him exonerated. "I don't accept payment. And I can't make any guarantees. I look for the truth, and if that turns out to incriminate Mike, I won't hide that fact. Sometimes, these cases don't turn out the way we would like."

They sat in silence until Mary said, "We know he didn't do it. I don't understand why anyone would harm Denise, but I know it was not my son. I have absolutely no doubt about that."

Robbie nodded in agreement. "We can handle it. No matter what you find. We know that Mike would never kill anyone, except in self-defense, which was clearly not the case here. It's true that he had access to Denise's insulin, but that doesn't mean anything. Loads of people have access to the insulin of their diabetic family members. I looked it up. Nearly seven and a half *million* Americans use insulin. Multiply that by their family members and friends who have access to it and that's an enormous number of potential suspects, even if you whittle it down to residents of Old Town."

"Very well. Thank you for being honest with us." Helena withdrew a checkbook from her purse.

I held up my palms. "Helena, I really don't accept payment. This isn't my profession. I've just gotten lucky a few times. I can't guarantee anything."

Annie tilted her head to the side and squinted at me. "You have never accepted payment for any of the cases you solved? My goodness! That's quite admirable. I'm glad that you live in Faye's beautiful home." She pointed a gnarled finger at me. "Rescue that boy for me. I'd do it myself, but I'm not as spry as I used to be."

"I hope I can be of assistance. Please don't hesitate to share anything that you know. Even small details can turn out to be helpful." I was supposed to be at the Inger House at eleven the Sunday morning that Denise died, but I'd been running a little bit early. So Denise must have been killed around ten thirtyish. "Where were each of you on Monday morning around ten thirty?"

Mary gasped. "You think it was one of us?"

"It's helpful to eliminate people."

Thurman chimed in with a booming voice, "I was at the golf club all morning."

"Which one?" I asked.

He smiled when he said, "Pine Grove. Ask for Jerry."

Helena said softly, "I was at the office. I can confirm that Robbie and Mike were working."

"We were at Synergy," said Jacky. "I take a yoga class there three times a week and Stu works out or gets a massage."

Everyone looked at Annie, who said, "I'm ninety-eight years old. I don't need an alibi."

For the first time since we entered the room, everyone smiled.

That left Mary. She sat perfectly still and said, "I was with my horses."

For one long moment, no one said a word. Almost as if her lack of a decent alibi convicted her of the crime.

But then Helena rose from her seat, signaling that we were done. I followed them out to the living room, where the family members engaged their guests. Annie settled in the same chair as before and eyed Rachel, who had an arm snaked possessively around Mike.

Annie rapped her cane on the floor. "Michael!" She beat the cane again. "Come over here."

She had everyone's attention now.

Nina sidled up to me. "What's happening?"

"I'm not sure. Just go along with it," I whispered.

"Walk this lady home," said Annie. "Her name is Sophie. Her husband's aunt was a good friend to me."

Mike looked at me in surprise. "Sure."

"I'll help you," said Rachel. "Just give me a minute to get my purse." She weaved through the guests to fetch it.

"Okay. Go!" said Annie. "Hurry now! It won't take that little tart long to come back. Run, y'all. Run!"

Chapter 7

Dear Natasha,
My living room is hardly ever used, so everything is
in perfect condition. But it looks stale. Hubby re-
fuses to waste (his word, not mine) money on new
furniture. How can I improve it on a meager budget?
Frustrated in High Point, North Carolina

Dear Frustrated,
Consider a new hubby with a looser grip on the
bank account. If that's not an option, then take a
hard look at the furniture. Is it matchy matchy?
One or two major new pieces can make a big dif-
ference. Maybe a new sofa? Or look around your
house for furniture you could switch around. Clear
all the lamps, art, and knickknacks out of the room
and start fresh.

Natasha

Nina, Mike, and I dashed through the crowd and out the front door.
"Which way?" asked Mike.
"Which way will Rachel go?" I asked.

"Rachel? Probably to the right."

"Then we'll go left." We scurried left toward the Potomac River, then turned left again and hurried along to the end of the block, where we paused and peered around the corner.

"We're good," I said, rushing across the street.

We continued in the same manner for four blocks, then turned left into an alley. The sun shone on gold and red leaves that covered the ground. An occasional iron gate allowed a peek inside a back garden.

"Does Rachel have your phone on Find My?" I asked Mike.

"Of course not," said Mike.

"Is that possible?" asked Nina.

I shrugged. "I think so. If she had access to his password, I think it would be pretty easy to set up."

Mike pulled his cell phone out of his pocket and scowled. "I'll turn it off, just in case."

"Good idea." It was getting way too easy to follow people. Sometimes it could be helpful, but it could also be misused.

"Sophie Winston," said Mike. "Why have I heard your name?" He gasped. "Are you the person who found Denise?"

I nodded. "I'm so sorry, Mike."

"How . . . how did she look?"

I didn't want to upset him. Fortunately, there hadn't been any blood or disfigurement. "Did you get to see her?" I asked.

"Yes."

"Like that. I wasn't sure if she was dead or alive. But I couldn't find a pulse."

"Do you think she suffered?"

"I don't know how an insulin overdose feels. I hope she didn't."

"What were you doing there?" he asked.

"I was supposed to meet Mitzi. When I arrived, I found Denise."

He stopped walking and looked me in the eyes. "Mitzi wasn't there?"

"I was early. She came later."

Nina held out her arm to stop us and peered out at the cross street. "Is that her?"

Mike and I leaned forward cautiously.

Mike slammed his back against the wall. "Yes."

Nina kept watch. "All clear. She's ahead of us now. That's a good thing."

"Where do you live?" I asked Mike.

"About two blocks from here."

"We'll walk you the rest of the way home," I said. "Hopefully she'll be heading to my house, and you can slip into your place."

Nina took a deep breath. "A piece of advice, if I might. Don't answer your door."

"She was one of Denise's friends," said Mike. "When Denise died, I thought she was as distraught as I was. But now she won't leave me alone. I just want to be by myself for a while. You know? Just sit in our condo and think about what happened and miss Denise. But nobody will let me do that. I guess they mean well, but I don't want everyone fussing over me. I just want to be alone."

"Everyone reacts differently. It's okay for you to feel that way. Hopefully, we'll manage to get you to your condo without her noticing and you can have the time alone that you need. Come on," I said. "Let's hurry before she goes to your place."

We continued walking along alleys for the next two blocks. The three of us looked around for Rachel before we emerged onto his street and walked to the front door of his condominium building.

"Thanks for helping me," said Mike.

"You're welcome. Let us know anytime you need an escort." Nina winked at him.

"Better go before she comes along and sees you." As soon as Mike was safely inside his building and stepping into the elevator, we headed home.

"So what was going on?" asked Nina.

"Rachel had her arm around him like an octopus and was offering to clean out Denise's clothes and belongings."

"Ouch! Too soon! Has she no sense? She needs to back away."

Nina peeled off at her house and I walked the short distance to mine. I was a little concerned because I hadn't heard anything from Mitzi. Obviously, she took laying low very seriously.

I spent the afternoon preparing an event proposal for the Society of Space Flight, which I thought would probably be a fun and interesting convention.

At four o'clock, Mars showed up, beaming. "Wolf just called me a genius!" He puffed up his chest. "Maybe I should have been a detective."

"What did you do that was so brilliant?"

"I took Mitzi's tracking device to a hotel! He wants me to casually show up at the hotel to meet an undercover cop and show him where I left it. They're setting up a sting operation."

"With Mitzi? Would you like some hot cider?"

"Like you have to ask?" He checked his watch. "I have a little time. Don't want to get there too early. Of course, Mitzi won't actually be involved. They're taking it over to the Inger House where a couple of cops will be waiting to see who shows up. Isn't that cool?"

I poured the cider into a pan and set it on a burner to warm up. "Very cool. I hope they catch him and that he's the person who murdered Denise."

"You say *he* as if you think it's a man."

I took out two mugs and a couple of cinnamon sticks that I tossed into the pot. "I guess I do think that. Although it could be anyone. Do you know a young woman named Rachel Powers?"

"Can't say I do. You should ask Bernie. He knows everyone. What did Rachel do?"

"She's chasing Mike Nofsinger. His wife hasn't even been buried yet."

"An early bird. I may not know her, but I can tell you one thing about her."

"Please do."

"She's after his money."

"He's in his twenties. I doubt that he has much money yet."

"The Nofsinger sisters have kept a low profile. But I've seen the kind of money they donate anonymously to political campaigns."

"How do you know it's from them if it's anonymous?"

"It's publicly called anonymous. Insiders know from whom it came. They say it was Helena who took that business to new heights. You'd be amazed by what they own. Her son, Robbie, is running the day-to-day part of it now, but someday, Mike will be the sole owner."

"Are you suggesting that a woman might have murdered Denise in the hope of marrying Mike?" I poured the cider into the mugs and handed one to Mars.

"It wouldn't the first time that happened. Especially if they're already involved, if you know what I mean."

"I don't think that's the case. He seems very upset about

Denise's death. I'd be surprised if he was seeing another woman."

"Maybe he's feeling remorse."

"Mars! That's an awful thing to say."

"It's possible. They always look at the husband first and there's a reason for that."

"I know, but I think his grief is genuine. Hey, there was a woman at Helena's house today whom she called Aunt Annie. Do you know her?"

"Never heard of her. Maybe a friend from out of town?"

"Could be. But she knew your Aunt Faye."

Mars drew his head back in surprise. "How old was she? Faye died years ago."

"Very old. In fact, she called you *little Marshall*."

Mars choked on his cider. "No one has called me that in decades. Now I really want to know who she is."

"She seemed . . . I don't want to say bossy . . . used to telling people what to do. If I see her again, I'll be sure to get her full name."

"Do you think Wolf will call and tell me the results of tonight's sting?"

"I seriously doubt it, but he'll let it spill when he's ready. Or maybe Mitzi will tell us."

Mars rose from his seat. "Want to come with me?"

"I would *love* to!" I thought for a moment. "But I'd better not. It might mess up their plan. Don't forget to act casual. Good luck, Sherlock!"

He hurried out the door. He was so excited that I wasn't at all sure he would be able to act casual.

He was back in an hour, wearing joggers and a long-sleeve T-shirt. He burst into the kitchen. "Hi! Has Daisy eaten yet? If not, I thought she might want to run with me."

It wasn't as though he'd never dropped by to take Daisy

for a run. Still my suspicion radar went on alert. "You want an excuse to go by the Inger House, don't you?"

"Shouldn't it be called the Nofsinger house?"

"Probably. I guess Helena and Jacky were Ingers before they took their husband's names. Good try at changing the subject."

"Okay, yes. I thought it wouldn't be as obvious if I ran by with Daisy."

"Do you want to ruin the sting? This is their chance at catching Denise's killer!"

"You don't know that. Mitzi's stalker might just be totally enamored by her curly hair. He might have been miles away from the Inger House at the time Denise was murdered."

"Or not."

Mars met my eyes sheepishly. "You could come with me. We could look like a couple out walking our doggie on a pleasant fall evening."

Daisy leaned her head against Mars's legs and looked at me with big puppy eyes.

"Did you teach her to do that?" I asked.

He fished a treat from his pocket and whispered, "Good girl."

"All right. But we stay on the sidewalk on the other side of the street. No sneaking through the alley."

"Daisy and I like alleys."

"So do murderers. Absolutely not."

"Okay. Hurry up. You'll want a jacket. It's getting cold outside."

I knew we wouldn't see anything. If I were tracking someone, I would be afraid that person might not be alone or might be armed. And I would certainly spy on the house for quite a while before making any move at all.

I pulled on a soft, fluffy jacket and slid Daisy's harness over her head. "Just for the record, I'm against this."

"Then why are you coming?"

"To prevent you from ruining the sting!"

"Oh, Soph! You're such a rotten liar. You know perfectly well that you're as curious as I am."

I locked the door behind us. "I admit that's true. But I don't want us to cause this thing to fail."

The three of us walked out to the sidewalk. The sun was setting, and lights were beginning to turn on inside homes and at their front doors, some of which still had gas lanterns with flickering flames. It was a lovely time to walk. A bit nippy, but the seasonal charm of pumpkins on stoops and harvest wreaths decorating front doors made the cold air worth it.

After a few blocks, we rounded a corner that would bring us by the Inger House. Mars questioned my insistence on remaining on the other side of the street, but I didn't waiver.

"There are lights on inside," Mars whispered. Unexpectedly, he flung his arm against me and stopped walking. "Look!" he whispered. "Someone is there, peering inside!"

We came to a complete halt. This was exactly what I had wanted to avoid. I grabbed Mars's sleeve and pulled him into a dark shadow. We crouched with Daisy between us. I hoped she wouldn't bark.

There was no question about it. Someone was peeking into the windows of the Inger House. The exterior lights hadn't been turned on, so all I could see was a figure in black.

Mars elbowed me. Without a word he pointed to a second figure moving stealthily past the house next door in a crouched position. If gunfire broke out, we were going to be shot. Why, oh why, had I agreed to this? Why hadn't I stayed home with Daisy and told Mars he should do the same?

The crouching figure drew closer. He rose to a standing position behind the peeper. We heard him say, "Hands up and against the window. Don't turn around."

But the person looking into the windows did turn around and screamed. It sounded like a woman! Could it be Rachel?

Chapter 8

Dear Natasha,
I'm expected to entertain six of my co-workers. Someone suggested a brunch because it would be easier and less formal. What will they expect?
Can't Cook in Two Egg, Florida

Dear Can't Cook,
At an absolute minimum, there should be coffee and tea, an egg dish, fruit, breads, and dessert. If you really don't cook, have it catered.
Natasha

The woman in black screamed again and tried to run. The cop tackled her and pinned her to the ground. I breathed a little easier because no bullets flew.

In spite of the darkness, we could see that the cop had handcuffed her.

"Could Mitzi's stalker be a woman?" I whispered to Mars.

The two of us rose. My legs were stiff from crouching.

The woman's angry voice floated to us. "What do you think you're doing? Do you know who I am?"

Mars looked over at me. I knew why. I recognized that voice, too.

"I guess we should help?" asked Mars.

Oh, but it was tempting to simply walk Daisy home.

"She'll call me from the police station," Mars muttered. "Or possibly you."

"We could turn off our phones." I didn't mean it, though, and knew we wouldn't.

We crossed the street to the sidewalk in front of the Inger House. The outside lights flicked on, confirming our fears.

Dirt and dust clung to Natasha's Peeping Tom outfit. "Mars, Sophie! Thank goodness you're here. Tell them who I am!"

"Hi, Anthony," I said to the officer. "Is Wolf here?"

"For heaven's sake! I have a TV show. Tell them, Sophie."

The officer ignored her plea. "Wolf is on his way. Do you know this woman?"

"I'm Natasha! Everyone who is anyone knows me."

Anthony rolled his eyes. "And I'm Anthony Watkins, Nala Watkins's boy."

I tried to hide my smirk. "How is your mom, Anthony?"

"Great! Gearing up for Halloween. You know how she loves ghosts."

"This is Natasha Smith," I said. "What were you doing looking in the windows?"

"I don't know what you're talking about. I was simply walking along, minding my own business when this brute of an officer tackled me!"

I leaned toward her and whispered, "It's best not to insult an arresting officer, Natasha."

"Arrest? You can't arrest me. In the first place I didn't do anything wrong. In the second place, I was minding my own business just taking a walk. I'm an upstanding citizen. You can ask anyone. Mars! Don't just stand there. Defend me already."

"I think you'd better stop insulting everyone and wait for Wolf," Mars grumbled.

"Some help you are! I'll never call you again if I'm in trouble."

"I would appreciate that." But he lessened the impact by saying it with a grin.

Thankfully, Wolf strode up to us. "Hello, Sophie, Mars, Daisy, Natasha." He casually looked around while he crouched to pet Daisy, who wagged her tail, happy to see her old friend.

If I hadn't known he was probably checking to see if the stalker might be watching, I wouldn't have realized that was what he was doing.

"Anthony, may I have a word?" he asked.

"Wait," cried Natasha. "Uncuff me first!"

Wolf ignored her and walked away with Anthony. We couldn't hear their conversation.

When they returned, Anthony removed the handcuffs.

Wolf's poker face had always annoyed me. I never could read him. But I knew him well enough to know he was a good man and would do the right thing.

"What were you doing at the Inger House tonight?" he asked Natasha.

"I was just passing by." She spoke in a haughty, annoyed voice.

"Show me where you were."

Natasha froze for just a beat too long. "Right here on the sidewalk. I don't understand why everyone is making such a big fuss."

Wolf crossed his arms over his chest and listened to her babble.

"You can see inside a lot of houses in Old Town.

They're close to the street. Honestly, that living room is so dated that it makes my skin crawl. Don't they know that less is more? Have they never heard of midcentury modern? Besides, no one is living here. Your officer has no business jumping people on the street. I have half a mind to lodge a complaint about this."

"Great. Then you won't mind coming down to the station so we can straighten all this out. Anthony, give her a ride, please."

I was in awe of Wolf's manner. He knew exactly how to get her to the station for further questioning. She thanked him and willingly stepped into the back of a police car as if she were taking a limo.

"Does she need a lawyer?" asked Mars in a low voice.

"That's up to her," said Wolf. "I seriously doubt that she had anything to do with Mitzi's stalker or Denise's murder. But it's my job to make certain. She sure blew our sting. Did the two of you notice anyone hanging around?"

"Just Natasha," said Mars.

"What were you doing here anyway?"

Mars gestured toward Daisy. "Walking the dog."

Wolf snickered. "Together? Yeah, right. And you just happened to pass the Inger House?"

"I came to be sure Mars wouldn't do anything stupid." I smiled and stroked Daisy.

Wolf shook his head and left. The lights in the Inger House went out, except for one in the kitchen.

"Well," said Mars. "At least *we* weren't the ones who blew the sting."

"They've left a light on. Think they're hoping the stalker might not have seen this and could still come?"

"It would be a long shot. But you never know. I suppose it's possible."

We ambled along the street, now quite dark. The lights on homes and streetlamps offered cozy glows. Mars insisted on walking me home and checking my house for intruders. There wasn't a reason in the world that Denise's killer or Mitzi's stalker would come after me. I thought Mars was being silly, but I went up to bed feeling safer because he had looked around.

THURSDAY

Early Thursday morning, someone knocked on my door. Daisy and Mochie jumped up and ran down the stairs. I slung on a bathrobe and followed them to the kitchen. Through the window in the door, I could see Mitzi, gazing around nervously.

"Good morning," I said cheerfully, as I opened the door.

Mitzi darted into my kitchen. "Is anyone else here?"

"No."

Her shoulders relaxed. "I woke you, didn't I? I'm so sorry. I felt as if I had to get here before people were up and about."

"You certainly accomplished that! Would you prefer coffee or tea?"

"Coffee, please. I need to be alert."

While I had my back to her, she gasped and ran for the stairs.

I whipped around just in time to see Nina walk in. "Good morning. You're up early."

"My husband had an early flight. Was that Mitzi?"

I nodded and set the kettle on the burner. "All clear, Mitzi!" I called.

Mitzi crept back into the kitchen. "Oh, it's only you, Nina. I'm sorry. I'm so skittish, but I have to be to stay alive."

"Mitzi!" Nina placed an arm around her shoulders. "Honey, I heard they caught someone last night."

Uh oh. "Whole wheat pumpkin waffles?" I asked.

Mitzi was far more interested in an arrest than what might be on the breakfast menu. Not that I could blame her. "They did? Wolf told me they didn't catch him. That something went wrong, and they'll try again tonight."

Nina poured hot water into my coffee press while I whipped together the eggs, flour, pumpkin, and heady, aromatic cinnamon, nutmeg, and just a touch of cloves for the waffles. I whipped cream with my immersion blender and poured maple syrup into a crystal creamer.

I turned the waffle maker to preheat and excused myself. I dashed upstairs and changed into comfortable stretch jeans and a deep green, mock-neck sweater. On my return, Mars had joined the group, and I caught the tail end of his version of the events the night before.

". . . Natasha willingly got into the squad car and was whisked away to the police station."

"Do you think Natasha could be my stalker?" asked Mitzi, her tone doubtful.

"Highly unlikely," I said while I made a quick fruit salad with thin slices of crunchy apples and juicy ripe pears, glistening red pomegranate seeds, tasty cantaloupe, grape halves, and chunks of walnuts. I sprinkled it with a tablespoon of sugar and a little fresh lemon juice and tossed it all together. Natasha had been known to do some odd things, but she would never be intentionally malicious. "What reason would she have?"

"Then why did she show up at the Inger House?" Mitzi looked worried.

"She made a snotty comment or two about the interior décor. I imagine she was snooping. Just very bad timing on her part probably."

"I'm so deflated. I thought for sure that the police would catch my stalker last night and I would be able to go home and live my life. Being in hiding has gotten old.

I'm going to lose my business if I don't get out there and work on the projects Denise and I had scheduled."

"I guess the important thing is to not be alone. Maybe you could hire an assistant for a while?" I asked. "You'll probably need someone anyway now that you don't have Denise."

"My husband is away. I'm not the best decorator in the world, but I could carry your samples," Nina offered as she set the table with Grace's Teaware Sage Green Leaves by Autumn Hill plates. I was thrilled that she chose them. The pastel blue and green pumpkins were a fun change from typical fall orange.

"You know," said Mitzi, "that might just be a good idea. There's a decorator in town who is driving me nuts. She must have called half a dozen times, but I don't care for her much. She's far too pushy. I've gotten clients because she drove them wild."

I served the waffles, placed the fruit salad on the table, and finally joined them.

"How interesting. Who is it?" asked Nina.

"Rachel Powers. Do you know her?"

I nearly dropped my fork. I tried to sound casual. "Did she call you before Denise died as well?"

Mitzi frowned. "Come to think of it, she did not. Our paths crossed once in a while. Old Town is like that. Most of the decorators are familiar with one another."

"What exactly is it that she wants from you?" asked Mars.

"She's interested in working together." Mitzi took a long drag of coffee. "It's . . . it's almost like she wants to step into Denise's shoes."

Nina's eyes met mine. I knew what she was thinking. The same thing I was. Rachel wanted Denise's life. More specifically, her husband and her job. "Mitzi, was Denise open about her diabetes?"

"What do you mean?"

"Did she tell people she was diabetic, talk about it with them?"

"She didn't hide it. But she didn't usually bring it up. I would guess most people didn't know. Her family did, of course. And I did. She handled it well and was quite low key. Why would anyone else need to know?"

It was possible to kill someone with an overdose of insulin even if they were not diabetic. But the fact that Denise had been diabetic made me wonder about the fact that her killer chose that method. "I think she might have been murdered by someone who knew about her diabetes and injected her with an overdose of insulin because it would appear to be accidental on Denise's part."

"Someone who knew her well enough to know she was diabetic." Mars helped himself to another waffle.

"That could be anyone," said Nina. "I bet a lot of people knew."

"Like Rachel," said Mitzi. "Oh my gosh! I asked her to help me! I might have hired my own stalker!" She stabbed another waffle, one of her eyes almost squeezing shut in a contorted expression. "I'm not hiding from *her*! Oh, that ticks me off. How dare she frighten me like this?"

Mars said calmly, "Don't go jumping to conclusions."

Nina elbowed him. "Are you kidding? I don't know why she would have been stalking Mitzi, but she's clearly interested in Mike Nofsinger and now she wants Denise's job? It does not look good for Rachel."

"I'm starved," declared Mitzi. "Now that I know who it is, my appetite has returned. Oh, what a relief! First task, Mike Nofsinger. He wanted to expand the primary bedroom. It's very small by today's standards and it needs a proper closet and a bathroom. Denise and I thought we could take the bedroom next to it and turn that into a bathroom and walk-in closet and still be able to give the master bedroom a little bit of that space."

"Denise just died," I said softly. "Have you spoken with Mike? Maybe he doesn't want to proceed with the renovations without her. He might want to sell the house."

The bright color in her cheeks drained from her face. "Of course. You're right. The Inger House must be the last thing on his mind right now. But there is someone I'm going to call. Wolf! This time we know whom we're after. And this time, we're going to get her."

"Hold on!" I said. "It's wise to mention her to Wolf, but her interest in Denise's job and husband don't add up to murder or stalking. It looks bad for her, but she could be completely innocent."

"Really? A woman who latches onto a man whose wife just died? I don't call that innocent," said Mitzi.

"Anyone want to split this with me?" Mars pointed at the last waffle.

"I will!"

Mars cut it and handed half to Mitzi. "You still need to be careful."

"If she hadn't called me, I wouldn't be suspecting Rachel at all. But Mike should know and be aware of what she's doing. Ohhh! What if I turned the tables on Rachel?"

Nina leaned toward her, clearly excited by the idea. "How would you do that?"

"What if I stalked *her*?"

Chapter 9

Dear Natasha,
My husband and I are building a retirement home.
I don't need a huge house. As far as I'm concerned,
the less to clean, the better. But a woman needs a
decent walk-in closet! Hubby just doesn't get it. He
says all he needs are shorts and couple of golf
shirts. How do I convince him that I deserve the
closet of my dreams?
                    Miffed Wife in Lady Lake, Florida

Dear Miffed Wife,
I understand completely! I bet he's not skimping
on the garage or space for his golf cart and golf
clubs. Put your foot down and tell him if you don't
get your closet, he can't have a golf cart.
                                        Natasha

"Whoa!" I cried. "Stalking is still illegal, even if you think you're turning the tables."

Mitzi stared at me. "You're a private investigator. I could hire you."

"I'm an event planner, not a private investigator. But I

can nose around a little bit and see what I might be able to find out."

Mitzi reached for my hand and squeezed it. "I'd appreciate that."

I turned down all offers to help me clean up and did the job myself when they left. There wasn't much to do, and it gave me some time to walk Daisy and think.

The police were probably going through Denise's computer and phone records right that minute to find out with whom she had been in touch before her death. As devastated as Mike seemed, there was always the possibility that Denise had an admirer who had murdered her when she didn't love him in return. I needed more insight into Denise's life. Preferably from someone close enough to have known what was going on, but not so close that he or she would clam up. Someone outside the Nofsinger clan.

Matt! Would he have talked with Denise about things other than the renovation in progress? I took a chance and called him. Mindful of the fact that he had high standards, I asked if he would like to join Daisy and me for brunch at an upscale café overlooking the river.

He sounded surprisingly happy that I had called. We agreed on a time, and I headed home with Daisy.

Matt arrived at the café precisely at eleven o'clock. He wore khaki trousers with a well-fitting, navy-blue sport coat. We sat at a table by the window, overlooking the Potomac River.

"Thank you for inviting me. It has been ages since I had brunch and I do enjoy it," said Matt. "I hope they have Eggs Benedict."

"Have you seen all the posts online about brunch in Old Town?"

"They almost make me want to cook. It feels so indulgent. We deserve it, don't we?"

We ordered our meal, Eggs Benedict for both of us. The server brought it promptly. The restaurant served it with asparagus and little rosemary roasted potatoes.

After a discussion about the delicious eggs, Matt said, "I'm fairly certain that we are not here because you're seeking etiquette advice."

I laughed. "If I *were* seeking etiquette advice, I would most certainly come to you. But you're quite right. I need some information. It sounds as if you may have been one of the last people to spend much time with Denise before her demise."

Matt looked out at the water. "You're probably correct about that."

"I was hoping she might have talked about her personal life a bit. Was she having problems with Mike?"

"No. She joked about him sometimes, but in the sweet way that wives do. She said that she and Mike were cramped in their condo, and she hoped to build a lot of closet space into the Inger House. But Mike would have a cow if she told him all her plans for the house. She was looking forward to renovating it and moving in."

"Did you get the feeling she phoned him a lot or was checking up on him?"

Matt raised his eyebrows. "Oh! You suspect the husband! No. Nothing like that."

"No mention of another woman or someone chasing him?"

Matt sipped his iced tea and thought for a moment. "She never took phone calls in front of me. Frankly, I thought that was simply good manners. When one is in the presence of another person, one ought not to take calls or even look at one's phone." He wiggled his forefinger in the air. "Unless . . . someone is about to give birth, and everyone is waiting for the call to rush to the hospital."

I laughed. That was definitely a good reason. "Did she seem upset about anything?"

"Given the nature of your questions, I must ask if it is true that the police believe her death was not an accident?"

"I'm afraid she was murdered."

"I see. Clearly, it is the height of impropriety to gossip. However, given the circumstances, it is incumbent on us all to share what we might know. She told me that her business partner, Mitzi, was prone to being needlessly hysterical and imagined danger. Apparently, her father is a police officer and constantly reminds her of danger everywhere. What to do if someone jumps into her car or tries to enter her home. Consequently, she was making Denise crazy imagining the worst. It was driving Denise nuts."

Had I fallen for Mitzi's hysteria? Maybe she wasn't being stalked at all. "Did Denise bring a purse when she came to work at your house?"

"What an odd question. She carried a large bag. You couldn't possibly miss it. A light tan, which I thought appropriate for the season, and it went well with most of her clothes. It was packed with samples and the like."

"Was she prone to misplacing it or leaving it behind?"

"Not that I recall. No, I'm certain that she didn't. She was very professional and pulled together. None of that where-did-I-put-something nonsense some people go through. It wasn't as though she had flung things into her bag. She was quite thoughtful and organized."

"Did she talk about her health at all?"

"My goodness. Health? No. I'd have remembered that. Most of my friends have reached an age where the main topic of conversation is their latest ailment with detailed and grotesque descriptions, and they insist on showing me parts of their bodies that ought not be made public."

The waiter brought us strawberry tarts for dessert. I took a bite, wishing Denise hadn't been quite so appropriately businesslike.

Matt gazed around surreptitiously and then leaned toward me. "I can tell you this, though. Thurman and I belong to the same golf club. The man thinks nothing of cheating. I wouldn't believe a word he says."

I walked home and had barely reached my door when Natasha hailed me and my phone rang.

I answered the phone while Natasha hurried across the street, slightly breathless. "Do you think you could get an invitation to the Inger House? I can't go there because of what happened. It was all a mistake, of course, but I'm dying to see the inside."

I held up a finger as an indication to wait a minute. But the call disconnected. It had been from someone called ML. Mitzi Lawson, maybe?

"You know Mitzi. Why don't you give her a call? She's working on the house."

"I've tried, but she's not answering her business number."

So she was still in hiding. She probably didn't want to take Natasha's call because there was a possibility that Natasha was her stalker. I didn't think so, but Mitzi was operating out of fear.

"Give me a second, please. I think that may have been Mitzi calling." I phoned the number that had just called. She answered in a whisper. "Sophie?"

"Hi, Mitzi. Is everything all right?"

"No." The line crackled.

"Where are you?" I asked.

"Inger" was all I heard before the call cut off.

"Something's wrong." I phoned 911 and asked them to respond to the Inger House. I started walking as fast as I could, and Natasha joined me. The operator asked all the questions she was supposed to ask, but I didn't have any answers. "Mitzi Lawson called me from there and said something was wrong. But the line went dead." I ended the call and broke into a feeble jog.

"Are we going to the Inger House?" Natasha asked eagerly.

"Natasha, I'm warning you. You will hate it. It's not minimalist and was probably last updated seventy years ago. I don't want to hear one word of criticism from you. Mitzi is in trouble."

"Oh come on! You're my bestie, but I hate it when you're bossy. You treat me like a child sometimes. Everyone thinks it's awful."

"Really? Who would *everyone* be?"

"My mother, my half sister, her mother, Mars, Nina . . ."

I laughed at her. "You wish! I happen to know that's not true. Good try."

"What if I promise to only make constructive suggestions?" she asked.

Ohh! I knew what that meant. She gave me those helpful instructions all the time. "No. Natasha, Mitzi is a professional and needs to make changes according to the tastes and interests of her client. You may say that you like something in particular, but you may not criticize or give any other opinion. Are we straight on that?"

"Nag, nag, nag," she muttered.

I knocked the bald eagle door knocker on the front door. No one responded.

"Maybe she's upstairs and can't hear the knocker," I said.

I tried the doorknob. The door opened with a creak worthy of a horror movie. "Mitzi?" I called. "Mitzi?"

Stacks of large boxes crowded the foyer. The dining

room had been changed, but I didn't have time to stop and appreciate it.

"Mitzi?" I called. It was a large house, and I was seriously concerned. I peeked into the kitchen. It remained untouched and Mitzi was nowhere to be seen.

Furniture in the living room had been bunched toward the middle. Everything had been removed from the walls. "Mitzi!" Surely she wouldn't have gone out and left the house unlocked.

"Ugh. This room should have been updated years ago," said Natasha. "I feel as if I walked into the 1950s."

I started moving faster, through the family room and into the first-floor bedroom. The pile of clothes on the bed had grown and more clothing lay on the floor in a large pile, topped by a lady's heavy red and black checked wool coat. I poked at the clothes to be sure she wasn't underneath them. "Mitzi?" I shouted, moving a big stack of them to the bed. I lifted more, until I was certain no one was underneath.

Natasha replied, "Coming. That conservatory is amazing." Her voice was distant.

The thud of the door knocker sounded through the house. "Natasha! Open the door!"

When the door knocker thudded again, I left the bedroom and ran through the house to the front door, which had just opened. To my relief, Wong had arrived, and the ambulance was just pulling up to the house.

I was leading Wong through the foyer when we heard a scream. We rushed to the back bedroom and found Natasha gazing at the piles of clothes on the bed and the floor. "What a mess. The duffle coat with toggle closures that's on the bed is ancient. That hasn't been in style in decades. Didn't this family ever get rid of anything?"

Wong and I exchanged an annoyed look. Natasha and I

accompanied Wong through the upper level of the house as she checked to see if anyone was hiding. As they went along checking the bedrooms, I came to an abrupt stop at a bathroom with old blue tile. Someone had left a toothbrush in a glass by the sink, along with a tube of toothpaste. I looked at it closely. The toothbrush looked damp. A tiny bit of water had rolled down to the bottom of the glass. Was someone staying in the house?

I hadn't paid much attention to the beds upstairs. I went back through the bedrooms for a second look. All of the beds were neatly made with pillows and comforters, ready for someone to nestle down and sleep.

While Wong checked out the attic, I looked in the basement, which was creepy. It lacked an exterior door, but offered a series of ancient rooms that gave me the willies.

I returned to the foyer, hurried through the dining room and kitchen to the door that opened to the backyard. It was a nice size by Old Town standards, but in spite of the trees and lawn furniture, it was easy to see that Mitzi wasn't there. I walked toward the gate slowly, searching the ground for anything that might indicate she had been there, or heaven forbid, had been dragged out of the yard. I opened the gate with my elbow, not an easy feat, but I didn't want to leave fingerprints. Her absence was beginning to make me fear she had been removed from the premises. I stepped into the alley and looked both ways, but didn't see anything out of the ordinary. I considered asking the immediate neighbors if they had heard anything, but that seemed like a job for the police, and I didn't want to step on their toes. If Wong didn't think it was necessary, then I would do it myself. I was still in the alley when I tried Mitzi's cell phone again.

She didn't answer. It rolled over to voice mail. "Mitzi, this is Sophie. I'm at the Inger House but there's no sign of you. If you're here, it's safe to come out. Wong is with us. Call me, please! I'm very worried about you."

I closed the gate and walked back to the kitchen.

Wong shot me an annoyed look. "We were beginning to think you fell down the same rabbit hole as Mitzi."

"Everyone is jittery. At least I have a witness that she called me."

"Your phone is better proof." Wong held her hand out for my phone.

I handed it to her.

"Is this the call? From ML?"

"Yes."

"How do you know it was from Mitzi?" asked Wong.

"It sounded like her. And she said 'Inger House.'"

"Do you not watch the news? With artificial intelligence, people can make it sound exactly like someone you know is calling you."

"I saw that on TV," said Natasha. "It wouldn't fool me!"

"Aren't *you* lucky," muttered Wong.

If I hadn't been so concerned about Mitzi, I might have laughed at Wong's sarcasm. "Did you notice the toothbrush in the upstairs bathroom? I didn't see it the first time I went through the house."

"You think Mitzi is staying here?" asked Wong.

"Someone might be."

"Look, Sophie. I don't know what's going on here, but it's a house. Maybe Denise left it there. Maybe her husband is sleeping over here. Maybe the people who moved out left it there. I'm going to send the ambulance away and write up an incident report." Wong left the kitchen. I could hear her telling the EMTs they could go.

"This is a dreadful kitchen." Natasha opened a cabinet that creaked. "I'm shocked that no one has updated it. This house could be beautiful. The room sizes alone are fantastic. It's hard to find a place with this much potential."

It was true that the kitchen needed a complete overhaul. I couldn't deny that. "Come on. Wong's probably waiting for us so she can lock the house."

We didn't make it far. The dining room stopped us. Mitzi had installed a stunning wallpaper with a white background. Woodsy vines in shades of brown wound up the wall accented by occasional apricot flowers. She had kept the antique table, chandelier, and buffets. The dark mahogany of the furniture worked beautifully with the browns in the wallpaper. And the white background prevented the brownish theme from being too dark. But it was the surprising addition of cranberry fabric on the seats of the Chippendale chairs that livened the entire room. I never would have expected that.

"I really should update my dining room," mused Natasha.

That was about the highest compliment I'd ever heard from her.

"Come on, you two. I have real work to do." Wong motioned to us.

When we walked out, I asked if she would be contacting neighbors.

Wong groaned. "I will not. There isn't a bit of evidence in that house that something happened to Mitzi. You know I have a lot of respect for you, Sophie, but I am not impressed with that phone call you received. In fact, whoever sent it as a prank is probably watching right now and laughing his head off at the commotion he caused."

I should have felt foolish, but I didn't. "If Mitzi wasn't here, then why was the front door unlocked when we arrived?"

Wong frowned as she considered that.

"Oh please," said Natasha. "How many Nofsingers are there? Any one of them might have dropped by the house and forgotten to lock up."

That was undoubtedly true. But I had a bad feeling about it. Why couldn't Natasha or I reach Mitzi by phone? If nothing was wrong, wouldn't she be answering? Or calling back?

Chapter 10

Dear Sophie,
My wife loves pillows. I don't have a problem with them in general. They can be very useful for an afternoon snooze on a sofa. But we have so many pillows on our bed that it has become a fifteen-minute nightmare to remove them each night. Frankly, I'm tempted to throw them out the window. How do I convince my wife to ditch the pillows?

*   Please Save My Marriage in Pillow, Pennsylvania*

Dear Please Save My Marriage,
Pillows are wonderful, but sometimes, less is more. Your wife is probably trying to bring more texture into the room. Make a deal with her. You'll take your wife shopping for a fabulous new comforter or duvet and a small throw as an accent if she cuts the number of pillows down to five. The new comforter and throw will add the plush look she's trying to accomplish. And she won't want to cover them up with pillows!

*   Sophie*

Wong reached inside and locked the door to the Inger House before pulling it closed. Rather reluctantly, she said, "Call me if anything else happens. My guess is that Mitzi will turn up and be astounded to hear about this." She hustled down the street.

I gazed at the neighboring houses, wondering who lived there. Hadn't they seen or heard anything the day Denise was murdered? They didn't notice anyone hanging around or sneaking into the house?

"Well? Are we going to stand here all day?" asked Natasha.

"Do you know who lives next door?" I asked.

We strode along the sidewalk and stopped in front of a red brick house with a coveted oval plaque by the front door, indicating it was a historic building.

The front door opened, and a bald man bounded out. "Natasha! To what do I owe this honor?"

Her face flamed red. "Jesse. I didn't know you lived here."

He ambled down the steps toward us. "Sorry I wasn't home the night you tussled with the cops. I'd have been the first one out here to help you."

"Oh. You heard about that?" Natasha sounded uncomfortable.

"You're a local star! What are you doing hanging out here?" His eyes widened. "Are you going to buy the Inger House?"

"I wish I could! Jesse McGuire, this is my best friend, Sophie Winston. Sophie, as if you can't tell, Jesse owns a local gym."

He wore a T-shirt with the name Synergy emblazoned across the front. Bulging muscles stretched the short sleeves. It was hard not to notice his ocean blue eyes. He smiled at me and gently shook my hand. "Sophie? Seems like I've heard your name."

"Possibly. Were you home the last couple of hours? Did you hear anything going on at the Inger House?"

"Sorry, I was at the gym. I came home to take care of a couple of things."

"How about the day Denise died?"

"I spend my days at work. You should come down. You'd like it. It's a more modern approach to taking care of your body. Some of my guys are into body building, but we also offer yoga and massages. It's a whole wellness concept that is spreading into the industry. We're not just workout machines anymore."

His physique was a testament to his business. But I wasn't sure if he was evading my question or just trying to get in a pitch for his company. "You were there the morning Denise died?"

He nodded. "I barely knew her. She introduced herself when she saw me on the street. Right about where we are now. I can't believe anything so awful could have happened to her."

I had rushed out so fast that I didn't have anything to write on. "If I give you my phone number, would you text me if you notice anything peculiar at the Inger House?"

"Sure." He rattled off his phone number so I could text my number to him.

"Thank you. I appreciate that."

"Does this have anything to do with Denise's death?" he asked.

"Maybe. We're not quite sure."

"I'm happy to help. I've got to run, but it was nice meeting you." He leaned toward Natasha and kissed her cheek.

She stiffened and blushed.

When we were out of hearing distance, I asked, "What's with you and that guy?"

Natasha groaned. "Why is life so complicated? If only Mars were as crazy about me as Jesse. It's not as if he stalks me or anything. He's just infatuated with me. It's under-standable, of course. He's not the only one. You wouldn't understand."

"He seemed nice enough. Maybe you should go out with him."

"He's not my type. I will win Mars back. Just watch me."

Poor Mars. Actually, if Natasha hadn't been with me, I would have stopped by Mars's house to find out if Mitzi still occupied his rental home. But, given the circum-stances, I thought it best to skip a visit to Mars.

At home, I put on the kettle for a bracing cup of black tea. I had a lot of respect for Wong, but she had been very quick to dismiss the phone call I received from Mitzi. Nat-urally, she knew a lot more about scams that were in progress, but I was the one who heard Mitzi's voice and I felt certain it had been a legitimate call. But where was Mitzi? Why had she said Inger House to me? She could have been trying to say a hundred things. I just hoped she was all right, wherever she was.

I poured boiling water over my tea bag and phoned Mitzi again. She didn't pick up at either number that I had for her. Unlike Wong, I tended to believe that ML could very well be Mitzi. She probably didn't want to put her full name on her new throwaway phone. And none of us should forget that we knew for certain that someone had placed a device in her purse so he could follow her.

To my way of thinking, all that added up to the possi-bility that Mitzi was in some kind of trouble. I wished I had an AirTag on her right now so I could find her.

I had a million things to do for work, but I couldn't focus. Instead, I dressed Daisy in her harness and took her for a long, leisurely walk. It was good for both of us to get out in the fall air.

We stopped at Mars and Bernie's rental property. I knocked on the door gently. No one answered. I didn't want to say Mitzi's name in case someone was listening. "If you are in there, please text me."

I steered Daisy away and walked on the other side of the street, keeping an eye on the house in case a curtain moved. No such luck.

Daisy and I continued by Mike's condo, where I couldn't see anything and had no idea which balcony might be his. The street where Helena lived was peaceful. We even walked by Mitzi's house, which sported a beautiful pumpkin-themed wreath on the front door. No one answered when I knocked.

I felt foolish. What had I expected to see? A hand pressed against a window? A note tossed down in my direction?

We passed the house where Mars and Bernie resided on our way home. I caught Mars on his way out to a dinner meeting.

"Have you heard from Mitzi?" I asked.

"Nope. I need to get hold of her. We have someone checking in on Monday."

"Let me know if she contacts you?"

"Sure will, Soph. Sorry, gotta run."

There wasn't anything I could do except hope that when darkness fell, Mitzi would be daring enough to visit me through my alley again. If she could. If she was alive. Or had she simply imagined something, as Matt had suggested?

FRIDAY

Mitzi didn't show up at my house that night. In the morning when I let Daisy out, I went with her, bundled up in a warm fleece bathrobe and fuzzy slippers. Hoping I had missed Mitzi's knock on the door while I slept, I checked around to see if she had left a note, but I didn't find anything. Daisy sniffed grass and moseyed along. I'd hoped she might follow a trail to the gate indicating someone had been there. We returned to the house. I fed Mochie and Daisy, then headed upstairs to shower and dress.

An hour later when I was making apple cider cranberry muffins, Nina showed up at the door, followed by Bernie and Mars. I slid the muffins into the oven. "Great timing. I'm testing a fall muffin recipe. How about some scrambled eggs?"

In no time at all, Mars nuked bacon slices, Nina prepared coffee and tea, and Bernie cooked the eggs. All I had to do was set the table with my pumpkin plates and set out a platter of fresh-from-the oven muffins.

"Did you find Mitzi?" asked Mars.

"Mitzi is missing?" asked Nina.

I filled them all in about the odd phone call from Mitzi. "I'm very worried about her. What if her stalker caught up with her and hurt her? What if she needs help? I have left multiple messages, but she does doesn't answer or call me back."

Bernie sipped his coffee. "She's working for Mike, right?"

"I think so, but I'm not sure. The whole Nofsinger clan went out of town for Denise's funeral. But someone went to a lot of trouble to update the dining room in the Inger House. I don't know if all that was planned before Denise died. I don't even know if he still plans to move into the house."

"Yeah," said Nina. "Knowing that someone had died in the house would be awful. I would consider selling."

"Nina," said Mars. "I hate to break this to you, but someone has probably died in a lot of these historic houses. Back in the day, most people died at home."

"Eww. Thank you so much for telling me that."

"My point is that while it would be upsetting to think about it every day, you have lived in your house happily for years," said Mars.

Bernie reached for a muffin. "Why don't you call Mike and ask if he has heard from her?"

"An excellent idea. And while you've got him on the phone, ask if he would mind if we looked around the house to be sure she's not there," said Mars.

"Wong searched the house yesterday." I bit into one of the muffins.

"Maybe we'll notice something she overlooked," said Mars. "It's really all we can do at this point."

That was the sad truth. I brought my phone to the table and called, putting it on speaker so everyone could hear.

"Hello?"

"Hi, Mike. It's Sophie Winston with Nina, Mars Winston, and Bernie Frei. How are you holding up?"

"Oh! Sophie. It's nice of you to call. I'm just putting one foot in front of the other. Trying to keep going. Denise was buried at her family's plot out of state. Now that I'm home, everything is scary quiet. I'm going back to work today even though I don't have to. I just don't want to be home alone. You know? It would be good to think about something else for a little while."

"That's understandable. Focusing on work might be helpful. I was wondering if you had heard from Mitzi."

"She called me a couple of days ago about the dining room and that little bedroom in the back. Wallpaper arrived or something. I didn't . . . couldn't care. I told her to do whatever Denise would have done. Maybe I'll come to regret that, but it's all so unimportant to me right now. Packages of things that Denise ordered keep arriving. I toss them in a pile unopened. It's as if the world stopped for me but not for anyone else."

"I think it's only natural to feel that way, Mike. Is Rachel still annoying you?"

"Day and night since I came back to town." He paused

for a moment. "Except for today. But it's early yet. I'm sure I'll hear from her soon."

"Hey, Mike! It's Mars Winston. How about grabbing a beer with Bernie and me tonight? Six o'clock at The Laughing Hound?"

"Sure. That would be good."

Mars continued. "Listen, no one knows where Mitzi is. We'd like to go over to the Inger House to look around for her. Is that okay?"

After a seemingly long moment of silence, Mike said, "You think someone killed her, too?"

"No. It's just odd that no one can reach her. Sophie received a strange call from her yesterday. We'd like to find her, so we'll know she's okay."

"Yeah, yeah. I'll meet you there in half an hour. Bye."

We skipped washing the dishes, but stacked them in the sink so Daisy wouldn't be tempted to clean them for us. I packed a couple of muffins for Mike, and we left Muppet with Mochie and Daisy. The four of us hurried over to the Inger House, which appeared sedate and majestic from the street.

Mike arrived a few minutes later, looking rough. He probably hadn't been sleeping. Maybe not eating, either. We exchanged greetings. I suspected that he hadn't shaved since he returned from the funeral.

"Mike, have you started to move over here?" I asked.

"No. But maybe I should. I see Denise everywhere I look in our condo. Mom thought I should give it a little time, but being here might be better for me."

I wasn't sure the building where his wife was murdered would be an improvement. But I thought I'd better keep that to myself.

He grabbed the edge of a plant urn and tilted it. "The key is gone."

Mars tried the door handle. The door swung open with a horrifying creak.

"We should look around in teams," said Mars. "I'll check the first floor with Sophie. Bernie, you and Mike take the upstairs with Nina."

"Hello?" I shouted.

"Are you insane?" asked Nina. "Why would you alert the person who broke in?"

"What if it's Helena or Jacky? Or Mitzi? They would be scared out of their wits if they heard a bunch of people tromping around inside the house."

"If they're afraid," said Bernie, "why would they leave the front door unlocked so anyone could walk in?"

He had a good point. Bernie led the way up the stairs, while Mars and I checked out the kitchen.

It looked just as it had the last time I saw it. I opened the door and gazed around the backyard. Nothing new there. When I returned, Mars asked in a whisper, "Is this where Denise died?"

I nodded.

His lips bunched together. "I think Nina is right. Getting up every morning and walking in here knowing what happened to Denise would be tough. If it were my wife, I don't think I could handle that."

"Not even if it were completely redone?"

He shrugged. "Maybe. But it would have to be completely different."

Remembering the toothbrush and toothpaste I had seen, I checked the trash can under the sink. I closed the cabinet and checked the fridge. Five bottles remained in a six pack of Heineken. "Do you think someone could be staying here?"

"Did you look in the refrigerator before? The beer could have been there before Denise was killed."

"Very true."

We headed for the living room, looked around the conservatory, which Mars loved, and walked into the family room. There was no sign of Mitzi. In fact, I didn't think anything had changed at all and that our visit was a complete waste of time as far as finding Mitzi. We went upstairs. The toothbrush and toothpaste were there, exactly as they had been before.

Downstairs, we peeked into the small first-floor bedroom. Mars looked in the tiny bathroom and I studied the heap of clothes. Something was different. The duffle coat with toggle closures was gone.

Piles of clothing had fallen off the bed and onto the floor. I thought back to the previous day. I was pretty sure I had heaped clothes on the bed in a manner that they wouldn't slide off. I didn't think for a second that the clothes had simply fallen off the bed again.

I walked over to the pile on the floor between the bed and the wall beneath a window.

"What are you doing?" asked Mars.

"I put most of these clothes back on the bed yesterday."

"So they slid off. There are so many. It was bound to happen."

I grabbed a bunch and placed them on the bed. And another bunch.

"Soph, we don't have time to clean up this entire house today. And maybe they wouldn't want us doing that anyway."

"I can't imagine that Helena knows about this pile of clothing. She wouldn't leave them in a mess like this."

"Whoever did it had a reason, I'm sure."

I doubted that. I picked up another stack and let out a little scream. I jumped back, holding the clothes in my arms.

"Mouse?" Mars chuckled.

I only wished it were a mouse. I dropped the clothes on the bed. My hands trembled. "Mars, I think there's some-one under the clothes."

"What?" He leaned over me. "Where? I don't see any-thing."

The space between the bed and the wall wasn't huge. I tried not to step on the garments when I wedged closer, but it was impossible. I lost my footing and pitched for-ward, my hand landing on silky blond hair. I couldn't help squealing.

Mars held out his hand and pulled me up toward him. "I still don't see anything."

Clearly, I needed to work on the pile from the end clos-est to us. I picked up clothes by the armful and tossed them on the bed in an untidy heap.

"There. Now do you see something?" I pointed at a foot in a sleek, high-heeled, black shoe.

Chapter 11

This time it was Mars who yelped and jumped backward away from the foot.

I was already on my phone with the 911 operator.

Mars snapped a photo with his phone.

"Gross! What are you doing?" I asked.

"Don't you want the cops to see how the body was hidden? We have to move the clothes off her. What if she's alive?"

I completed the call, left my phone on the nightstand, and helped Mars toss clothes on the bed.

Bernie raced into the room, with Mike and Nina on his heels. "What's with all the screaming?"

"Give us a hand, will you?" asked Mars.

The two of us pitched clothes to Bernie and Mike until we could see the entire body.

I squeezed past Mars, bent over, and moved blond hair off her face. For a moment I was stunned.

"Is it Mitzi?" Nina asked breathlessly from the other side of the room.

I looked up at Mike. "It's Rachel."

I reached for her neck, hoping to find a pulse. "I'm not getting anything." I lifted her hand and sought a pulse on her wrist. Nothing.

"Hello?" It sounded like Wong. "Sophie? Nina?"

Nina dashed out of the room.

Mars tried to find a pulse on her ankle, but he had no luck, either.

The heavy sound of EMTs walking across the hardwood floor came near. We cleared out of the way to make room for them.

Wong followed them in for a look.

One of the EMTs asked the standard questions about who she was and whether she had any medical conditions.

We all looked at Mike, who shrugged.

"Her name is Rachel Powers. She's an interior decorator. I don't think any of us know her well enough to tell you anything about her medical situation," I told them.

He thanked us and went to assist the others.

Wong emerged from the bedroom. We exchanged looks when we heard her calling Wolf. When she was finished with that, she said, "Perhaps you can tell me what you're doing here?"

"I still haven't heard from Mitzi. No one has," I said.

Nina piped up. "We thought we should come back and have another look. See if there was anything that we might have missed yesterday."

Wong sighed. "Well, I guess that was a good thing. I better search the house again."

"Mike is the new owner. Mike, have you met Officer Wong?" I asked.

"Not personally. I've seen you around, though," he said.

Wong reached out to shake his hand. "Want to come with me?"

"Sure."

The two of them headed for the foyer. I could hear her asking, "What's all this in the boxes?"

Bernie, Mars, and Nina disappeared somewhere, but I stayed and listened as one of the EMTs reported finding Rachel dead and was told the medical examiner would be on the way.

I honestly didn't want to jump to conclusions or think badly about anyone, but I couldn't help remembering how we had to sneak Mike away from Rachel. Why had she been here anyway? Had she come to meet Mitzi and work with her? Had she walked in on her own using the key that was under the flowerpot? Was she curious like Natasha and wanted to see the house? Or was she dreaming of living in it with Mike? It was pretty audacious to just walk into a house, even if you thought no one was living there. And how did she know about the key? Or did someone leave the door unlocked and she happened into a trap?

Poor Rachel. I hadn't liked the way she went after Mike when he had just lost his wife, but I felt certain she didn't deserve this. And I was just a tad queasy about the possibility that Mike might have been responsible for her death. I hoped he had a very good alibi.

Wong returned from her run through the house and met me in the dining room.

"What are you thinking?" asked Wong.

"That someone hit her over the head and then took the clothes out of the armoires and used them to cover her body."

"In the hope that no one would notice her," said Nina.

"Exactly."

"It's a different modus operandi than before," said Wong.

I nodded. "Her purse. Did he take her purse?"

Wong and I rushed toward the kitchen with Nina on our heels.

But the kitchen counters looked just as they had days ago. "It's possible that Rachel didn't bring anything with her, but that seems unlikely."

"Okay, hold everything," said Nina. "People steal purses for money or to use the credit cards. It was probably some guy who was walking by. Why would you think it wasn't?"

"It could have been," I said. "Wong, maybe you should ask the doctors to look for injection sites and test her for an insulin overdose."

Wong blew air out of her mouth. "Whoever it was clearly expected her to die. Otherwise he wouldn't have hidden her body under all those clothes."

"You keep saying *he*, but an insulin injection might be the kind of thing a woman would do, you know?" said Nina. "It wouldn't require much strength."

Wong shook a finger at her. "We need to keep this quiet. No blabbing, you hear me? The less the assailant knows, the better."

"You don't have to tell *me* that," said Nina. "I don't socialize with any murderers."

Good grief. "Nina, it could be anyone."

At that moment Wolf walked in and shot me a not-you-again look. "Hello, Sophie."

"Hi, Wolf, right through here." I led him to the EMTs with Rachel.

The medical examiner arrived on Wolf's heels. I pointed him in the right direction. It must have been getting crowded back there.

Wolf asked Wong to gather us in the family room and take down the names of everyone who had been present. Then he shooed us out the door so we wouldn't get in the way of the forensic team. A crowd had gathered outside. They peppered us with questions. We had no answers and simply walked away.

I worried about Mitzi and wondered aloud if I should ask the police to do a wellness check.

"We could pay her a visit," said Nina. "Let's try that first."

The five of us headed for her home. It seemed to me that Mike came along because he didn't want to be alone. He had to be in some degree of shock about Rachel's death, even if he wasn't crazy about her. I suspected I wasn't the only person wondering if Mike had been responsible for Rachel's demise, but we couldn't talk about that in front of him.

At Mitzi's, Mars knocked on the door. "Mitzi?"

When she didn't answer, I tried pounding on the door. "Mitzi!"

"Maybe we should try the alley," said Mike.

An older man with a dour face opened the door of the house next to Mitzi's. "What is all this racket?"

Mars introduced himself to the neighbor and apologized for disturbing him.

"You get out of here and leave Mitzi alone." His eyes narrowed. "One of you fellas following her around?"

"No, sir!" said Mars. "We're checking up on her. Making sure she's all right."

The man leaned toward him. "If she wanted to see you, she'd open the door. Go away!"

When we turned to leave, Mars said in a loud voice, "We'll simply call the police for a wellness check. They'll come over right away and park a couple of police cars outside the building while they look around."

The old man bellowed, "That will not be necessary."

We stopped in our tracks. Mars's back was to him, and I caught his big grin before he turned around.

The man pointed at Mars. "You, big mouth, and the lady to your right come with me. The rest of you wait on the sidewalk."

The old grouch went inside his house and returned with a key.

"We're worried about her. Thank you very much for letting us in. I'd hate to think she might be hurt or sick. I don't believe I caught your name?"

"Cromwell," he grunted.

"Thank you, Mr. Cromwell," I said.

Cromwell unlocked the door. Mitzi had decorated her home in Nancy Meyers style. Natural light flooded in through tall windows. The walls, sofa, and chairs were white, but colorful pillows and books adorned the living room. I knew she had chosen them carefully, but it didn't appear that way. A giant bunch of blue, white, and purple hydrangea in a French watering can were classic Nancy Meyers. The two bedrooms on the second floor had a similar aesthetic.

In the kitchen, two small bowls were on the floor. "I forgot that she has a cat!" I opened a cabinet and found cat food, confirming that fact. "Poppy!"

I breathed a little easier when we didn't find Mitzi. She hadn't fallen or become too ill to call for help. "Do you see a cat anywhere?"

"Nope. But it's a nice place," muttered Mars.

I went through the house again in search of the cat. I knew from experience that cats were experts at hiding, especially from strange voices. I looked under the beds but didn't find it.

"Do you think she's staying in a hotel?" I asked.

"She's not at my rental house. We had it cleaned and someone from out of town is staying there now."

"She didn't return the key?"

"Not yet."

We thanked Mr. Cromwell, who, after all his grouchiness, also appeared relieved that he didn't have an emergency situation next door.

But the question remained. Where was Mitzi? I might have overlooked her cat but was now hopeful that the absence of a cat meant she had taken it with her.

Mike seemed to be at a loss. Bernie suggested we grab some lunch at a new restaurant he wanted to check out.

It wasn't far from where we were, and Mike was game to come along. The scents of basil and garlic hit us the minute we walked inside. Basic wood tables and chairs occupied the space, but one's attention immediately went to the art on the walls. Each painting bore a price tag along with the name of the local artist.

Bernie ordered meals for the table to share, and it wasn't long before fresh-from-the-oven pizzas showed up, one vegetarian, one for meat lovers, and one with barbecued chicken. Our server also brought us salads, as well as lasagna and manicotti to try. It was far too much food, but we loved sampling bites of everything.

It took our minds off Mitzi and Rachel for a while, but eventually, the conversation drifted back to the house.

"Why do they call it *the Inger House* when most of your family are Nofsingers?" asked Bernie.

"It was built by my great-great-grandfather, Willie Inger. My great-grandfather lived there after that, and he was an Inger, too. I guess the name caught on then and just stayed that way."

"You're very lucky to have a house like that in your family." Nina took another bite of her pizza.

"That's what Denise said. My grandmother, Helena, was very happy that Denise was an interior designer because the house is in dire need of updating."

"Did your parents ever live there?" asked Bernie.

"Dad lived there as a kid. But my mom has horses and wanted a place with land, so I grew up in Great Falls and they still live there. My great-aunt Jacky and her husband, Stu, have lived in the Inger House for as long as I can remember."

"That's so sweet," said Nina. "They handed it over to you to start your family."

It was the wrong thing to say.

I thought Mike might break down, but he took a deep breath and muttered, "It's not quite as thoughtful as that. Jacky and Stu have knee problems and can't do stairs like they used to. They don't much care for the tiny first-floor bedroom, so I guess I was next in line."

"You could always sell it." Mars sipped ice water.

Mike finally grinned. "And be disowned by the entire family? Actually, I think it's kind of cool to still have the house. I'll probably move in soon. I don't cook, so it wouldn't matter if the kitchen was being renovated. And I've always loved the conservatory. I spent a lot of time playing in there as a kid. I'd like to bring it back to the amazing place it used to be."

I watched him as he spoke. Clearly, he felt a strong connection to his roots, which was laudable. As much as I hated to do so, I couldn't help wondering if Rachel pushed him too far. Had he flipped out and killed her? He was clearly struggling with the loss of his wife and Rachel had been relentless in pursuing him. And there was that one other little thing that I couldn't dismiss. Mike seemed at a loss, as if he didn't know what to do without Denise. But there was a reason that the police considered spouses first. Was it possible that he had designs on someone else and had killed his wife?

I pushed that ugly notion out of my head. It wasn't until we were walking home that I wondered if he killed Denise because he was in love with Mitzi. The mere thought sent shivers through me.

I should have worked that afternoon. But I found it difficult to focus with Denise and Rachel dead, and Mitzi missing. I could only hope that Mitzi was still alive somewhere. After cleaning up the kitchen from breakfast, I baked an apple cider cake to test the recipe for our upcoming brunch.

Each time the phone rang, I jumped, afraid it would be bad news about Mitzi. I set the cake on the counter to cool while I ventured up to my attic.

It contained a bedroom, a small bathroom, and a huge storage area. I ventured under the old beams and poked around in search of fall décor for the party. I located a set of three mercury glass pumpkins that had lights inside them. They would be ideal for the buffet.

I made two trips down the stairs holding them carefully and set them on the buffet in my dining room.

The cake had cooled. I considered how I could dress it up a little for the party. Powdered sugar? Would that look too Christmasy? Icing? I generally preferred a simple look, but before I could try anything, someone pounded on my front door.

When I opened it, Helena and Jacky stood on my stoop with their husbands and Mike's parents behind them. "Hello! To what do I owe this lovely visit?" I invited them in my foyer.

Helena gazed around and led everyone to the living room as if she knew the way. They settled comfortably.

"I hope we're not interrupting anything. It's just that it's so urgent," said Helena.

"Would you like a cup of tea? I have a fresh-from-the-oven apple cider cake in the kitchen."

I thought Thurman might trip over his own feet in eagerness to try the cake. "I'll give you a hand."

"Thurman!" Helena scolded. "This isn't a party."

"Apple cider cake, Helena. It would be rude to turn it down."

I hurried to the kitchen, cut the cake, and placed the pieces on vintage Haviland dessert plates I had picked up at a yard sale. The barely scalloped shape and delicate swirls of tiny beads around the edges were perfect for showing off the cake. Thurman tried a piece, declared it superb, and helped himself to another while I put on tea. He helped me carry trays of cups, cake, forks, spoons, napkins, cream, and sugar into the living room.

When everyone had been served, Helena said, "We heard that you found Rachel. Such a tragedy! And now . . . surely you understand how this complicates Mike's situation."

Mary glared at her mother-in-law before shifting her focus to me. "They've arrested Mike!"

Chapter 12

Dear Natasha,
I got roped into having a brunch for out-of-town
guests. Sigh. I'm not a morning person. What's the
easiest way to do this?
                              Night Owl in Owl City, Tennessee

Dear Night Owl,
Buy all ingredients and alcohol in advance. The
night before, prepare overnight French toast that
you can bake in the morning. Use my recipe for
chocolate hot pepper bread. Prepare a pasta and
squid ink casserole that can be baked in the morning. Set the table and arrange an area where guests
can help themselves to coffee and drinks. Use the
crystal and china you save for guests. Go to bed
early and rise with the songbirds to finish all the
things you put off the night before.
                              Natasha

"What? When?" I asked. "I had lunch with him a few hours ago."

Helena didn't touch her cake. "Arrested is not quite accurate. Detective Fleischman took him in for questioning."

"Alex German will tell him what to do. Be sure he's there when Mike is questioned."

Thurman cut Helena's piece of cake in half and helped himself to it.

"It seems Rachel was murdered in exactly the same manner as Denise," blurted Jacky.

"With insulin?" I asked.

"I'm afraid so. From behind. Two jabs, just like Denise," said Jacky.

Daisy seemed infatuated with Mary. I wasn't sure if it was because Mary stroked her and tickled her under the chin or because Daisy could smell the intriguing scent of horses on her.

Mochie, on the other hand, had jumped up on a side table, where he watched our visitors with wary eyes and swished his tail from time to time as if he were assessing them.

I noticed that no one claimed Mike wouldn't have murdered Rachel and found that interesting if disturbing.

"Are you making any progress?" asked Stu.

I watched Thurman calmly sip his tea, his eyes on the remaining half piece of cake on Helena's plate.

"Not yet. But I will be coming around to visit with each of you."

"We're all here now." Stu smiled at me.

Indeed they were. It would be complete folly to interview them in a group. Their family bonds were tight. "I'll need a little more information first."

"Anything," said Robbie.

"Do you know where Mike was last night?"

Mary was quick to answer. "Yes. He came out to our

house and spent the night. He's been so bereft and finds it difficult to be in their apartment. He says it feels empty."

Robbie's quick glance at his wife told me she was lying. Either that, or Robbie hadn't gone home last night. Which led to new possibilities.

"What time did he get there?"

Robbie watched his wife carefully.

"Around eight, I believe."

An interesting choice of words because I didn't believe her for a second.

My reaction must have shown because Robbie quickly added, "Or seven? Was it seven?"

Mary looked away.

"Tell me about Mike's relationship with Rachel," I said.

They all looked at Robbie and Mary.

Mary folded her hands in her lap. "I don't think they had a relationship. Do you, Robbie?"

Robbie seemed uncomfortable at having the question thrown his way. "I don't believe so. We didn't know of Rachel until she showed up after Denise died. She appeared to want to comfort him, but Mike acted as if he wanted her to leave him alone."

Mary nodded. "I don't think he had any interest in her."

"Your cake is delicious," said Thurman.

"Is it one of Faye's recipes?" asked Helena.

"No. Sadly, I don't have any of her recipes."

"Did you have an opportunity to meet Faye before she died?" asked Jacky.

"I'm sorry to say that I did not."

Helena gazed around the living room. "She would like you very much. May I see the painting of her?"

"Yes, of course! It's in the kitchen. Follow me." I led her into the kitchen where the portrait of Mars's Aunt Faye hung over the fireplace mantel. The others followed along.

I was certain it was only my imagination, but the slowly

setting fall sun appeared to make Aunt Faye's portrait glow as if she knew her old friend was looking at it.

Helena was fixated by the painting. "It's lovely. It brings back wonderful memories. Faye was so kind to Jacky and me. We lost our mother at a very young age. Our father was an intimidating man, but Faye was an extraordinary woman who challenged him with aplomb. A natural diplomat. I am so thankful to the women who surrounded us with love. I don't know what would have become of Jacky and me without Faye."

"I loved coming over here." Jacky smiled as she gazed at the portrait. "Faye used to arrange teatime for us in her elegant dining room. She served cakes and tiny sandwiches, and other goodies. Those parties were always so much fun! I can still hear her saying 'Pinkies in, ladies. Pinkies in.'"

Helena turned to me. "I hope you will keep us informed of your progress."

"Of course. I will need access to the house. Which one of you should I call in that regard?"

Helena fished a key out of her purse. "This is the key. The police have done a thorough investigation. I can't imagine that you would find anything of interest at this point."

"Perhaps not." I took the key she offered. "But you never know."

Thanking me profusely, the family filed out of my house.

I checked the time and wondered whether it would be more beneficial to phone Wolf or Alex.

Mars had once told me that Wolf only gave me the information that he wanted me to know. I didn't particularly like that, but I appreciated that it was necessary in his position as a police detective. And I knew he would never intentionally mislead me. He couldn't tell me everything. Alex might be more forthcoming, but would likely know far less about what the police already knew at this point.

It was nearly dinnertime. With any luck, Alex might still be in his office. I cut a chunk of the cake and wrapped it, tying it with a little bow. I slipped Daisy's harness over her head, clasped the leash to it, and set off on a walk toward the courthouse. The lights were on in Alex's office, but the door was locked. I knocked on it.

Alex came to the door and unlocked it. "Sophie! What brings you here?"

"Mike Nofsinger."

"Ahh. Yes, that makes sense. I should have realized that his family would reach out to you."

He petted Daisy and locked the door behind us. He always would, I supposed, having been attacked once by someone after hours.

He showed us into his office. Alex had been in the military and the neat, organized office reflected that. No sloppy piles of files cluttered the desks. Most of the furniture was mahogany, a tasteful combination of antiques and knockoffs.

"You know I can't tell you anything."

I took a deep breath. No matter. He might reveal something useful anyway. "Has he been arrested?"

Alex sat back, ramrod straight. "Not yet. I'm hoping that he won't be charged. They don't have a firm time yet on Rachel's death, but it appears that it was in the morning. Possibly around nine-thirty. He doesn't have an alibi for either death."

I tried not to smile. Alex had already said something useful. Now I knew the approximate time of death.

"That's difficult for those of us who live alone," I said. "Any motive that you know of?"

"Wolf's questioning leaned toward the possibility that Mike had an interest in another woman, possibly Rachel."

"I presume he told you that Rachel was pursuing him?" I asked.

Alex raised his eyebrows. "He mentioned something about Rachel wanting to help someone named Mitzi decorate the house. I gather Mitzi was his wife's friend and business partner? I've put in a call to her but haven't heard back."

"No one can find her."

"That's odd. Are you saying she could be dead, too?"

"I honestly don't know. She thought someone was stalking her. We did a quick wellness check of her home today, but there was no sign of Mitzi, or of a struggle, or anything out of order."

"What in the world is going on? Three women. Is Mitzi the same age as Denise and Rachel?"

"I would think so. And they are all interior decorators or designers. I don't think that's a career that usually aggravates people or incites ire."

"Probably not. There must be some connection other than Mike." He paused before asking, "Why didn't Mars come in?"

What a curious question. "Come in?"

"He's sitting outside on a bench as if he's waiting for you."

I turned to look out the window. "He must be meeting someone else." I rose to my feet. "Keep me posted about this?"

Alex tilted his head. "You know I have a duty to keep my clients' matters confidential."

"I know," I said with a smile. "I would never expect you to reveal anything of that nature. But I might be able to help you and some things aren't confidential."

Daisy and I walked out of the office. She tugged me straight to Mars, who ruffled the fur on her neck and cooed sweet nothings to her.

"What are you doing here?" I asked.

"A guy can't sit on a public bench? I thought I'd take a little rest."

Uh huh. I didn't believe that for a minute. Mars ran every day. "Are you coming down with something? I hope you're not getting sick."

"I'm fine. Where are you headed?" He rose and we began to walk.

"Home. We just took a little evening stroll."

"Right into Alex's office?"

I couldn't help ribbing him a little bit. "Why, Mars! You can't be jealous."

"I'm looking out for you. That's all. Tease me if you like, but two women are dead and a third is missing."

"No one is after me, Mars."

"You don't know that."

"I don't fit in the equation."

"Maybe not. But you need to be careful. Someone out there has a syringe loaded with insulin and he's not afraid to use it."

Mars saw me to my door and then insisted on a quick run through of the house to be sure no one lurked inside. I objected, but deep down, I knew I would feel better knowing that he had checked it out.

After he left, I fed Mochie and Daisy, and poked through the fridge for leftovers. I took my plate of cheeses, grapes, macaroni salad, olives, and a baked pear, and settled in the sunroom. Distant lights twinkled in the darkness. Faux candles glowed in lanterns I had brought downstairs.

I pondered Mike's situation while I nibbled on cheese. I could understand why his family was concerned. If I were the police, I would be thinking one of two likely scenarios. The first would be that Mike had murdered his wife and Rachel. Could there be a third woman in that equation? Someone I didn't know about yet? There would have been easier ways to get rid of them if Mike was in love with someone else. Divorce for starters. And he could have been upfront with Rachel and told her he wasn't interested.

But what if Rachel murdered Denise?

Mike might have killed Rachel out of anger. It wasn't that far-fetched. If Rachel saw Denise as standing in the way of her having a relationship with Mike, she might have gotten rid of Denise.

The other possible scenario scared me a bit. What if Mike used Rachel? Convinced her to murder Denise? Maybe he told Rachel that the two of them couldn't be together because of Denise. Then, when Rachel murdered Denise, Mike killed Rachel so she couldn't testify against him for asking her to murder his wife. Sort of a murder-for-hire scheme except no money changed hands. He duped her.

There might be even more reasons for Mike to be involved with the murders. Reasons that hadn't yet become apparent.

Something was going on with his parents. They were eager to protect Mike, which was perfectly natural. But something didn't feel right there.

Normally, I appreciated the value of a closely knit family. Everyone dreamed of having supportive parents, siblings, and cousins. But when it came to murder, I had to wonder if any of them would tell the truth.

Maybe I should begin with Rachel. I looked up her social media. She had worked at Silver Dog Designs, and I happened to know the owner, Lillith Rollins. I would start with her.

SATURDAY

I wasn't sure if Lillith would be working on a Saturday, but a quick check of Silver Dog Designs indicated that the shop associated with her business was open on weekends.

No love was lost between Lillith and Natasha. I found that rather humorous because they reminded me of each other. Lillith dressed impeccably. Lest she find my wardrobe as awful as Natasha did, I skipped my lovely comfortable clothes and donned a fluid skirt with a pattern of black leaves on a brown background. A black mock turtleneck sweater and black flats matched it nicely. I added a belt with a gold buckle, which made all the difference.

I wasn't sure if Daisy would be welcome in the store, so I let her out before feeding her breakfast. Mochie finished his salmon quickly and hopped up in the bay window to clean his whiskers.

I skipped breakfast and stopped by Big Daddy's Bakery for vanilla lattes and fresh apple doughnuts doused with cinnamon sugar. When I saw Lillith's assistant, I was glad I'd thought to buy extras.

Lillith had swept her deep brown hair back into an elegant chignon and wore a close-fitting cream knit dress that made me glad I hadn't worn jeans. "Sophie," she said in a soft voice. "It's lovely to see you."

"Hello, Lillith. I'm so sorry about Rachel."

Her eyes widened ever so slightly. "We are broken-hearted."

"I brought some goodies." I turned to her assistant. "Would you like a vanilla latte and an apple cider doughnut?"

The young woman rushed over, caught Lillith's eye, and slowed down, trying to mimic Lillith's suave mannerisms. "This is very thoughtful of you. Thank you."

Lillith took the others from me. "Please come into my office."

A chandelier hanging from the ceiling set the tone for the room. Without it, the room would have been nice but perhaps a tad blah. Everything, from the desk to the filing cabinets, was white with a touch of gray in it. For her purposes it provided a perfect background for the colorful samples on tables and displays.

"I should have realized that you would be stopping by," said Lillith. We sat in uncomfortable white chairs that would have been at home in a formal living room. "But I'm afraid I don't know anything about Rachel's death." She handed me a latte and took the top off the other one to drink it.

"Did she mention Denise to you?"

Lillith rose and closed the door.

Chapter 13

Dear Sophie,
My in-laws are coming for a visit and Hubby thinks we should host a big family brunch. I'm in a panic. Dinner seems so doable, but with brunch I'm afraid I'll end up in the kitchen frying eggs for twenty people.
Chicken in Egg Harbor City, New Jersey

Dear Chicken,
If you have that many people, set it up as a buffet. Have a coffee, tea, and alcohol station set up away from the food. It's okay to buy your favorite indulgent sweets like breakfast breads, croissants, and cinnamon loaves. Get hubby involved in making a huge bowl of fruit salad. For the main course, bake sheet pan frittatas. They're quick and easy.
Sophie

When Lillith was seated, she took her time sipping latte, as if she was contemplating how to respond. "Rachel had eyes for Mike. There's no denying that. During his engagement to Denise, I almost fired Rachel. I brought her in here, where you sit at this moment, and explained that I have a reputation in Old Town, and I would not have an employee destroy what I had worked so hard to achieve."

"I'm not following. What was she doing?"

Lillith let out a sigh and gazed around the room. "Bad-mouthing Denise. Spreading vile rumors about her professionally. I knew they weren't true and told her that had to end immediately. To be honest, I wanted to hire Denise. She had real talent. Rachel, well, I don't like to speak ill of her now that she's gone, but she didn't have Denise's vision. She couldn't see the possibilities like Denise could. Denise had an amazing knack for tonal development. She could see the hues and brought them together beautifully, like an artist. To Rachel, blue was blue was blue."

"She was still working for you, though. Does that mean Rachel stopped denigrating Denise?"

"As far as I know."

"And it was all about Mike?"

"I'm afraid she didn't hide her feelings very well, but . . ."

"But what?"

"I don't think it was Mike she wanted. Rachel came from an unstable family background. I think she sought to belong. To have the feeling of security that comes from being part of a family and knowing they have your back."

"Not their money?"

"Oh well!" She flung her hand back dramatically. "I'm sure that had something to do with it. Everyone wants money. But Rachel felt alone and saw Mike as the person who could offer her what she longed for. She was like an abandoned dog, never feeling that she belonged anywhere. Always sniffing around for a place to call home."

In spite of her behavior toward Mike, I now felt sorry for Rachel. "What about her own family? No siblings?"

"She didn't like to speak about her family. I gathered that her parents had issues with alcohol and the only sibling she ever mentioned to me died many years ago."

I leaned toward Lillith. In as soft a voice as I could muster, I asked, "Do you think she might have murdered Denise?"

Lillith's chest heaved as she took in deep breaths. She

held her chin high and closed her eyes briefly when she said, "Possibly."

"Did she work here the day Denise died?"

"Oh! So, I might be her alibi after all." She rose ever so elegantly and typed something into her keyboard. "I'm afraid I can't help you. Rachel took that day off. I don't know where she was. I went to see a client that morning. They're putting in a breakfast nook."

"Did Rachel have any friends I might speak to?"

"I would think so, but I don't know them. With the exception of Mitzi Lawson, of course. You might check with her."

Swell. If only I could find her!

I thanked Lillith and browsed around her shop before leaving. She had some lovely fall arrangements. I bought a couple of sets of candle holders in weathered white that could serve in any season. Lillith had wound delicate vines of small pale orange leaves around them, which were perfect for fall, so I purchased those as well. Like so many other stores, her selection leaned heavily toward white, green, and blue pumpkins, which appeared to be all the rage.

One corner was devoted to large bags. Unlike the totes that were often given as promotional items, these were well constructed and full of pockets, inside and out. The sort of thing one might take boating or on a day-long excursion. They came in cheerful colors and could be monogrammed. A black-and-white horizontally striped bag sported a bright pink monogram, RPA, in a beautiful swirling font. I made a mental note to come back to do some holiday shopping.

Carrying my purchases, I headed for the door. Lillith walked over and held it open for me. In a voice so low that I almost thought I was imagining it, she whispered, "Don't underestimate the power of Helena Nofsinger."

I turned to look at Lillith, but she said nothing more. She merely met my gaze and waited for me to depart.

What was that supposed to mean? What an odd thing to say. Could she have meant that Helena arranged for the demise of Denise or Rachel or both? Did Helena have someone watching Mitzi, or heaven forbid, me? Or watching over the Inger House? That was an awful way to end our conversation.

It didn't make any sense, though. If Helena had something to do with the deaths of Denise and Rachel, why would she ask me to look into them?

I turned at the corner, still thinking about what Lillith had said, when I heard a car door slam. A sleek black Lincoln sedan shot out of the alley and turned right in haste. I thought I saw Lillith driving, but wasn't certain until I saw LILL on the license plate. Maybe I had made her late for an appointment. Or maybe not. Maybe she had more to do with Rachel's demise than she let on.

I walked along and came to Nofsinger & Lawson. Inside the window, the shop seemed desolate. I could make out a small kitchen in white with alternate tiles and cabinet styles on the countertop. The front door was glass, and the name of the shop was repeated on it in an artistic arch that also served as their logo. Just below it, someone had taped a sign. It wasn't handwritten. Someone had taken the time to create and print it.

WE ARE TEMPORARILY CLOSED TO HONOR THE LIFE OF DENISE NOFSINGER. CURRENT CLIENTS WILL BE CONTACTED REGARDING THEIR PROJECTS. THANK YOU.

It was short and to the point. Mitzi must have posted it. I wondered when she had done that. Before or after she was last seen?

I pulled out my phone and called her home number. I didn't expect her to answer, but hopefully I could leave a voice mail. It rolled over as I had hoped.

"Hi, Mitzi. It's Sophie calling. I don't have to know where you are. I just want to be certain that you're all right. If there's anything I can do for you, I hope you'll call me. Do me a favor and leave me some kind of sign that you're okay. Thanks, Mitzi."

I had barely put my phone away when it chimed. I hoped it was Mitzi! But when I glanced at it, Bernie had texted me. **Stop by for lunch? Have someone here whom you might want to meet.**

How could I turn that down? I changed directions and strode over to The Laughing Hound. Bernie waved to me from the bar. I made my way to him.

"Feel like a fall sandwich? A Fuji apple, Havarti, and smoked turkey melt. Want to give me an opinion?"

"Who could pass that up?"

Bernie grinned at me. "I hoped so. Hot cider or iced tea?"

"Tea, please."

He spoke with a server briefly, then walked around the end of the bar. "Do you know Tom Simmons?"

"I don't think so."

He wiggled his eyebrows. "He's a friend of Mike Nofsinger." He led me to a table where a young man ate.

"Tom, this is Sophie Winston, the woman I was telling you about. Mind if we join you for lunch?"

"Please do."

Tom looked to be in his early thirties. Sorely in need of a haircut, he pushed mouse-brown hair out of his eyes. He wore a light gray hoodie with jeans and didn't appear to be the kind of fellow who worked out at a gym. I liked his easy smile and calm expression. We had interrupted him in the middle of eating his lunch.

Our sandwiches and tea arrived just as we sat down at his table.

"Tom is a good friend of Mike Nofsinger," Bernie said by way of introduction.

"Oh! Mike seems like a nice guy," I said.

Tom nodded. "We go way back. Mike and I met in grade school. We're a lot alike. Sort of nerdy. We were really into Harry Potter back then."

"Who doesn't love Harry Potter?" I asked. My sandwich smelled heavenly. Melted cheese was always so hard to resist. "So you must have known Denise, too." I bit into my sandwich and savored the wonderful combination of salty cheese and sweet apple.

A gloom fell over Tom's face, and he winced. I felt horrible for even bringing Denise up in conversation.

"Yeah. I hope they find who did it. I mean, it won't bring her back. Nothing will ever be the same again, but of all the people in the world, she didn't deserve that. I don't know if Mike will ever recover. How do you get over something like that?"

"Do you know of anyone who was angry with Denise?" I asked.

"No, Denise was cool. I've been thinking about this. It had to be someone she knew, right? Because Denise was smart. She wouldn't have opened the door to a stranger."

"Someone might have overpowered her," said Bernie.

Tom nodded. "I guess so."

I took a chance when I asked, "Did you ever date Rachel?"

Tom seemed surprised. "How did you know that?"

Just a hunch on my part. "So you must be hurting, too."

"It was a shock. I still can't believe that she's gone. But it never worked between us. Mike and Denise kept throwing us together. They meant well, but I'm not Rachel's type."

"No?" I asked. "Was she your type?"

He sat back and thought about it. "No. I hate to say it now that she's dead, but she wasn't very nice. I thought she was self-centered and superficial. That probably sounds funny coming from an ordinary guy like me, but I think I saw a side of her that they didn't know about. To tell the truth, I think she wanted to have an affair with Mike."

"Did she?" asked Bernie.

Tom shrugged. "You'd have to ask him. I doubt it, though. He and Denise were tight. I don't think he had any interest in Rachel at all."

I finished my delicious sandwich. "Do you think that Rachel could have murdered Denise?"

Tom didn't hesitate. "Yeah. I've thought about that a lot. I wondered if I should go to the police, but I don't have any evidence. And now that Rachel is dead, too, I guess it's more likely that the same guy killed both of them."

"Do you suspect anyone?" I asked.

"It couldn't be Mike. He loved Denise. They had the kind of relationship I only dream about. Lots of joking and laughs. They were the perfect couple."

"They didn't have issues with anyone?"

"Not that I know about."

"How about Mike's parents? Did they have problems with someone?"

"I wouldn't know. I don't see them much these days. When I was growing up, I spent a lot of time at their house. They had horses, and a really funny rescued goat who would follow us around." He shook his head. "They were nice to me. I never saw anything weird going on there."

"Do you have any friends who might know something

helpful about the deaths of Denise and Rachel?" asked Bernie.

"We've talked about it. I mean, how could we not? Two women from our group murdered? And in Mike's new home? What are the odds of that? But we can't figure it out."

I gave Tom my number. "If anything comes to you, even something that seems very minor, would you give me a call?"

"Sure."

"Lunch is on me, today, Tom." Bernie smiled at him. "Thanks for your help."

"Wow. Thanks for lunch! I wish I could tell you something helpful. I'd like the killer to be caught." Tom rose and thanked Bernie again before he left.

"Do you ever feel like you're going around in circles?" I asked Bernie.

"Every day!"

"What do you know about Helena and Jacky and their husbands?" I asked.

"Thurman is here a lot. He's the life of every party as far as I can tell. He's a hugger and loves to buy a round of drinks for his pals. Everyone seems to like him. But in spite of that, Helena calls the shots. She's very nice and tips well. My servers almost trip over each other to get her table. I'm under the impression that she likes to help young people who are starting out. She's known to give very big tips to servers who are in university or working on a graduate degree. Much quieter and not as huggy as Thurman, but she seems really great."

"How about Jacky?"

"She makes Helena appear subdued. She's talkative with a great sense of humor. She overshadows her husband, Stu. He's the quiet one in that marriage, but you can see how much he adores her."

"Lillith told me not to underestimate Helena. Does that mean anything to you?"

"Helena is clearly the brains behind the family business. When you run a business, sometimes you have to be tough. I don't like it, but I know from experience that there are times when I have to be firm. I'd like to be Mr. Nice Guy all the time, but you can't run a business that way. Maybe that's what she meant?"

"Do you think she meant that Helena killed Denise and Rachel?"

"Lillith. Hmm, who knows? Maybe she meant Helena is covering up for someone?"

Chapter 14

Dear Sophie,
I'm the worst at decorating my fireplace mantel. It always looks like a jumble of stuff. I see pictures of books stacked on mantels but mine look like clutter that I forgot to put away. Help, please!
Hopeless in Triangle, New York

Dear Hopeless,
Some decorators refer to a triangle concept for mantels. The peak doesn't have to be perfectly in the center. It can be a bit to one side or the other. That's a great place to start. Hang or place the largest item there. It could be a mirror, a wreath, a large painting or picture, or even a rustic piece of memorabilia. Now add other items in the same colors or theme with the smallest at the outer edges of the imaginary triangle.
Sophie

I walked home, let Daisy out, and unpacked my purchases. Daisy returned to sniff everything and I spent the next hour setting out the new candleholders, placing pet-safe battery operated candles on them, and winding the leafy vines around them. But all the while I was thinking about who might have more information on Mike, Denise, and Rachel.

Bernie's notion that Helena might be covering up for someone made some sense to me. But it didn't limit the number of suspects, because she would certainly be protective of the entire Nofsinger clan.

I wound a little vine loosely around the tallest candleholder while debating who would be the weakest link in that family. Helena was clearly in charge. But that wasn't a bad thing. It meant she was the boss of their real estate company, which employed most of them. They were a close family. Of course, if you could work for your successful family business, why would you wander very far away? They must get along because as far as I knew, none of them had opted to be in a different profession.

But one of them had managed a bit of distance. Robbie worked for his family, but his wife, Mary, had moved them out of Old Town. She might be the weak link I sought.

I retreated to my office where I Googled Mary and Robbie Nofsinger. After poking around a bit, I located an address that appeared to belong to them. While it might be rude to simply show up at their doorstep, I thought it better to do exactly that. If Helena was as powerful over her family as Lillith had indicated, it would be wise not to forewarn anyone of a visit.

I changed into dark green jeans, a maroon turtleneck sweater, and a vest in the same green as my trousers.

I slid Daisy's harness over her head. "You're my magic to get close to Mary today. We're going to see horses!" I wasn't sure if Daisy had ever met a horse up close and personal. I hoped she would behave. I grabbed a few small apples from the fridge and tucked them into a tote bag.

Daisy was thrilled to go for a ride. The sun shone brightly, taking off a bit of the fall chill. I rolled the windows down in the back just far enough for Daisy to sniff the air without sticking her head out the window.

Part of the greater Washington, DC, area, Great Falls offered land to roam. Daisy squirmed and sniffed the air as we drew closer to farmland. I slowed near the drive I thought led to Robbie and Mary's property, then spied Mary near a fence stroking a horse.

Perfect!

I parked on the side of the driveway, far enough over to be passed if someone else should need to drive in. Farther along, a modern farmhouse-style home and a large white barn were at the end of the driveway.

I stepped out and latched Daisy's leash to her harness, then called out, "Hi!" I grabbed my tote bag of apples.

Mary crouched and held her hand out to Daisy. "Hello, pretty girl."

Two brown Labradors came to greet her.

Daisy waggled her tail and exchanged dog sniffs with the Labradors, but quickly turned her attention to the horse.

"This is Dobby," said Mary. "You should have seen him when they brought him to us. He was a mess. All skin and bones. I can't understand why people are so cruel to animals."

"He's gorgeous!" The sun shone on his rich chestnut coat. "Do you often take in rescue animals?"

"Everyone here is a rescue. I tease Robbie about that."

"I'm sure he appreciates you rescuing him," I laughed.

She responded with a doubtful expression.

"Do you get along with Helena?" I dared to ask. After all, mothers-in-law could be difficult.

"Get along with her? I admire her!"

"Oh?"

"I guess most people don't realize what she and Jacky went through as children. People see the big house and the business that Helena built and assume that they always had a lovely life. But the truth is that they lost their mother when they were very young. Their father was a cold man. All business, I gather. He put Helena to work when she was ten! If it hadn't been for Annie and some women in Old Town who took them under their wings, I don't know what might have become of them."

"Annie was the elderly lady I met at Helena's home?"

"She's like a mother to them. To this day! There isn't anything they wouldn't do for her. She went to work for their father, cleaning and helping with the cooking and such, when Helena was born. Annie is a remarkable woman with a lot of guts."

"Everyone must have doted on Mike."

"They did! Is that what brings you out here? Is there news about Mike?"

"I hope you'll forgive me for coming unannounced."

"If Mike is off the hook, then all is forgiven."

"May the horses have apples?" I asked.

"Sure! They'll love you. We don't often get company that brings treats for them."

"I came to see you because you may have a little more distance from them and see them differently than they see one another."

"The outsider who married into the family and then stole Robbie and whisked him out to Great Falls?" Mary laughed.

"Something like that. You and Robbie turned down the Inger House."

"I have my horses and Robbie likes it out here, too. No neighbors to complain when he plays the piano."

I nodded. "I thought you might have some insights about the deaths."

"I wish I did. I have wondered if someone wants to buy the Inger House and thinks the murders will drive the price down. Is that crazy?"

I was horrified by the mere thought that anyone would do something so incredibly brutal. "Does someone have an interest in buying the house?"

"Too many to name. And I don't work in the office where they would know all of them."

"Do you think someone in the family wants to sell the house?" I asked. "Maybe for the money?"

She faced me. "Not a chance. It has some kind of birthright hold on them. They will cling to that place until the very last Inger-Nofsinger takes his dying breath."

I stroked Dobby, wondering if I wouldn't feel the same way about a house my ancestors built.

"It's all so odd," said Mary. "If only we could identify the deranged person who murdered Denise and Rachel, then Mike would be off the hook."

Unless it *was* Mike. I wondered where he had been the days of the murders. I could only hope he had a good alibi. "Do you have any idea who it might be?" I asked.

"It has to be an outsider. Someone who dislikes the Nofsinger family for some reason. I'm sure they have angered tenants over the years. Or it could be someone who is jealous of their financial success. Some people harbor grudges."

"Is there anyone who feels that way about Mike?"

Mary gazed out over the pasture. "It's possible. To be perfectly honest, I thought Rachel murdered Denise. My daughter-in-law was kind and gracious whereas Rachel could be . . . grating. Pushy. I thought she had flipped out because Mike and Denise would be moving into the Inger House. Apparently, I was wrong."

"Not necessarily. The fact that Rachel was also murdered does not mean that she didn't kill Denise."

Mary's eyes locked on me. "No. That cannot be the case. Absolutely not."

I understood why she was adamant about that. The person most impacted by Denise's death, the one who had lost his love and watched his future crumble, would be Mike. I had come to Great Falls under the impression that Mary might be more forthcoming about the Nofsingers. But as I looked into her eyes, all I saw was a mother who would do anything to save her son. Maybe even murder.

On that uneasy note, I thanked her and headed back toward Old Town musing about Mary's character. Mothers were protective. And that was a good thing, but there had been something about the set of her jaw that worried me. Who was to say how she spent her days? Dobby wouldn't mention it to anyone if she left her home for a few hours.

My path took me through the beautiful countryside where trees were turning red and gold.

Thurman had claimed to be at Pine Grove Golf Club the morning of Denise's death. I didn't know if they would be receptive to Daisy, but I could swing by there on my way home.

Forty-five minutes later, I pulled into the beautifully manicured lawns of the Pine Grove Golf Club. I stepped out of my car, latched a leash onto Daisy's harness, and told her to be on her very best behavior.

As if she understood me, she walked like a well-trained lady. I spied a gentleman in a golf shirt embroidered with the name of the golf club and asked if he could direct me to Jerry.

"Who is this?" he asked.

"Daisy."

He petted Daisy and told me that Jerry worked in the pro shop.

"Thank you. Are dogs allowed there?" I asked.

He smiled. "Well-behaved dogs like Daisy are welcome."

We located Jerry right away. He was asking another man to sweep up a mess of popcorn someone had left on the floor. "I dread seeing Mrs. Framblin, because I know she'll bring the twins in here and they touch everything with their dirty little hands!"

"Excuse me, Jerry?" I introduced myself. "I'm sure you heard about the terrible murders of two young women. I'm looking into it."

"What a nightmare. I hope they catch that guy. I know the father-in-law of one of those girls."

"Thurman Nofsinger?"

"Exactly. Great guy and an excellent golfer!"

"He told me that he was here the morning that his daughter-in-law died."

"Oh yes. Most definitely." Jerry smiled broadly. Almost too happy, I thought.

"He played a round of golf?"

Jerry didn't pause for a second. "Mr. Nofsinger booked one of our meeting rooms for a business meeting that morning."

"You're sure about that? Whom did he meet with?"

Still smiling, he drew back his head as if I was out of line. "I don't know the nature of the meeting or who attended. And if I did, it would be highly inappropriate to divulge his personal business."

"Fully understandable." He was correct, of course. But I planned to aim one little last zinger at him.

He relaxed and shot me an annoyingly self-satisfied grin.

"I'll have the cops come out and get that information from you."

He wasn't grinning when I left.

I strolled out of the shop and heard a hissing sound. I glanced to my left and spotted the man who had been sweeping.

He motioned to me, and I walked over to him. "Hi."

"You are asking about Mr. Thurman, yes?"

"Thurman Nofsinger."

He nodded, held up his hand, and rubbed his thumb against his forefinger and middle finger. "Mr. Thurman has paid Jerry to tell you he was here."

"How do you know that?"

He snickered. "My English is not so good, and Jerry thinks I do not understand."

"Your English sounds pretty good to me."

"Thank you. I go to night school and watch movies in English on the TV."

"Did you actually hear Thurman ask Jerry to cover for him?"

"Oh yes. I am standing right there. I even see the money he gives to Jerry." He handed me a piece of paper. "Here is my name and phone number. If you need someone to help you sometimes, I am good at fixing things in the house and in the garden."

I glanced at the name he had written. "My name is Sophie. Sophie Winston. It was a pleasure to meet you, Mr. Estrella." I held out my hand and he smiled when he shook it.

Daisy and I headed home. I couldn't recall having run into anyone who had paid for an alibi before. Thurman zoomed to the top of my list of suspects.

I parked the car in my garage. Daisy ran around the yard for a few minutes, but soon hurried into the house and sprawled on the kitchen floor, apparently exhausted from our excursion.

SUNDAY

Sunday passed too quickly. I spent the day trying out recipes and decorating my house for the big brunch. I sent a text to Nina. **Breakfast for dinner tonight? My place, 6PM.**

She responded and showed up promptly.

Nina unpacked a pitcher and poured a red liquid into tall glasses. It wasn't until she added celery stalks for garnish that I realized she had made Bloody Marys.

"What other kind of cocktail would one drink with breakfast for dinner?" she asked.

I served my Butternut Squash Sheet Pan Breakfast, which we thought made a fine dinner.

"I did a little snooping today," said Nina.

"Me too. I hope you learned something useful. The only big thing I found out was that Thurman paid someone to give him an alibi."

"That's huge! So Thurman killed them!"

"I'm not certain yet. But I'm going to take a closer look at him."

"Gosh. Mine is boring. I found out who lives in the house across the street from the Inger House. It's Agnes Hampton!"

"You say that like she's someone we should look into."

"Oh, I doubt that she killed anyone. But I know her. I'm going to drop by the house tomorrow on the pretense of visiting her cat. Maybe she saw something!"

After indulging in Applesauce Spice Sheet Cake for dessert, Nina went home with Muppet.

MONDAY

I spent Monday morning catching up on work that I had been putting off. Lillith's harsh words about Helena weighed on me. I wondered when I might be able to question someone in the Nofsinger offices without Helena hanging around. Late afternoon, maybe?

I made a quick salad for lunch, rationalizing that it would make up for the dessert I had the night before, then returned to my home office to work and answer some questions for my column.

At four in the afternoon, I strolled over to Inger Property Management. The red brick building was larger than I had thought. Retail stores and a restaurant occupied the bottom floor along the waterfront. I took the elevator up to the third level where I was greeted by a receptionist whom I judged to be in her sixties. A name plate on the top of the desk said *Hazel Davenport*.

Her face lit up when she saw me. "Sophie Winston! We've been expecting you. I'm to send you back to Mrs. Nofsinger's personal assistant. But first I have to tell you how much I enjoy your column."

"Thank you so much!" I didn't like being sent to the personal assistant. I leaned toward her. "I'd rather speak with you."

"Oh! All rightie."

I'd clearly caught her off guard, which was exactly what I wanted.

"What can I do for you?" she asked.

"Were you working the morning that Denise Nofsinger died?"

"That poor child. I was here all right. You can imagine the horror we felt. Such a lovely young woman. Could I get you a cup of coffee?"

"I would love that."

She hurried away and was back in a flash. "Let's sit over here. I can hear the phone if it rings."

She showed me to a settee with a coffee table in front of it and handed me a plate and napkin. A mug sat on the plate. The lovely aroma of cinnamon and nutmeg floated to me. Two small rounds that looked like doughnut holes rested next to it.

I took a sip. "Wow! This isn't regular office coffee! It's delicious!"

She beamed. "It's my own fall blend. Since Helena was

kind enough to hire me, the least I can do is make proper coffee."

"You're a very conscientious employee."

Hazel studied her hands. "My husband died rather abruptly from a heart attack. He had a good job and I stayed home to raise the children. I didn't know that he had a gambling addiction until after his death when people wanted to be paid for the money he had borrowed. I was in a terrible fix."

Chapter 15

Dear Sophie,
Is it possible to cook everything in advance for brunch so I won't have to work, and I can have fun with my guests?

Hungry in Friendsville, Maryland

Dear Hungry,
You'll have to do a few things on the day of the event, like make coffee and tea. But you can do a lot ahead, especially if you make a breakfast board. You can prepare hard-boiled eggs (or deviled eggs!) in advance. You can also prepare sliced fruit, and wash grapes. That morning, you can slice breads and cook sausages or bacon. But most of it will be done!

Sophie

Hazel looked me in the eyes. "I'm a wiz on Facebook, but I don't know all those fancy computer programs. And I can't stand on my feet all day anymore. I thought I would have to sell the house and then out of the blue Helena called me and offered me this job. I had known her just about all my life. Someone mentioned to her that I was looking for work and she hired me!"

"I'm so glad she did."

"I still don't know any fancy computer things, but I know about phones and receiving people when they come in. I keep an eye on the cleaning crews. And I bring in a homemade cake for everyone's birthday. I'm the go-to gal around here if anything needs fixing. If I can't do it myself, I have a whole Rolodex full of reliable people. Whatever anyone needs, a new chair or desk or office supplies, I get it for them. And I make sure we have excellent coffee, not that horrible stale stuff they have in most offices. She hired me when I was in need, and I make myself useful."

"What are these?" I asked, picking up one of the sugar-coated balls.

"My pumpkin doughnut holes, except they're not fried. They're baked!"

I tried one. "Fantastic! Do you share your recipe?"

"I would be delighted to share it with you."

I gave her my e-mail address. Hazel was so nice that I wanted to just chat with her, but I had come on a mission. "So how did you hear about Denise's death?"

"Helena shot out of her office and told us Denise had been hospitalized. She was on her way to the emergency room."

"Did you put the call about it through to her?"

"Um, no. I hadn't actually thought about it. I guess Mike must have called Helena's cell phone number."

"So Mike wasn't here at work?"

She shook her head. "Mike usually comes in around seven thirty or so. He answers e-mail and whatnot, then collects what he needs and leaves."

"He works from home?"

"No. He inspects buildings that they might buy or sell.

He meets with people who do maintenance on buildings for us. Takes care of tenant problems. That sort of thing."

Helena had said Mike and Robbie were working. Stunned by her clever dodge, I realized that they weren't necessarily in the office. "You're certain he wasn't here?"

"Yes. I remember Helena saying he was on his way to the hospital."

"Do you remember what time he left this building?"

"I would say around nine."

Plenty of time to kill his wife. "How about Robbie. Was he here?"

"As I recall, he had a meeting somewhere and didn't come into the office at all that day."

A second lie from Helena.

"What time did Helena come to work?"

She turned a worried face toward me. "They're all suspects?"

"I'm afraid so. I'm trying to eliminate everyone I can to narrow it down."

"I see. That makes sense. Helena was here that morning. No question about it. But she left as soon as she heard the news about Denise."

"Do you know of anyone who holds a grudge against one of them?"

"There are a few people who are angry because the Nofsingers bought a property they wanted. But I haven't heard anything outside of business dealings. And they all sounded fair and square to me."

"Does Thurman have an office?" I munched on the second doughnut hole.

"Yes. But he rarely comes in. It's really a waste of space. Jacky and her husband have retired. You'd think Helena would turn everything over to Robbie so she can retire. I suppose she has given him much more responsibility for the day-to-day management, but she's still the head honcho."

"Is there a conference room?"

"Oh yes. It's beautiful, with glass walls overlooking the river."

"Do they sometimes rent meeting rooms elsewhere?"

"Why would they? Oh! They rent the entire restaurant downstairs for their annual Christmas party. Is that what you mean?"

Not exactly. I was wondering why Thurman would rent a meeting room at the golf club. But I said, "That must be lovely."

Hazel sat quietly and appeared to be thinking. "Why would any of them want to murder Denise?"

"I wish I knew. Are you aware of any squabbles? They must disagree from time to time. No one agrees about everything."

Hazel whispered, "Robbie has been worried about something. I thought it was Denise's murder. We've all heard that the police interrogated him. If my son were accused of murder, I think I would flip out. I don't know if I could function at all!"

"Did you ever hear Mike complain about Denise?"

"Oh my, no. He was so sweet on that girl. Last Valentine's Day, he asked me where I would want to go for dinner. I booked a table for them at the cutest little French restaurant. Do you know what that boy did? He sent *me* a dozen red roses for Valentine's Day to thank me! They made me cry."

On that sweet note, I asked Hazel to let me know if she picked up on anything that might be helpful, gave her a hug, and left.

I was walking home when Nina phoned. "Where are you? Can you come to Agnes Hampton's house?"

"Across the street from the Inger House?"

"That's the one. We'll be waiting."

It didn't take me long to walk there. I banged the oak

leaf door knocker and could hear someone inside walking toward the door. I had the eerie sensation of being peered at through a peephole in the door. It swung open.

Agnes glanced around nervously. "Come in quickly."

She pushed back light brown hair and closed the door behind me. The lock snapped shut.

"Hello." I smiled at her.

She motioned for me to follow her into the living room. All the curtains were drawn as if it were nighttime. "Can I get you something? A drink?"

"No thanks. I just had coffee."

"I would offer you some cookies, but I've been too worried to bake and store-bought cookies can't cut it if you ask me."

I sat on the settee beside Nina.

"Tell Sophie what you told me," said Nina.

Agnes wrung her hands. "I'm scared to death. My husband is gone now, you know, so it's just me in this big old house and I'm terrified that I will be the next victim."

Very gently, Nina said, "I mean tell Sophie what you saw."

"Oh. On the day Rachel was murdered, I saw someone running from the house."

"Who?" I asked.

"A young woman." Agnes gestured toward her own hair. "She had blond curly hair."

I exchanged a look with Nina, who said, "I don't have a photo of Mitzi. Do you?"

I quickly looked up Nofsinger & Lawson Fine Interiors on my phone and clicked on the *About Us* section of their website. Photographs of Denise and Mitzi popped up immediately. I handed my phone to Agnes.

"That's her! That's definitely the woman who murdered Rachel, except she was blond."

"Murdered?" My head spun. Was that possible?

"Why do you think she murdered Rachel?"

"I have no idea. Over a man, maybe? Why does any human murder another human?" said Agnes.

She misunderstood my question. I tried to frame it differently. "What makes you think she killed Rachel?"

"Because she was running from the house."

"Did you see anyone chasing her?"

"No. Rachel was dead."

"Have you told the police this?"

Agnes shot an angry glance at Nina. "You promised me you would not tell the police. You promised!"

"Sophie isn't the police, Agnes."

Poor Agnes was so agitated. I sought something comforting to say. "I don't think you will be the next victim, Agnes. Whoever murdered Denise and Rachel had a reason that didn't involve you."

Agnes shook her forefinger at Nina and me. "You listen here. I do not want to be involved. I don't want the killer knowing that I'm the one who turned her in to the police. Then she'll come after me for sure. No ma'am. The cops came around knocking on the doors and I pretended that I wasn't home. I should have done that when Nina came over. I don't want you two dragging me into this mess. I have a calm, peaceful life and I'm not ready to join my husband yet."

A long-haired, solid white, blue-eyed cat walked in and appraised Nina and me. She mewed and then wound around Agnes's ankles. "Now you've gone and upset Snowflake."

"We would never want to do that," said Nina. "Agnes adopted her from the shelter."

Agnes shook her finger at us. "I'm not opening the door to you again. I don't want that killer thinking I saw something. She will come and get me. She will. She's over there watching me."

"Why would she watch you?" I asked.

"Why would she murder people?" Agnes asked back.

"Have you seen her coming and going from the house?"

"I just told you I saw her running away. I promise you, if you send the cops around, I won't open the door. They will have to drag me down to the police station and I will lie through my teeth."

"Agnes, is there anyone who could come and stay with you for a while?" I asked.

"No! It's just Snowflake and me against the forces of evil that exist beyond the walls of this house."

I tried to speak in a soothing voice. "The woman you saw is an interior designer named Mitzi. She is as scared as you are. If you saw her running from the house, it's probably because she was trying to get away from the murderer. In fact, no one has seen her since."

Agnes placed her palm against her neck. "She's over there. Early every morning, I see the light turn on upstairs in the bedroom. She's there waiting to kill again."

I hoped she was wrong about that. "I'm actually glad that you told us about seeing her. I can sleep better knowing that she's in hiding. Have you seen anyone else coming or going from the house?"

"I wish Jacky and Stu had never moved out," she grumbled.

"They were good neighbors?" I asked.

"They sure were. And quiet, too."

"How long have you lived here?"

"Going on fifty-some years now. But nothing like this has ever happened. It was a nice, calm neighborhood."

"I believe it still is. Do you have Nina's phone number?"

Agnes scowled at me. "Probably. Somewhere."

I pulled out my little notepad and wrote Nina's number on it along with her name. Handing it to Agnes, I said, "If you see or hear anything at all that scares you, I want you to call Nina. Okay? She'll come over here and make sure you're all right."

"You won't call the police?" asked Agnes.

"Well—"

I nudged Nina with my elbow.

"Of course not. We girls have to stick together. Right, Snowflake?"

As if she understood, Snowflake mewed.

"All right. Can I call you if I see someone spying on me? Trying to look in my windows?"

"By all means!" I said. "We don't want that!"

"Okay." Agnes didn't look any happier, but at least she didn't seem as agitated anymore.

Nina and I thanked her and left.

I paused to gaze at the house. "Want to visit the Inger House with me in the morning?"

"Who is going to be dead this time?" asked Nina.

"That's not funny!"

"Sure. I'll bring breakfast."

On the way home, we ran into Mars and Bernie, who asked for an update. The four of us walked on to my house where I whipped up a quick sheet pan dinner of marinated pork loin with baby potatoes, shallots, carrots, and sweet potatoes. While I chopped up the veggies, Nina made apple cider cocktails.

I slid the tray into the hot oven and halved pears for an easy dessert before settling on the banquette to munch on an hors d'oeuvre board that Bernie had prepared from cheeses, olives, crackers, and fruit in my fridge.

Nina told them all about Agnes and how frightened she had been. "The important part, though, was that she saw Mitzi fleeing from the Inger House on the day that Rachel died."

"Consequently, Agnes thinks Mitzi is the killer," I added.

That got their attention.

Mars's eyebrows raised. "No. Is that even possible? She *could* have put the tracker in her purse herself and made up the story about being stalked. That would explain a lot! Then she goes into hiding, and she's on the police wavelength but as a potential victim."

Chapter 16

Dear Natasha,
I want to have brunch for my girlfriends, but we're all on diets and don't want to eat anything rich or sugary. Avocado toast is so done. No bacon, pancakes, waffles, or casseroles. Suggestions, please?
Watching My Weight in Bacon Springs, Mississippi

Dear Watching My Weight,
How about a yogurt buffet? Set up cute parfait glasses. Buy your favorite plain yogurt and offer an array of fresh fruit toppings, nuts, granola, and a little bit of chocolate!
Natasha

Mitzi was scaring me. Had Mars and I bought into her story and assisted her? "I don't think the police are actively looking for her, either."

Mars rose and fetched a notepad and pen. He wrote Mitzi's name on it with a question mark. "I feel like an utter fool."

"She played the frightened victim very well," I pointed out. "And neither Denise nor Rachel would be wary of her. In fact, she said she was supposed to meet each of them at the Inger House."

"Ahh, but why murder them?" asked Bernie. "What would she have to gain?"

"For starters, I guess she's now the sole owner of the design business," said Nina.

Mars scribbled that on the pad. "But she could have accomplished that by buying Denise out."

"Maybe she didn't have the cash to do that." Bernie popped a grape in his mouth.

"And Rachel?" I asked.

"I know Rachel was interested in Mike, but maybe Mitzi is, too." Nina poured herself another cocktail.

"Then why would she be hiding?" I asked. "Once Denise was dead, she wouldn't have to hide anymore."

"To continue with her act?" Mars loaded a cracker with Gouda.

Bernie smiled. "What if I phoned her tomorrow and asked her to come and decorate a room at my house?"

"How would that help?" Nina placed a piece of cheese in her mouth.

"She would have to come out of hiding to see the room. And if she needs money, she might just do that," Bernie said.

"Oh great. She'll kill you, too," Nina said.

"No she won't," said Mars. "Let's give it a try. The two of us can overpower her."

"Not if she comes equipped with insulin," I pointed out.

"We'll think about it," said Mars. "What have you learned, Sophie?"

I rose to serve our dinner. Nina handed me Spode Woodland dinner plates. The brown floral pattern on the rim invoked fall, and woodland birds and animals were featured in the centers of the dishes. I had been picking them up here and there when I saw them.

I sliced the pork loin, which had developed a light crust from the marinade. I placed it on the plates, then spooned on heaps of the vegetables. The marinade scent mingled with the shallots and smelled enticing.

I slid the pears into the hot oven and closed the door.

We sat down to eat, and for a short time, it was all about the food. But it didn't take us long to come back to the murders.

"Any developments on your part, Sophie?" asked Mars.

"Helena and Thurman lied to me."

Everyone stopped eating.

"Why would they kill their grandson's wife?" Bernie poked a bit of sweet potato with his fork.

"I don't know that they have. Helena said that Robbie and Mike were at work the morning Denise was murdered. According to the very chatty receptionist, that's not the case. Mike was in the office early in the morning but left by nine o'clock. And Robbie didn't come in at all that day. Allegedly, he had meetings outside the office."

Mars fumbled for the notepad and wrote their names down. "What about Helena?"

"She was in the office and didn't leave until she received word that Denise had been taken to the emergency room."

"Mark her name out," said Bernie. "So we won't get confused."

"However, her husband went a step further. He claimed to be at a meeting at his golf club. Not only was he not there, but he paid someone to lie about it. Which I think looks really bad for him because he anticipated that someone would be checking up on his whereabouts."

"Motive?" asked Nina between bites.

"I truly don't know. But I don't think Helena suspects him. If she thought her husband was guilty, she wouldn't have had to cover up for Robbie and Mike." I savored a bit of the soft shallots.

"Did you have a chance to visit Mike's mom?" asked Mars.

"Daisy and I took a trip out to Great Falls. Mary takes in rescue horses."

Nina gasped. "No! Then she's not the murderer."

"But she is very concerned about Mike. She went into Mom mode immediately and was very protective. So far, I haven't gotten the feeling that any of them disliked Denise. In fact, she said she thought Rachel murdered Denise."

"So Mike might have killed Rachel in retaliation. She took Denise from him. That's a powerful motive." Mars helped himself to more pork tenderloin.

"One other thing. Mary, Mike's mom, has absolutely no alibi and readily admits it."

Mars added her name to the list of suspects.

"We're going over to the Inger House tomorrow morning. Want to come?"

"What for?" asked Bernie.

"I'm not sure. I feel like we must have missed something or overlooked a clue. It's not easy to murder someone, let alone two people. Yet someone or two people pulled that off."

When everyone was done with our main course, I removed the pears from the oven and took out four bowls. I scooped the core out of the softened pears and topped them with a scoop of vanilla ice cream. I drizzled chocolate sauce over the ice cream and topped each pear with just a spoonful of whipped cream.

Nina took them to the table. "Mmm, so indulgent."

I laughed. "It's fruit. It's good for us."

My phone rang after my friends left, and I recognized Holly Miller's voice. I had known her when she was a fund-raiser in Washington, DC, and had organized several events for her.

"I'm in town for a couple of days. Would you be free for a brief visit tomorrow morning around ten?"

"Holly! Perfect timing." She had solved some murders at a mountain resort called Wagtail. "How would you like to check out a murder scene with me? It's in a fancy historic house."

"Murder?"

"I'll fill you in tomorrow. Want to come for breakfast?"

"I would love to, but I can't. Holmes wrangled me into a breakfast that I can't get out of. Well, not without upsetting him."

"Too bad. Meet me at my house at ten then!"

That was a lucky break. I looked forward to seeing Holly.

I checked all the doors to be sure they were locked before I went up to bed. I felt like Agnes. Had the murderer accomplished what he wanted? Or was he planning to kill someone else?

TUESDAY

The first person I thought of on waking was Mitzi. Was she in hiding because she was the killer? Or was the killer looking for her? Whatever the reason, she had to be hiding out somewhere. I tried texting her. **Who is feeding your cat?** Maybe that would get her attention.

I padded down the stairs in a fluffy bathrobe, noting that the temperatures were beginning to drop. I let Daisy out into the backyard, then put on the kettle for tea. Mochie mewed at me and rubbed his head against my ankles. "Breakfast is coming up, Mochie."

I spooned turkey cat food into his bowl. He settled to eat it just as Daisy was ready to come back in. I hurried upstairs to shower and dress in comfortable stretchy jeans and a sweater before Nina brought breakfast. I was feeding Daisy when Nina delivered lattes and avocado and egg bagels.

Holly arrived at exactly ten o'clock. We hugged and chatted nonstop, especially after Nina noticed her beautiful engagement ring. She and Holmes hadn't set a date for the wedding yet, but I hoped I would be invited.

Nina and I filled her in on the deaths of Denise and Rachel as we walked over to the Inger House.

Holly was impressed by the mansion, especially the beautiful conservatory. "I don't even know Denise, but it breaks my heart that she died before she ever had a chance to live in this home. I can't even imagine it. Do you think her husband will sell the place? It's awfully big for one person."

"I honestly don't know. It has been in the family for so long that I'm not sure any of them want to give it up," I said.

She gazed at the kitchen floor where Denise had died. "I guess everyone is worried about someone bumping into them with an insulin injection. It could be done so easily."

"I think Denise knew what had happened. She looked like she was trying to get out the door but couldn't quite make it."

"Where did Rachel die?"

I led her to the back bedroom. "She lay on the floor right here. The killer had covered her with piles of clothes." I stared at the spot where Rachel had lain. There wasn't a thing on the old floors that indicated she had ever been there. No bloodstains, no hair, no tiny bit of ripped clothing.

"Most likely to hide her body," said Nina. "But where did the additional clothes come from? And why hide Rachel's body when Denise wasn't hidden at all?"

"Because someone was coming in? Had knocked on the door?" I guessed. "What I would like to know is why Rachel was in the house. Denise had every right to be here. She was renovating the house and she planned to live here with her husband. But unless Mitzi gave Rachel a key and asked for her help, I don't know how she got inside."

"Unless the killer opened the door for her," said Holly.

It was such a simple and logical response, but the hair on my arms prickled at the thought of Rachel's murderer inviting her into the house.

I opened the double doors of the armoire. It was empty. The interior reflected its age, particularly the way the rod for hanging clothes had been mounted, which I had never seen in a modern armoire. It was in remarkably good condition. I was not expert on antiques, but I suspected this piece would fetch a good price.

"The first time I saw this house, there was a pile of clothes on the bed, and more inside the armoire."

"Which the murderer must have needed to cover Rachel adequately," said Nina.

"My thoughts exactly. Unless . . ." I studied the hardwood floor. It was old and creaky underfoot, which was typical of historic homes in Old Town. My own stairs squeaked like crazy. I kneeled for a better look.

"Unless what?" asked Nina.

"There is another reason one might empty an armoire—to move it. Look at the floor down here. The feet had been in the same spot for a long time. See the slight indentations? Here on the front leg, you can see that it didn't go back exactly where it belonged and there's a very light scraping along the floor where it was moved."

"I think you're right. Shall we move it?" asked Nina.

She didn't have to ask twice. The three of us managed to swing the heavy armoire away from the wall.

Nina peered at the wall behind it. "Something's there. Like a big patch on the wall."

Holly and I peeked behind her. A piece of old plywood

appeared to have been torn off the wall. It leaned against wood slats that had been screwed onto the wall, parallel to the floor with no gaps between them. We slid the armoire to another wall. The three of us stood back and studied the unusual boards.

"Plumbing access?" suggested Holly.

"It's very big for that. I'll go outside to see what's there. Maybe they had to connect something modern, like a heat pump?" I doubted that, but in old buildings patchwork addition of modern fixtures was always possible.

In the backyard, I located the window of the bedroom and knocked on it to let Nina and Holly know I was there. But I didn't see a heat pump or other appliance outside the bedroom wall. As far as I could tell, the brick rear of the house showed no signs of having been disturbed. I supposed the beige paint could have covered up signs of replaced bricks. After all, the house was well over one hundred years old. There must have been a lot of changes to it over the years as modern inventions came along. I ran my hands over the section where I thought the wood planks had been added inside. I couldn't feel any aberrations. I returned to the house. But when I walked through the dining room into the foyer, I stopped dead.

The door to the basement hung open. My breath caught in my throat. Had someone been there with us the whole time? Heard us moving the armoire? My heart pounding, I edged toward the bedroom door, listening for voices.

A floorboard creaked behind me. I shrieked.

"What's with *you?*" asked Nina, brandishing a battery-powered screwdriver.

"Someone is in the house with us," I whispered. "The basement door was open."

"That was me." She held up the screwdriver. "I saw a bunch of tools in the basement when Wong was searching the house the other day."

Nevertheless, I peeked into the bedroom before entering. Holly was trying to unscrew a board with a Swiss Army Knife.

Nina passed me. "Look what I found! This should make it easier."

"Great!" Holly took it and made quick work of unscrewing the first board. "These screws have been here a long time. They're not rusted, just really tight."

She removed the board and handed it to Nina, who handed it to me. I laid it on the floor outside the bedroom.

When the second board came off, the three of us exchanged looks.

"Does anyone else think those look like . . . ?"

Chapter 17

Dear Natasha,
My husband's boss and his wife are coming for
brunch. My husband thinks I should decorate the
fireplace mantel with fall junk. I loathe fussy décor.
All that stuff to dust! How can I achieve a fall am-
biance without pumpkins, foliage, books, or can-
dles?
                    Keeping It Clean in Plain City, Ohio

Dear Keeping It Clean,
Tell your husband that you don't need to dress it
up. I have never understood why people put books
on the mantel. Just set a painting on the mantle.
You don't even have to hang it.
                                          Natasha

"Ribs?" asked Nina.

Holly swallowed hard. "I would have to agree."

I reached for the screwdriver. "Let's take off two more boards before we call Wolf. I read somewhere that a woman intentionally hid a plastic skeleton behind a wall in her house to spook future owners."

"I'd really like to think that's what happened here," said Holly. "But it doesn't look good."

I unscrewed the boards. A skull wasn't visible yet, but tattered cloth hung off bones.

Holly's phone rang. She glanced at it. "Oh no! I forgot all about Holmes." She walked away saying, "Hi, honey!"

Meanwhile, I placed a call to Wolf.

His voice mail answered.

"Wolf, this is Sophie. Call me as soon as you can. Nina and I found a skeleton. At least, that's what we think it is."

Holly returned spouting apologies. "I am so sorry, but I promised Holmes I would meet him for lunch and I'm already late. I really want to stay and find out what that is. Promise you'll keep me in the loop?"

Nina and I hugged her and promised we would come to her wedding in Wagtail. And that we would bring Daisy, Mochie, and Muppet. It seemed very quiet when she left.

We returned to the bedroom and began the unscrewing process again.

I told Nina about my call to Wolf.

"I think it's a fake," said Nina. "It doesn't smell like much. Just musty, like an old attic."

"We can only hope so." I handed her a board. "But the bones don't look like they're plastic."

"Shh," said Nina. "Did you hear that?"

We listened but didn't hear anything.

I resumed the process of removing boards until I was looking into the eye sockets of a skull. "I don't think this is fake," I whispered.

"Me either," Nina whispered back before snapping a photograph.

A shiver ran through me. The skeleton was both frightening and mesmerizing. "How old do you think it is?"

"Don't know. This house is ancient."

The sound of something being dragged across a floor somewhere in the house reached us.

"Someone is in here," breathed Nina.

A door slammed in the house. "I heard *that*!"

The two of us fled the Inger House as if we were running for our lives. When we were safely across the street, we paused to catch our breath.

"A prank," said Nina. "A Halloween prank?"

"It's too early for that."

"We should watch the front door to see who comes out."

"An excellent idea, but there are other exits. Whoever it is could leave through the kitchen or the conservatory and go out the back gate."

Nina froze, then said boldly, "Maybe someone opened a window for air and a gust slammed the door shut."

"And what was that sound of something dragging across the floor?"

Nina took a deep breath and shuddered. "I'm not going back in there."

"Not until someone is with us. But we have to lock the door," I said.

"I'll wait here."

"Some friend you are!"

"Okay, okay."

We crossed the street. I slid the key into the lock and heard it clank. For good measure I tried to open the door. It held fast.

Nina was already in the middle of the street, heading for the other side.

I followed her. "Do you think Mitzi could be hiding in the house? There is a toothbrush in a bathroom."

Nina gazed up at the windows. "It would be difficult to do that without leaving any sign of your presence. Right? Like a coffee cup or crumbs from something you ate? Or a dim light on at night?" She stopped talking for a moment. "But I am not coming back at night to see who shows up!"

I wanted to laugh at her, but I understood how she felt. I wasn't planning to return to the house unless someone was with me. Preferably Wolf. We started to walk home.

"I do, however, want to be there when the cops come. Call me for that, okay?"

"Of course."

I phoned Wolf again from home but had no luck. I spent the afternoon decorating my house for the brunch. The kitchen, dining room, and living room were probably the rooms where most photos would be taken. Maybe my sunroom as well. Given our bizarre morning, I found I was a bit reluctant to enter my attic room. Fortunately, no one lurked there. No humans nor human remains. Not that I knew of anyway.

As I opened storage boxes in search of dried autumn flowers, my mind still dwelled on Mike, the Inger House, and the skeleton. Why would someone have moved the armoire to begin with?

I perched on a storage box. There were several possibilities. One of the Nofsingers might have moved it, discovered the planks attached to the wall, and moved it back. Maybe Jacky and Stu decided they wanted it in their new home after all, but when they saw the planks, they knew it had to stay to cover them up. Maybe Denise, Mitzi, or Rachel had moved it, planning to use the room in another way, like a library or a study. Or they wanted the armoire in a different room. It was very handsome.

What would I do if I moved a piece of furniture in my house and found planks like that? I would probably push the armoire back in place until I was ready to seal the opening with drywall. So it wasn't all that remarkable that whoever had moved it had also returned it to the original position.

But in the back of my mind, as I resumed searching for harvest décor, I had to entertain a more sinister reason. What if Denise, Mitzi, or Rachel had moved the armoire and discovered the planks sealing the wall? But someone in the Nofsinger family didn't want them to know about the skeleton?

I wished I had a floor plan of the house. I had a very strong feeling that the little bedroom and bath on the first floor might be located behind the kitchen or dining room. Someone thinking about enlarging the kitchen might have been interested in clearing out the bedroom. I shook my head. Unless I missed my guess, that skeleton had been hidden for a very long time. It was entirely possible that none of the Nofsingers even knew of its existence.

At that moment, I put my hands on a stack of napkins with precisely frayed edges. They were a wonderful color, sort of an orange that leaned toward a faint pink. And right next to them was an entire box of carefully preserved dried blue and green hydrangea, which would be perfect in tall vases in the living room.

Clutching everything in my arms, I carefully walked down the two flights of stairs. I set the napkins on the kitchen table to remind me to wash them, and carried the dried hydrangea into the living room where I divided them among vases. I returned to the attic and retrieved more fall decorations. For the next three hours, I ran up and down the stairs moving summery accents to the attic and bringing autumnal lanterns, baskets, and throws downstairs.

Wolf phoned as I was admiring the results and thinking how to dress them up more.

"A skeleton?" he blurted.

"Hi, Wolf. Yes. Most definitely."

"This is going to be a long day. I should be there in about fifteen minutes."

I thanked him and phoned Nina. We hurried over to the house but waited outside.

Nina studied the windows. "Do you think someone is still in there?"

"I hope not! But we'll have Wolf with us."

He walked up to us as I spoke. "Why are you out here?"

"We heard someone in the house earlier and left in a big hurry," I explained.

"Are you two spooking yourselves or is there actually a problem?"

Nina pulled out her phone and showed him the picture she had taken of the skeleton.

As always, Wolf remained calm. "All right. Let's go in and see this."

I unlocked the door. It squeaked a little when it swung open. We walked into the foyer and stopped. I didn't hear a thing.

I motioned to Wolf to follow us and led him to the bedroom.

Nina gasped.

Chapter 18

Dear Natasha,
My mom loves your show and said you would
know the answer to this. I'm having a brunch party
for my friends from work. Mom says I need to mail
invitations to them. I think that's cheugy! I say just
telling them is all I need to do. Who's right?
                              Rizz Girl in Cool, Texas

Dear Rizz Girl,
Words may change but good manners do not. One
must always send written invitations to a party.
Otherwise, how will your guests know when and
where to go?
                                      Rizz Natasha

The armoire was back in place!
The clothes that had been piled on the bed were gone.
I ran to the armoire and flung open the doors. Clothes
hung neatly on hangers again. "Well! That proves someone was in the house. When Nina and I left, the armoire
was against that wall"—I pointed at it—"and the clothes
were on the bed."

"It's true, Wolf," said Nina. "The skeleton is in the wall behind the armoire."

He studied us. "Is this a prank? Because I really do not have time for games."

"What about the photo I showed you?" asked Nina. "That's proof of what's behind the wall."

I began to remove the clothes from the armoire.

Nina and Wolf pitched in.

When the clothes had been removed, the three of us pulled the armoire away from the wall.

This time I gasped along with Nina. Every single old slat of wood had been screwed back onto the wall.

"That's not how we left it," I said. "All the slats were in a neat pile outside the bedroom door."

"I am *not* going into the basement to get the rechargeable screwdriver again." Nina crossed her arms defiantly.

"Let me see that picture." Wolf held out his hand for Nina's phone. He studied it as he walked out of the room.

"We are so lucky that the person who was in the house didn't attack us," I said to Nina.

"I think there were two people. How could one person get all this done so quickly? It's only been a few hours."

Wolf returned to the bedroom. "Wong is on her way over here along with a forensic crew that will take down the planks. This is your last chance to tell me that it's all a joke."

"Wolf! Why don't you believe us?" I asked. "Have I ever pulled a prank like this on you?"

"That's the trouble. This isn't like you. But two young women have been murdered here. That means people are getting hysterical about this house. It's a grand old place. Not a house of murder. This is a very old home, but people find things like letters, and coins, and photographs in the walls. Not skeletons. I've been in a lot of historic houses. Some people think they have ghosts. Others find oddball things in houses that they just bought. But it's kind of hard to believe that families have lived here for decades yet no one discovered a skeleton."

His attitude made me want to remove the planks myself so he could see it. I probably sounded impatient when I said, "But I have never lied to you."

"You may have refrained from telling me the whole truth."

I winced. That was probably true. I may have done that. But sometimes it was necessary.

Fortunately, Wong and the forensics team arrived shortly. Wolf departed for some other case he was working on, while Wong, Nina, and I watched as the planks were removed again. Halfway through the process, I knew we had a problem.

There was no skeleton.

Chapter 19

Dear Sophie,
My boss thinks brunch would be a great way for
employees to get to know each other. There are
thirty of us! She doesn't want to go to a restaurant
because we won't be able to mingle. I think she's
nuts. Help!

Need Aspirin in Boss, Texas

Dear Need Aspirin,
Find a nice outdoor park with tables and make it a
potluck brunch! Good luck.

Sophie

Nina elbowed me in the ribs. "How can that be? Have we lost our minds? Is it possible for three people to imagine they see the same thing that isn't there?"

Wong raised her eyebrows at us. "Wolf will not be happy about this."

"I don't understand. Maybe the person who was sneaking around the house carted the skeleton away," I said.

"And why would they do that?" asked Wong.

It was a good question. "So we would look incompetent? So no one else would see it? Because that person placed the skeleton in the wall after killing him or her? Nina, show Wong the photo you took."

All the planks were off the wall now. Wong stepped closer. "Looks like the same space. Did you use AI or some other technique of inserting a skeleton?"

"No!" Nina and I chimed.

"Do you want us to replace the planks?" asked one of the guys.

"No!" I said it before giving it any thought.

Wong shrugged and said, "I guess you're done. Thanks, everyone."

While they collected their gear, I edged closer to the wall. I could hear Nina defending us to Wong.

I had never carried, lifted, or touched a real skeleton before. Other than silly songs like *the knee bone is connected to the thigh bone* I didn't know a thing about what might or might not be connected after years in a wall. Probably nothing. All the tendons and whatnot would be gone. So basically, everything would collapse like the blocks in a game of Jenga. The skeleton had fit between two pieces of lumber. It seemed to me that as the years went on, the bones would have been propped up by virtue of being squeezed between the wood. Once a piece was removed, everything could collapse.

I took a deep breath and poked my head between the two-by-fours. It was too clean. "Wong! Look."

"I am *not* sticking my head in there."

"But look. If this hadn't been opened for years, don't you think there would be dust at the base? Or dead bugs or something?"

"Thank you, Sophie. Now I really don't want to look in there."

I gazed at Nina. "Someone took it away."

"Yeah, duh!"

I shone my phone flashlight where the skeleton had been. And there it was. A tiny glimmer. I reached for it and managed to pick it up. I felt triumphant and almost giddy as I held it out to Wong nestled on my palm. "Voila!"

She wrinkled her nose. "What is that?"

"I believe they're called collar pins. Or collar bars, perhaps."

"What does that prove?" she asked.

"It must have dropped off the skeleton's shirt."

Wong pressed her hands against her waist and shook her head at me. "Sophie, you have lost your mind. You don't know how that filthy thing came to be there or to whom it belonged. Besides, it probably slipped out of something when they were packing and moving. Leave it here for them to find."

She could be right, but I found it inside the wall. Nevertheless, I set it on the windowsill. "Wong, I know for a fact that there was a skeleton in that space earlier today, and we have another friend who can back us up on that because she saw it, too. Someone came and got it in the interim. Now I don't know where they put it, but I'm willing to bet it's somewhere in this house."

"Well, if you find it again, you call me." She turned to leave the room.

"You're not even going to search the house?" asked Nina.

"I have searched this place twice already. Not even a pencil has ever been moved."

"A toothbrush has appeared," I said. "And food in the fridge."

Wong sighed and left. We heard the front door close behind her.

"We'll get Mars and Bernie to come over here and search the place with us," I said, undeterred. "There's safety in numbers. Real or fake, we're going to find that thing."

"Bernie has some guys working for him who are pretty strong."

I nodded. "You call Bernie. I'll phone Mars. See if they can come over now. It shouldn't take long if we divide up into teams."

We were in luck. The two of us sat outside on the stoop while we waited for them.

The next-door neighbor, Jesse McGuire, spied us and came over.

I introduced him to Nina.

"I heard the cops were here this morning," he said. "Please don't tell me someone else died."

"Not exactly." I told him about the disappearing skeleton. Nina showed him the photograph.

"Whoa!" He stepped back and looked up at the house. "And you think that someone is still inside?"

"We don't know," said Nina. "We have reinforcements coming to do a search."

"I'm game," said Jesse. "I'd be glad to help."

As if they had timed it that way, Bernie and several weight-lifting bartenders arrived, followed shortly by Mars and Daisy. From the way they greeted one another, I gathered that Jesse and the bartenders were already acquainted.

"Daisy!" I exclaimed as she ran toward me.

"I thought she might sniff out something. She is a hound, after all," said Mars.

We divided into two groups and split up the house. Nina led one group upstairs, and I took the other group through the main floor and the basement.

The main floor was easy to search. Closets and trunks were opened. Everyone raved about the almost empty conservatory. I dreaded going into the basement, but it had to be done.

Several of the men on our team stopped to admire the workshop someone had built in the basement. I hoped the

other group was having luck because we weren't! My dismay must have shown.

One of the muscular young men said, "My great-nanny,
Annie, used to work in a house like this. She said a lot of
them had back staircases that led to the kitchen. Have you
seen anything like that?"

"Great-Nanny Annie!" laughed Jesse. "Is that really what
you call her?"

"Oh yeah. She's a hoot," he said. "She's almost one
hundred and still sharp as they come."

That sounded familiar. Could there be two Annies who
were almost one hundred? "That wouldn't be the Annie
who raised Helena and Jacky, would it?"

"Yeah. I know them. They're like aunts to me."

I gazed at the walls with fresh interest. I bet there were
back stairs in this house at one time.

As I looked around, it dawned on me that I hadn't seen
a washer or dryer. Given the age of the building, they would
likely be in the basement. I ambled behind the workshop
area and flicked on an overhead light. A washer and dryer
were in a large unpleasant space with a table for folding. It
was grim. Dreary concrete blocks and giant stones lined
the walls. I'd seen basements in Old Town where similar
walls had been dressed up so I knew the basement could
be improved upon. This wasn't a place where anyone
would want to spend much time. I was willing to bet Denise planned to move the washer and dryer upstairs somewhere.

A narrow panel in the wall had a latch on it. I flicked it
open and found a staircase. At first, I expected it to be
creepy and loaded with spiderwebs, but it was obviously
still in use. The air inside smelled of licorice and it didn't
contain any creepy crawly creatures.

I walked halfway up the dark stairs and screamed. The
uppermost stairs were littered with bones.

Bernie raced up the stairs behind me. "Ugh. Are you okay?"

"I'm fine. I think we found our skeleton."

"Unless there are two," he said. "That's a lot of bones."

I didn't want to entertain that possibility. "Look! Do you see that bit of dark cloth? I think it's the same one."

"Do bones smell of licorice?" he asked. "That must be a landing ahead. Where's the door?"

"I don't think we can reach it without disturbing the bones. We should probably leave it like it is for Wolf to see."

"Good idea. The less we touch, the better."

We retreated down the staircase and I called the main number at the Alexandria Police and asked for Wolf.

He showed up half an hour later and gave Mars and Bernie a curt nod before following me down to the basement. I let him walk up the small staircase alone and waited for him at the bottom, which wasn't much nicer, but at least there wasn't a dead man in the room with me. Not that I knew of anyway.

Wolf joined me at the bottom of the stairs. In a soft voice he said, "I'm sorry. I should have believed you." He strode past me and made a phone call.

I followed him upstairs, where everyone else waited in the living room.

Wolf ended his call and gazed around at everyone. "I'll need all of your names, home addresses, and phone numbers in case I need to reach you. Who found the bones?"

"I did," I said, raising my hand slightly.

"Of course it would be you."

If anyone else had said that I would have seen it as a snide comment, as if he meant to imply that I knew where to find the bones because I had placed them there. But I knew Wolf wouldn't think that of me.

I sat down on the floor and stroked Daisy.

One by one, Wolf allowed people to leave until only

Bernie, Mars, Nina, Daisy, and I remained. "Do I understand this correctly? None of you were with Sophie when she found the bones?"

"She called me over when she found them," said Bernie. "We didn't disturb them. We thought it best to leave them exactly as we found them."

Thankfully, the forensics crew arrived. As they descended to the basement, I phoned Helena, to inform her of the developments.

"Helena, it's Sophie. I'm very sorry to tell you that we discovered a skeleton in a wall at the Inger House."

I heard the quick intake of her breath through the phone. "You what?"

"The police are here, gathering the bones. I thought you should know because people will probably hear about it."

"Yes. Yes, of course. Thank you. That's just horrible. Can you tell who it is?"

"No. It's just the bones and a very small amount of fragile fabric. The forensics crew is here collecting it."

"I see. How old do they think it is?"

"I don't know yet."

"Civil War, perhaps?"

"Helena, I'm not an expert on dating bones. I guess they could go back that far. Are there stories about the Inger House during the Civil War?"

"Yes. I just, well, I can't imagine . . . are you sure they're human? Maybe a dog fell into a crevice?"

"I'm afraid not. I saw the skull. It's definitely human."

"How awful."

"I expect Detective Fleischman will be dropping by to keep you informed."

"Do you think there could be a connection between Denise's murder and the skeleton? No, of course not. How could there be?"

"I don't know. It seems like a stretch. But Rachel's body

was found in the room where the skeleton was originally found."

"Which room was that?"

"The first-floor bedroom."

"I see. Oh, Sophie! This is a nightmare. Has Mitzi turned up yet?"

"Not that I know of."

"I live in fear that she'll be discovered dead somewhere," said Helena.

"Let's hope that's not the case." I said goodbye and disconnected the call.

Everyone appeared to be waiting for me. We filed out of the house rather somberly. "I suppose we should be glad that we discovered the remains." I locked the door. "I don't know how long that person was in the wall, but I'm sure someone missed him or her and wondered what became of that person."

"Like Mitzi," said Mars.

I turned quickly to look at him. "Do you know something?"

"I wish I did! I know she's not where she was staying. We should have slipped an AirTag of our own in her purse."

"That's illegal," said Wolf, sounding tired.

"I didn't say I did it. But if we had, we would be able to find her." Mars turned away from Wolf and shook his head.

Wolf stepped into his car and drove away. Bernie headed back to his restaurant. Nina, Mars, and I agreed to have dinner together the next evening at my house.

By the time I walked into my home, it was dark outside. I had trouble focusing on anything other than the skeleton and the deaths of Denise and Rachel. For once in my life, I didn't head for the fridge. I pulled on a cozy sweater and took Daisy for a walk.

The windows of the charming old homes glowed in the night. Lamps lighted entrances to the houses and the occasional Halloween ghost had begun to make an appearance. Daisy greeted other dogs and I relaxed as we walked. Just off King Street, we walked past Nofsinger & Lawson Fine Interiors.

I stopped cold. Nofsinger was now dead, and Lawson was missing. What had happened to those two lovely women? As far as I knew, they had had a thriving business. Denise had done a beautiful job on Helena's kitchen. I couldn't imagine what they might have done to drive someone to murder.

We walked home. I was emotionally exhausted yet feeling restless. Mochie was happy to see us. At least I thought so by the way he yawned and stretched before turning over and ignoring us. Daisy was ready for a nap, too.

I snacked on leftovers for dinner, fed Daisy and Mochie, and hit the sack early, which turned out to be a good thing because my phones started ringing at four in the morning.

As far as I could make out, reporters had called Helena, who referred them to me. I didn't have much to tell them, but I confirmed that a skeleton had been found and suggested they call the police for more information.

The phones didn't stop ringing. I finally turned them off, wrapped up in my fuzzy robe, and padded downstairs to make a cup of tea. There was no going back to sleep now.

The lights were on in Nina's house, too. I pulled two mugs out of the cabinet. I knew she would want Lady Grey tea.

Inspired by Hazel's Doughnut Holes, I whipped up something similar and slid them in the oven to bake.

Nina arrived minutes later, wrapped in a cozy purple bathrobe and fuzzy slippers. She turned on the TV in the kitchen immediately. Muppet seemed excited to be up and about so early in the morning.

Cameras showed the Inger House, which was completely dark—not a single light shone in the windows.

"Agnes must be having a fit right about now with all the reporters outside her house." Nina cringed.

The reporter said, "We have confirmation that a skeleton was found in the house locally known as the Inger House. The site of two murders recently, one has to wonder what's going on there. No one has been able to confirm any connection between the recent deaths and the skeleton, which is believed to have been in the house for quite a while, perhaps decades."

Chapter 20

Dear Sophie,
My wife thinks my very practical desk is too dark
and heavy. I like it and there's plenty of storage, in-
cluding a file drawer on each side. She showed me
a picture of a white desk that is nice enough, but
the only thing you could store in it is a paper clip!
Need Pens & Files in Penn Argyl, Pennsylvania

Dear Need Pens & Files,
Make a deal with her. You will accept the new desk
only if you can build an entire custom storage wall
full of file drawers, nooks, and crannies for all your
work needs.

Sophie

"You wouldn't believe what they can figure out from ancient bones these days," said Nina. "I called my husband last night. He says they bring in forensic anthropologists in cases like this. They can tell whether it's male or female, when the person was born, what kind of diet they had, and quite often the cause of death."

"Does he have any connections with local anthropologists?" I pulled the doughnut holes out of the oven, dipped them in melted butter, and rolled them in cinnamon sugar.

Nina laughed. "That's exactly what I asked him! As a matter of fact, he knows some of them very well."

"Will he be making inquiries?" I brought the warm doughnut holes to the table.

"Of course." Nina helped herself to a doughnut hole. "Mmm. What are these?"

"They're called doughnut holes, but I think they're misnamed. They're more like a little round piece of cake." I tried one, too.

"You have to make these for the brunch!"

"I probably will."

The TV station shifted to a discussion of what bones could reveal, including some poisons that were administered as medicines at various times in history.

Nina stretched. "At least we know there's no connection between the skeleton and the recent murders. Those clothes on the bones were nothing but tattered remnants. I'm betting that person died a very long time ago."

"He was probably murdered though. Otherwise, he'd have had a decent burial and wouldn't have been hidden in the wall."

"How did Helena take it when you called her?"

"Pretty well. All the Nofsingers who lived there must be creeped out to imagine they went about their daily business and never knew the skeleton was in the wall. She said something about the Civil War."

Nina nodded. "That would make sense. A lot of crazy things happened then. Some of the larger buildings in town were used as makeshift hospitals."

"One would hope they didn't hide all the bodies inside walls. Something terrible must have happened to that person. Think about it. Let's say you murder someone in your house. What would you do with the body?"

"Dig a grave in the backyard, drag it outside, cover with dirt, and plant a garden."

"You answered that way too fast."

Nina laughed. "Wouldn't that be the easiest thing to do?"

"Maybe. If it were a time of year when the ground was soft, and you had the strength to dig an appropriately large piece of ground. People are pretty big, and rigor mortis sets in fast. That could be a lot of digging."

"I hadn't considered that. My concerns would be that a nosy neighbor might see me or that it would develop an odor and neighborhood dogs would come and dig it up."

"Second choice?"

"I guess the wall would be safer in some respects. But the odor! I've read about people who let a dead family member just lie there. I can't imagine how it must have reeked. Isn't that how a guy was caught in New York City a long time ago? The neighbors complained about the smell and a body was discovered in a closet?"

I had read about that incident as well. "Whoever that skeleton is, someone went to great lengths to cover up his death."

After I fed the dogs and Mochie, we ate a breakfast of scrambled eggs and doughnut holes. Nina went home, and I shot upstairs to shower and dress. My destination was Synergy, the gym owned by Jesse McGuire. I had a bad feeling that he wouldn't tell me if Jacky and Stu had been there when Denise was killed. He would probably say it was private information. All the same, I thought I should try. I dressed in all black, hoping I would look slimmer and more fit. As if! It would be cool in the morning, so I added a camel-colored jacket.

I took off at a brisk walk. Old Town was just waking up. Stores weren't open yet, but cafés and gyms were already in full swing. I found Synergy in a renovated building with huge glass windows. Inside, patrons rode stationary bikes, lifted weights, and tortured themselves on various exercise machines. I could see Jesse helping someone in the back of the room.

I entered the building and couldn't help gazing around and wondering if one of the people sweating away could be the murderer. Some of them wore Synergy pins, not unlike the one I had found.

The young woman at the front desk eyed me with doubt. I couldn't blame her. I had joined two exercise clubs in my life with the best intentions, but had soon given up on them. I felt as if that information was written on my forehead. "Good morning!" I said cheerfully. "I would like to see Jesse, please."

"Maybe I can help you," said the young woman.

I fudged. "He asked me to stop by."

"This is a busy time of day for us. Maybe you could come back later for your tour."

I eyed her name badge. "Heather, would you please tell Jesse that Sophie is here to see him?"

"And what would Sophie's last name be?"

Well, that was just plain rude. She had no reason to be so snotty. "Winston," I muttered through gritted teeth. "Sophie Winston."

"He's busy right now. I'll let him know Sophie Winston came in."

I had had about enough of her. I skirted the desk and walked toward Jesse as fast as I could. Heather scurried along behind me. "You can't go back there. Do you hear me? Stop! You cannot go back there."

"Jesse!" I said with far more affection than I normally would have shown.

"Sophie! It's good to see you. I heard what happened. It was all over the news this morning. That was something! Now I'm wondering what's behind the walls in *my* old

house. Come in my office. Can I get you an energy boosting drink?"

Boosting my energy sounded like a great idea on its face.
But I was afraid it might be some kind of hyped-up caf-
feine that my cupcake-loving system wouldn't tolerate. "I'll
pass on that, thanks."

"How about carrot and apple juice?"

"Okay, sure. That sounds good."

He handed me a glass bottle. "Are you here to see the
facilities?"

"Actually, I need a favor."

"Sure. Just name it."

"Members of the Nofsinger family informed me of their
whereabouts on Sunday around nine to ten thirty in the
morning, when Denise died. It's so I can eliminate them as
suspects. I've been able to confirm almost everyone's
whereabouts except Jacky and Stu Finch. They claim they
were here. I wondered if you could confirm that?" I smiled
at him, hoping I'd made it sound innocent enough.

He typed something on his keyboard.

I looked around his office. A board on the wall featured
a host of badges, not unlike the one I had found at the
Inger House.

"Normally I wouldn't share that kind of information,"
he said. "You never know what someone is up to. But . . ."
He broke into a huge grin. "I can confirm that they were
both here. Whew! I wouldn't want any of my clients to be
murder suspects!"

"No! That would be terrible. Thank you so much." I
pointed toward the little pins. "What are those?"

Jesse grinned. "Inspiration."

"What? I don't get it."

"Do you remember your first-grade teacher giving you
stars when you did something well?"

"It has been a while, but yes, I do remember that."

"Same concept. Working out is hard. When you join you get the basic round pin with the triangular top in yellow. Then you get other pins as rewards. For instance, the purple one is for people who come in at least four times a week for one month. It's all about developing the habit of working out. The more you do, the higher the pin. So many people give up and drop out that we try to make it fun and give rewards for achievements."

"I see," I said. The pin I found probably belonged to Stu or Jacky and was lost when they moved out of the house. But whoever lost the pin that lay under the china cabinet was a member of the club, including the man sitting right in front of me. I smiled at him. "Was it a zoo outside your house this morning?"

"It was wild. The news trucks arrived first. Then as people began to cluster around, the lady across the street, Agnes, came out with a broom and started smacking everyone with it trying to move them away. She was very upset. I hate to say this, but it was kind of funny. She probably resented me for laughing." He placed his elbows on the desk and intertwined his fingers. Leaning toward me, he asked, "Who do you think the murderer is?"

As tempting as it was to say I thought it might be someone who used his gym, I thought better of that. "I'm not sure yet. But you helped me narrow down the suspects. I can't thank you enough." I truly was grateful.

A man with bulging muscles came to the door. "Excuse me, Jesse, one of the treadmills is out of commission. I can't figure out what's wrong with it."

When he left, I said, "His muscles are so big they look painful. What happens if he gets a charley horse?"

Jesse nodded. He lowered his voice. "I'm worried about him. He's using insulin to build muscle. A practice I don't care for."

Chapter 21

Dear Sophie,
I'm buying a new nightstand with built-in outlets
for charging my phone. But they come in all kinds
of sizes. Is there some rule of thumb to go by?
Sleepless in Midnight Thicket, Delaware

Dear Sleepless,
Any height that suits you will work. However, as a
rule of thumb, nightstands should be level with the
height of your mattress.
Sophie

"Insulin? Is he diabetic?" I asked.

"No. It's not that at all. There are theories that it increases muscle mass and improves performance."

"I'm a little bit confused. If he's not diabetic, how would he obtain insulin? I thought insulin was only available by prescription."

"It was," Jesse murmured. "But there are a couple of brands you can buy without a prescription now. I feel like it's being misused when it's taken to build muscle, but some people don't listen. Everyone likes quick and easy fixes, but whether it's building muscle or losing weight, everything takes time. You have to work at it."

"Let me get this clear. So a doctor doesn't have to write a prescription for the insulin?"

"No. You can buy over the counter insulin. I understand it varies from state to state, but some stores sell insulin and syringes without asking any questions."

My mind reeled at the revelation. I had assumed the killer would have difficulty getting insulin and would either be diabetic or have access to insulin through a diabetic friend or family member. "Thank you, Jesse. You have been very helpful!" It was true, but now my pool of suspects had grown.

I rose from my chair, and he escorted me to the front of the gym. "Let me know if there's anything else I can do to help."

I thought Heather turned a little bit green when he kissed me on the cheek. As I walked out, someone opened the door and held it for me. "Stu! And Jacky! What a nice surprise. I was planning to get in touch with you. There's a cute café around the corner. Could I buy you a cup of coffee or a latte?"

They shared an uneasy look. "Helena said you might want to speak with us." She glanced at her husband. "Let's get it over with."

"You make it sound like going to the dentist," I teased.

They smiled and reluctantly walked with me to the little café. When we were seated with steaming cups of coffee before us, I said, "Jesse seems very nice. I met him for the first time the other day."

"He was our neighbor for years," said Stu. "He's a good guy. Always ready to lend a helping hand. Um, why are we here?"

"Mostly I'd like to know if you're aware of anyone who might be angry with Mike, Denise, or Rachel."

"We barely knew Rachel," said Jacky. "Denise was a lovely person. I can't imagine anyone having a beef with her that couldn't be resolved in some way. We were delighted when Mike married her."

Stu nodded in agreement. "It could have been so much worse."

"Oh?"

Stu appeared at a loss. "He could have married someone like Rachel."

"So you did know her?"

"Not well," said Jacky. "But when Denise died, she zeroed in on Mike like he was a target. It was upsetting. The poor boy had just lost his wife. Unseemly, is what your Aunt Faye would have called it. One just doesn't do that!"

"I felt sorry for her," said Stu. "I could relate because when I met Jacky, she was dating someone else and didn't give me the time of day."

"I was just out of college, handling rental properties when Stu applied for an apartment. He was relentless!" She smiled at him.

"I wasn't about to let her get away. She's just as beautiful today as she was then."

"Oh, Stu!" Jacky flapped her hand at him, but I suspected she thrived on his adoration.

I changed the subject. "I suppose you heard about the skeleton?"

Their eyes met briefly and both of them stiffened. "We can't believe we lived in that house for the better part of our lives and had no idea," said Stu.

I wanted to joke that a skeleton wasn't exactly going to knock on the inside of the wall to make his presence known, but I didn't think that would go over well with them. For all I knew, they might believe in ghosts, and it might be perceived as disrespectful to whoever the skeleton was. "I guess you're glad you moved out."

"I'm horrified," said Jacky. "How did you find it? I never imagined that you would be tearing down the walls in our home."

"Me either! It wasn't exactly like that. In actuality, we didn't tear anything down. I noticed that the armoire had been moved."

Stu's eyes widened. "Who moved it?"

"I don't know. Denise or Rachel, I suppose."

Jacky winced. "To renovate, honey. That little bedroom was always just a catch-all." To me she said, "If it had been a decent size, we would have stayed in the house. The stairs were getting to be too much for us. It was either put in an elevator—"

"—But that would have been a big undertaking and such a mess—"

"So we decided to move out and let the next generation tackle the house. There was a lot that needed work. These old homes, you know," said Jacky.

"But it skipped a generation," I pointed out.

"Mary," sighed Jacky. "She has always been the rebel in our fold. Robbie was eager to take the house. I wish—"

"—He had," said Stu. "He loves that old place."

"Do you think Mike will still move in?" I asked.

"Poor Mikey," Jacky moaned. "He doesn't know what to do."

"He's lost without Denise. Just like I would be if anything happened to my Jacky." Stu bestowed a smile on her.

"Are there any old family stories that suggest who the skeleton might be?"

Jacky thought for a moment. "The Ingers go way back. There's even a family crest with a wolf head on it. Who knows what chaos might have taken place there centuries ago?"

"The Civil War, you know," said Stu. "That's what I think

it is. As the house was quite large, it may have been used as a headquarters or a hospital."

While that might be true, I didn't think a wartime hospital, with many dying patients, would have bothered to hide a corpse in a wall. But stranger things had happened, and we knew it was a turbulent time.

"Do you have any thoughts on who murdered Denise and Rachel or why?"

"We have discussed all kinds of crazy scenarios." Jacky paused to sip her coffee. "I mean, really, some of them are so off the wall."

"Like Denise having a jealous lover," Stu laughed.

"Was that a possibility? Were there problems between Denise and Mike?"

"They were the sweetest couple. Truly in love with each other." Jacky reached out for her husband's hand. "Like Stu and me."

"But a spurned lover from Denise's past is certainly a possibility," Stu said. "Who knows what kind of obsessed man might have pursued her?"

"Has Mike told you anything to that effect?"

Jacky was quick to say, "No. Not at all. We've been speculating, just like everyone else. I'm afraid that some stranger managed to get inside the house and could be living there. He could be deranged and imagine that it belongs to him. One hears about such things on the news."

"Do you have any reason to think that's the case?" Maybe she was right. Could it be Mitzi? Maybe Agnes across the street wasn't as loony as I had thought.

"Probably not. It's just odd that the two murders took place in our old home. I lived there all but three years of my life! We've been so busy setting up our new home that we haven't been over to the old place," said Jacky. "Mike told us that Denise and Rachel knew one another so it stands to reason that they would have mutual acquaintances. Like Mitzi, for instance. Has anyone checked to see where she was when they were murdered?"

Mitzi's name always came up. I had to find her. "Do you know Agnes across the street?"

Jacky and Stu exchanged a look and grinned.

Stu said in a low voice, "I wouldn't go by anything she says."

"We have known her for many, many years. Frankly," Jacky tsked, "I'm afraid she's losing it. She's all alone now and really needs to move to a place where she can be cared for. Oh my, the things she has told us. You just wouldn't believe. She's actually a very sweet woman, but she has quite the imagination. She watches entirely too many true crime shows on TV. They make her skittish and afraid. We joke about it, but it's actually very sad that she lives in fear like that." She checked the time on her watch. "I hate to break this up, but we're due at Helena's house soon."

I thanked them for taking the time to meet with me. They were most gracious and even apologized for being hesitant about speaking to me and invited me to call them if they could be of help.

I still had the key to the Inger House that Helena had given me. But the last thing in the world that I wanted to do was go there alone. If Mitzi or someone else was living in the house and killing the people who entered, it would be folly to go inside by myself. I called Wolf and asked if he could accompany me.

"Sorry, Soph. But I can check with Wong. I think she's on her shift. Hold on." Wolf came back to the phone. "Wong will meet you there in ten minutes."

It must have been a slow day for Wong.

I walked over to the house and examined it from Agnes's side of the street. It was so beautiful. The original Inger who built it hadn't spared any expense. I studied each of the windows for signs of life, like a soda can on a window-sill, or any sign of movement inside.

"See anything interesting?" asked Wong as she walked up to me.

"I'm afraid not. Thanks for coming."

"No problem. Why are we going inside?"

I explained about the beer in the refrigerator. "I wonder if Mitzi is living there."

"And knocking people off?"

"I hope she's not doing that!"

We crossed the street, and I unlocked the door. As if pre-arranged, the two of us stepped inside the foyer and stood quietly, listening.

"I don't hear anything," whispered Wong.

"Me either. Let's check the fridge and the trash under the sink."

We entered the kitchen, where I opened the refrigerator while Wong looked in the trash bin.

"It's been emptied," she said. "And there's dishwashing soap under the counter. Was that there before?"

"I don't think so. Neither was the package of sliced cheese or the takeout from The Laughing Hound. And a couple of the beers are gone. Shall we check the bedrooms?"

"You walk behind me."

I followed her upstairs. Both of us tread as quietly as we could. The main bedroom didn't look any different. We searched each one until we reached the far corner bed-room at the front of the house. The latest John Grisham book lay on the nightstand alongside a small lamp.

"That definitely wasn't there before," I whispered.

"The extra blanket either," Wong observed.

Wong opened the closet door. A warm hoodie, a pair of jeans, and workout clothes hung inside.

"Someone is definitely living here," said Wong.

"You think it's a man?" I asked.

"Could go either way. But women usually have more stuff. Makeup, curling iron, face cream. Things like that."

We checked the bathroom. A damp towel and wash-cloth hung on a bar. And a slightly wet toothbrush stood upright in a glass next to a tube of toothpaste. Wong pulled the shower curtain open. A bottle of bodywash sat on the edge of the tub.

"I think we have definite confirmation that someone is staying here," I said. "Agnes across the street was right."

"Who?"

"A little old lady. She said the light goes on in the bed-room early every morning. I hoped it was Mitzi, but I think you're right about it being a man."

"I'll go talk with her."

"She might not answer the door. She's scared witless and thinks if she talks to the cops the killer will come and murder her."

"That's crazy!"

"She comes across a little addled in person. But it looks like she was right about this. She also claims that she saw a blond Mitzi running from the Inger House the day Rachel was murdered."

"Have you told Wolf that?"

"No. I thought she was probably confused and didn't put much stock in what she said. But this changes things."

"I think we'd better get out of here before this person returns. I'll let Wolf know."

We walked down the stairs in a hurry.

When my phone rang, Wong turned around and looked at me, her eyes wide. "Hurry!"

The day Nina and I heard noises upstairs came back to me. The two of us ran out of the house onto the front porch. I locked the door and was a little bit relieved to see that I wasn't the only one breathing heavily.

"Which house does Agnes live in?"

I pointed it out to her and checked my phone. "That was Wolf calling." I hit the button to call back.

"That was quick," said Wolf.

"Wong and I are at the Inger House. Someone is definitely staying here."

"How do you know?"

I told him about Agnes and the items we had discovered in the house. "We think it's a man."

"Mike?"

"That could be. I thought it would be difficult for him to stay in the building where his wife was murdered, but maybe it's worse to be home alone with all her possessions and so many memories."

"I'll look into that. I'm actually calling about the skeleton. The forensic anthropologists jumped on that right away. I wish I could get other people to work as fast. They haven't completed their tests yet, but it's definitely a man."

Chapter 22

Dear Sophie,
I rarely buy light brown sugar but usually have
dark brown sugar on hand. Can I use that instead?
Does it really make a difference?
                    Grandma in Sugar Beach, Missouri

Dear Grandma,
Light brown and dark brown sugar can often be
switched without ruining a recipe. Dark brown
sugar contains almost twice as much molasses as
light brown sugar. If a recipe calls for light brown
sugar, use half white sugar and half dark brown
sugar.

                                        Sophie

"I'm putting you on speaker so Wong can hear. Civil War era?"

"Not even close. He was about forty-three years old when he died. Here's the real kicker. He had a broken neck, and they are putting his date of death around 1969."

"A broken neck? How can they tell? Whoever moved the bones tossed them around like sticks."

"They have methods of determining that from micro-scopic markers in the bone in question."

"So he was murdered!"

"Well, there *are* accidental ways to break your neck, but most people aren't hidden in a wall when it's an accident."

"Is there a way to find out who he is? DNA in the bones?"

"The short answer is yes. Teeth are a better source and they found a few of those, so they're working on it."

"Have you called Helena or Jacky?"

"I'm meeting with them this afternoon."

"Thanks for letting us know."

I disconnected the call. "How old do you think Jacky and Helena are?" I asked Wong.

"Old enough to have been alive when that man was hid-den in the wall."

I accompanied Wong across the street. She politely tapped the door knocker. "What's her last name?" she whispered.

"Hampton. Agnes Hampton."

No one answered the door.

Wong tried again.

There was still no answer.

"Mrs. Hampton?" I called. "It's Sophie Winston. Do you remember me? I was here the other day."

"Maybe she's not home," said Wong.

"Or maybe she is!" cackled a voice from above.

Wong and I looked up.

Mrs. Hampton watched us from a window, her entire head outside. "You think I don't recognize a police uni-form? You're not taking me anywhere. And I'm not talking." She reached a hand out of the window and pretended to zip her mouth shut.

"Mrs. Hampton, I'm Officer Wong and I would love to talk with you for a few minutes."

"Nope. I am not involved. You people brought vans and crowds. And yesterday when I woke up in the morning,

the street in front of my house was swarming with reporters. I had to go outside and get rid of them. Leave me
in peace!"

"You know I can get a warrant to come in and see you,"
said Wong.

"Can you do that?" I murmured.

"No," she whispered. "But Agnes doesn't know that."

Agnes slammed the window shut.

"I have an idea," I whispered. I motioned to Wong to
walk away with me.

When we were out of Agnes's earshot, I said, "I'll go
home and bake some cookies. Can you ditch your uni-
form?"

"I'm not supposed to. Not while I'm on duty anyway."

"Do you get off at three?"

She nodded.

"I'll meet you back here. Wear something that won't in-
timidate her."

"Like a tutu and a tiara?"

I giggled. "That might work!"

Wong went off to do her job and I hurried home trying
to make sense of someone living in the Inger House and
the fact that the skeleton was of relatively recent vintage.

While Daisy went outside, I made a mug of tea and
stroked Mochie, thinking all the while of the skeleton. Had
Helena and Jacky's father murdered someone in their home
and hidden the body? Surely, they would have noticed the
smell. By my calculations, the girls would have been in
their teens. Certainly old enough to know what went on in
their home. But maybe they were in school that day and
everything had been cleaned up by the time they came
home in the late afternoon.

Daisy returned, and I made a ham sandwich for lunch,
sharing a little bit of it with Mochie and Daisy. I took my

meal to my office. Settled in the chair, I searched *missing man Alexandria, Virginia, 1969*. The names of missing people popped up. Far too many! But as I scrolled, I realized that many of them were not in 1969 nor were they from Old Town or Alexandria. As I searched, it dawned on me that the man in the wall could have been from anywhere. The greater Washington, DC., area encompassed parts of Maryland and a broad section of Virginia. He could even be a visitor to the United States. Odds were good that he was from Old Town, but I didn't find anyone. No leads at all.

Debating what else I could search to find a missing person announcement, I typed in *Oliver Inger*, but found no reference to Helena and Jacky's father, only the website of their real estate office. I scrolled down, but didn't find anything of interest. I tried *Oliver Inger Obituary*. There were a few entries, but none of them were local. That was odd. When I tried *Nofsinger Old Town*, lots of articles came up, most of them about the family, donations, and civic contributions.

Could Mr. Inger still be alive? It was possible, I guessed. After all, Annie was quite old. Maybe he was, too.

I checked the time and whipped up some chocolate chip cookies. Sometimes I felt like they were the only thing I baked, but they were universally popular. I placed a large tray of them in the oven and stashed the rest of the dough in the freezer for unexpected visitors.

The aroma was heavenly as they baked. When I took them out of the oven, I hurried upstairs and changed clothes. Agnes might be more comfortable with me if I wasn't dressed in solid black like a cat burglar. Looking a bit more normal in stretchy jeans, a white turtleneck, and a puffy vest, I packed up the cookies and walked over to Agnes's house.

Wong arrived at the same time, but she had swapped

her uniform for jeans and a sweater. We were about to rap the knocker when I saw a man jog up the steps to the Inger House. "Wait," I whispered.

Wong turned around and saw him, too.

I checked for traffic and dashed across the street. "Hi!" The man turned to look at me. It was Robbie Nofsinger.

"Sophie. Hi!" He ambled down the stairs to me. "Mmm. Do I smell cookies?"

"Yes, we're having trouble getting Agnes Hampton to talk to us. She's afraid of the police. And scared to death because of the two murders here. I thought cookies might convince her to open the door."

"I can help you with that."

We walked across the street.

Robbie banged the knocker in a short rhythm. "Knock, knock! Who's there?"

Agnes opened the door and shrieked, "Robbie Nofsinger! As I live and breathe. Come in, come in!"

We walked inside and I closed the door.

Agnes hugged him and then pushed him away. "Let me see how you look. Oh my! As handsome as you ever were. Why didn't my Ruthie marry you instead of the jerk that moved her all the way out to Seattle?"

"It was my loss. How's Ruthie doing?"

"Come sit down. Cold cider? I bought some yesterday."

"I brought chocolate chip cookies." I handed them to her. She uncovered them. "Homemade?"

"Yes." I smiled at her.

Wong asked, "Could I help you with the cider?"

"Are you the big horse rider?" asked Agnes.

Wong was visibly surprised by her question.

Robbie grinned. "She means my wife. No, this is—"

There was a long pause until I said, "Rosa."

Wong shot me a look. That was her name, even if she didn't use it professionally.

"I have always loved that name. I can't remember why I named my daughter Ruthie."

Wong followed her to the kitchen. I could hear them chatting.

"You're like magic. You obviously know her very well," I said to Robbie.

"Her son Brad is my age. We did everything together. I spent half my time over here and when we weren't here, we were across the street at my house. Even when we moved out, Brad and I were best friends all the way through high school."

"Here we go!" Agnes was remarkably different in Robbie's presence.

I watched the two of them interact. They were clearly fond of each other. The fear Agnes had previously displayed vanished in his presence. I finally interrupted their reunion as delicately as I could when they both had mouthfuls of cookies. "Agnes, are you still seeing the light go on early in the morning?"

Her mouth pulled tight, and I felt guilty for bringing it up.

"Yes. Every morning at five thirty. I know she's there. I'm terrified that she's watching me."

Robbie frowned at her. "Are you talking about a light in my old bedroom?"

"Yes! How did you know?"

"Aww, I'm so sorry I frightened you. That's me. I've been staying in the house," said Robbie.

"Well, why didn't you come over here and say so?" Agnes demanded.

"I didn't realize you were watching the light."

"What about the light in the kitchen?" she asked.

"That would be early in the morning, too. Or sometimes I hit the fridge for a snack in the evening. I guess it could be anytime. I haven't been sleeping very well lately."

"Of course you're not. How can you sleep when the murderer could come in and kill you?" she asked.

He took her hand into his. "We are very upset and sorry that Denise and Rachel were murdered in our beloved old house. I thought I should move in there to keep an eye on things."

"But the killer could go after you!"

"I have a gun." He held up a forefinger to his lips as if they should keep that their little secret.

"Do you have a license for it?" asked Wong in a stern voice.

"Yes, of course." He focused on Agnes. "Not a thing has happened since I moved in. It's quiet and peaceful."

Agnes said, "You had better be careful. I bet the killer sits outside, upset that you're in there."

Robbie smiled sweetly. "Don't worry about me. I'll tell you what! Remember how Brad and I used to place toys in our windows to send signals to each other?"

"That was the cutest thing!"

"You and I can send signals to each other. Okay? Every night when I turn on the light and every morning when I get up, I'll put something on the windowsill, so you'll know everything is fine. You do the same in Brad's old room."

"I like that. We'll be watching out for each other. Who do I call if I don't see anything?"

"Me," said Wong. "I'll write down my phone number for you."

"And what will you do?"

"I'll go to the house and make sure Robbie is okay."

"And the killer will get you, too."

"I have a gun, too," Wong said softly as if it was in confidence.

"What is this world coming to with all the guns? Do you have one?" she asked me.

"No. I have to rely on cast-iron frying pans."

Agnes laughed. "I don't have the strength to pick one up anymore!"

"How long have you lived here?" I asked.

"We moved here in 1972. I remember that because Brad and Robbie were the 'two in their terrible twos'! Oh, they kept Helena, Jacky, Annie, and me on the run. But I wouldn't have traded those years for anything." She smiled at him.

I was disappointed. I had hoped she might have lived in her house in 1969 when the man in the wall was murdered.

Wong asked her about seeing someone fleeing the house the day Rachel was killed.

Agnes stuck to her story about Mitzi. "Absolutely. That curly-haired woman ran like the devil."

"Have you seen her since then?" I asked.

"No. But no one else has been murdered, either. Maybe it was Rachel the killer was after the whole time."

That was a twist I hadn't considered. Had the killer mistaken Denise for Rachel the first time? It seemed unlikely.

"Thank you for the cider, Agnes." I tried to sound very casual when I asked, "Do you happen to know where the Inger family is buried?"

"Oh sure. They're at Christ Church Cemetery. I see it when I take flowers to my husband's grave. There are a few Inger graves and one with a very elegant monument on it."

Robbie stared at me with concern. "Denise is buried out of state in her family's plot."

I simply said, "Thanks." There was no point in upsetting anyone. I suspected word would get back to the entire family about my question very soon. I shouldn't have asked in front of Robbie.

He gave Agnes his phone number. "I want you to call

me if you get scared or are worried about anything. Okay? Remember that I'm just across the street. I can be here in a minute."

She clung to his hand. "I feel so much better knowing you're there."

I couldn't get over the change in Agnes. Fear was a powerful stimulus. She changed to a sweet lady the moment she heard Robbie's rhythmic tapping on her door.

The three of us left. I had mixed feelings about Robbie living in the Inger House. Aside from the fact that the killer might return, there was the chance that *he* could be the killer. Either he was incredibly brave or very clever. I wasn't sure which.

I walked home and ran into Nina, who was outside with Muppet.

"We just came from your house," she said.

"I was over at Agnes Hampton's. You won't believe this. Robbie is staying at the Inger House."

"He's not afraid?"

"That's exactly what I wondered. It was a lucky break, though. I was planning to go over to the Inger gravesite. Want to come?"

"You do such fun things. Don't tell me. You think an Inger ghost has returned."

"Wouldn't that be amazing? I'll explain on the way over."

Nina agreed and I went home to let Daisy out for a bit before leaving in the car. I stopped in front of Nina's house to pick her up. As I drove, I told her about our visit with Agnes.

"I was worried about her. She was frantic and verging on hysterical," said Nina. "I wonder how long Robbie will be there?"

"He didn't say."

"Mmm," Nina murmured. "Trouble in paradise?"

"He didn't mention Mary much."

We stepped out of the car at the graveyard. "Agnes said there's a small monument."

We found it quickly. A small obelisk bore the name *Robert Inger* and beneath it the dates *1835-1935*.

"Wow. Robert lived to be one hundred years old! Do you suppose they named Robbie after him?"

"Probably. He must be the one who built the house. There are older Inger gravestones over here."

"Do you see one for Oliver Inger?" I asked.

"Nope."

I followed along behind her, double-checking to be sure. Nina stopped cold. "That's it for the Ingers. I know you, Sophie. Something's up. What's going on?"

"The person whose skeleton was found died in 1969 at the age of forty-three."

Nina nodded. "So?"

"So where is Helena and Jacky's father?"

Chapter 23

Dear Sophie,
My husband and I live where we can walk most
places, so we share a car. But he's notoriously bad
about leaving the keys in a pocket. I have tried a
hook in the kitchen, but he never puts the keys back.
I need help!
          Restaurant Critic Hayley in Key West, Florida

Dear Restaurant Critic Hayley,
A small bowl where you enter your home appears
to be the best solution for most people. When we
enter our homes, we're often carrying something.
If you have a place near the door for a small table
with a bowl, both of you can deposit the keys there
instantly. It's also a great place to set down the
mail so it doesn't get lost in the shuffle elsewhere in
your home.

                                                    Sophie

"Are you saying the skeleton in the wall was their father?"

I struggled with a response. "Possibly. I have nothing to

go on other than his age, which would be about right. I looked for an obituary but didn't find one. It's possible that I missed it or didn't do a proper search. But if he was deceased, wouldn't he have a grave marker here like the rest of the Inger ancestors?"

Her eyes wide, she stared at me. "Maybe he's alive?"

"That's entirely possible."

"Maybe we should ask them."

"I'm planning to have a chat with Annie. Given her age, I think I'd better call ahead."

We returned to the car. I was waiting for the light to turn green so I could turn right and pull into traffic when Nina howled, "Left! Turn left!"

"Why?" In spite of my question, I did as she said.

"I think I saw Thurman driving by. Look for a chic Alpine White BMW."

"Okay. But why are we looking for him? He's probably just going to his golf club."

"And who paid someone to lie to you about his where-abouts the day Denise died?"

She had a point. Not much of one, because it was a very long shot. He could be taking the car for servicing or going to a doctor for a checkup.

It wasn't difficult to catch up to his car. I stayed a short distance behind so Thurman wouldn't get suspicious. But honestly, we had every right to be driving on that road. Even if he saw us, there was no reason he should think we were tailing him. It was just a coincidence.

The BMW turned right into the parking lot of a dry cleaner.

"Turn! Turn!" Nina shrieked.

"He's just picking up laundry," I said, hastily turning right onto the adjoining property, a local drive-through fast food business that I happened to know had great milkshakes. We were caught in the line of traffic to the takeout window.

Nina fussed at me. "We've lost him now."

"Want a milkshake? There's no way to get out of the drive-through lane."

"Might as well. Double chocolate, please."

I drove around the small building, ordered, picked up our milkshakes, and handed them to Nina. I was afraid she was right. We'd probably lost Thurman. But luck was with us when we exited the takeout lane to a perfect view of the back of the dry-cleaning building. Thurman embraced a woman. She leaned into him so that I couldn't see her face.

I parked the car. "Have you got sunglasses?" I asked, slipping on a pair.

Nina gasped and reached into her purse for giant sunglasses. "He could still recognize us, you know." Nina handed me my milkshake and dipped a spoon into her thick double chocolate while watching them.

"I don't think they're picking up laundry." The woman in Thurman's arms wore heels and a pale blue dress that clung to her shapely figure. When she pulled back and gazed up at him, I promptly spilled a spoonful of ice-cream-thick strawberry milkshake on my sweater. Lillith! The same interior decorator who had told me that Helena ruled the family. I wasn't mistaken, either. I spotted her black Lincoln sedan parked next to Thurman's car.

My mind reeling, I ate the thick ice-creamy-like milkshake and watched them. "Do you feel guilty? Like a voyeur?"

"Guilty? Thurman is the one who should feel guilty. Shame on him!"

"Thurman could be out here for business reasons. He certainly is a hugger."

"Oh right. Do you see the way Lillith is clutching him?"

Nina snorted. "Looks like a different kind of business to me."

"They're having an affair," I conceded. "Do you suppose he was with Lillith on the day Denise was murdered?"

At the exact moment I said that, they engaged in a kiss that left absolutely no doubt in my mind about the nature of their relationship.

"Didn't you talk to Lillith?" asked Nina.

"Yup. She said she was with a client who was putting in a breakfast nook."

Nina chuckled. "I heard you're supposed to give a detail like that when you're lying. Makes it sound like the truth. They might have done it together!" Nina gasped again. "What if they went to the Inger House to—you know— and Denise caught them?"

I turned to Nina. "You have a very wicked mind. Sadly, that's a possibility. He paid that guy at the club to lie to me and she probably lied to me, too, but I bet they didn't plan to murder anyone. They thought the house would be empty."

"That doesn't explain Rachel's death, though."

"True. Well, well. It may or may not have any bearing on the murders, but it's certainly suspicious." I felt for Helena, of course, and wondered if she was aware of her husband's infidelity. One never knew what secrets people had and what they might be willing to do to protect them. Was it possible that Denise had stumbled upon their affair?

Nina slurped the last of her milkshake. "Do you suppose—I'm just throwing this out there—that Lillith and Thurman were planning to get rid of Helena and move into that house? With Helena gone, Thurman would be loaded and in charge of the family. He could boot Mike and Denise right out and move in with Lillith."

"I don't want to think that's the case. But that could be what happened."

As we drove home, Nina asked if we were still on for dinner that night.

"I'd forgotten all about it. Sure. Why don't we both make our contributions to the brunch to try them out? I don't think Mars and Bernie would mind eating brunch for dinner."

"Ugh. I have to cook?"

I laughed at her. "You'd think that someone who likes to eat would enjoy cooking. No problem. I'll thaw some salmon and roast veggies. You make the cocktails."

"That kind of cooking suits me much better."

I turned onto our block and the first thing I noticed was a skeleton in front of my house. He sat on a pile of bones. Gourds in all shapes, sizes, and colors surrounded him.

I parked on the street. People on the sidewalk stopped to gawk at the odd decoration.

At exactly the same time, Nina and I muttered, "Natasha."

I phoned her immediately. "What did you do?"

"Don't you love it? I was inspired by the skeleton in the Inger House."

"I do not love it and I would like you to come over here and remove every last bone and gourd."

"You always overreact," said Natasha. "Your style of wispy dried branches won't cut it. I'm sorry to have to be the one to tell you, but they look like trash that blew in. Besides, you said I could decorate the front of your house."

Had I said that? What was I thinking? "Nooo. I believe I suggested that you make some beautiful arrangements for the living room. Natasha, if you don't come take this away, I will put it all out for the trash collectors. Need I remind you that the producer specifically did not want a Halloween theme?"

"You don't even like the gourds?"

"They're not terrible," I admitted. "But they look like someone dumped them there. How are people supposed to get to the door?"

"You're so picky. I'll be over tomorrow to make some changes."

I said goodbye and drove to the alley to park in my garage. I grabbed two huge lawn bags and handed one to Nina. "In light of the murdered man found in the Inger house, I can't imagine anything more offensive at my front door right now. I don't think I can even tolerate a skeleton for Halloween this year. Too close to home for me."

Nina and I collected the plastic bones and set the bags by my kitchen door for Natasha to pick up the next day. Nina went home, and I started dinner.

Two hours later, Nina arrived with pumpkin spice cocktails. Mars and Bernie walked in right behind her. Bernie carried something in a white bakery-style box.

"Is that dessert?" I asked.

"It is. We're trying it out for our fall and winter menu. It needs to be in the freezer. I'll go ahead and stash it if you don't mind."

"Be my guest."

"We're all testing things! I'm trying these out for our brunch, so I want you to be honest with me." Nina poured a sparkling amber liquid into double old-fashioned glasses and garnished them with apple slices.

I feared the typical combination of pumpkin spice might be at odds with alcohol, but the drinks were delicious.

I had set the table with an Autumn Orchard tablecloth from Pomegranate that looked just right in shades of rosy apple and green. My square white dinner plates were inexpensive, but they looked high end on the colorful tablecloth.

The vegetables were almost finished. I quickly swiped a

mixture of mustard and maple syrup over the salmon and popped the tray into the oven. Minutes later, we were seated and eating.

"You won't believe what happened today," said Nina. She regaled them with the details of catching Lillith in Thurman's arms.

"You're not joking?" asked Bernie.

"Absolutely not," Nina assured them.

"Where's my list?" asked Mars.

I fetched it for him along with a pen.

"Did you confront them?" asked Mars.

I looked at Nina. "Maybe we should have."

"You're right. What would be the downside? They'd have been embarrassed but so what?" asked Nina.

In his droll British accent, Bernie said, "Maybe Thurman would have pulled out his wallet and paid off the two of you!"

When we stopped laughing, I said, "It explains him paying off the guy at the golf club, but we don't know that he was with Lillith that day. He could very well have been at the house, murdering Denise."

"I know it's a wild guess, but I thought Denise might have caught them meeting at the Inger House," said Nina.

"Wow. Or Rachel, for that matter." Mars wrote on his list. "I had no idea. Then Thurman is a contender after all. I thought we would be excluding him."

"And now you can add Lillith to the list," I said. "But you can cross off Jacky and Stu because Jesse was able to confirm that they were at Synergy that morning."

"How about Robbie?" asked Mars.

I told them how sweet he was with Agnes. "I don't know what's going on in his marriage, but he's staying at the Inger House."

"How about Helena?" asked Mars.

"The receptionist at her office says Helena worked that morning. She remembers her rushing out when she got word that Denise was on the way to the hospital. However, Mike claims he was checking out property. He has no alibi."

Bernie stopped eating. "So Mike could have killed his own wife?"

"Maybe it was an accident," said Nina.

"An accident with insulin?" I said doubtfully. "If that was the case, why did he run off and leave her? Why wouldn't he have called nine-one-one immediately?"

"Good point," said Nina. "I hope you brought a great dessert, Bernie. All these veggies and fish are too healthy for me!"

While I collected the dishes, Mars said, "So here's the rundown as of now. Helena, Jacky, and Stu have solid alibis for Denise's death. Thurman, Mary, and Mike have no alibis at all. Robbie remains to be seen. Does that sound right?"

"Correct," I said as I opened the box Bernie had brought. "It's a pumpkin roll?"

Bernie grinned. "I'll cut it for you."

I handed him dessert plates and put on the kettle for tea and decaf coffee. As he cut the slices, I delivered them to the table. "Who wants tea and who wants coffee?"

Mars rose and helped carry the mugs to everyone. We joined the others and conversation came to an immediate halt. It was a Pumpkin Spice Ice Cream Roll!

"Delicious!" Nina said. "This is how vegetables should be served."

"I'd order this," said Mars.

"Me too." The Bourbon pecan ice cream inside was a perfect match for the cake roll.

"Good to hear. We tried frosting the outside, but it was

too much, and we didn't like the way the buttercream texture competed with the ice cream. Plus, we serve it sliced, so no one is looking at the whole cake anyway."

Mars cut another slice for Nina and helped himself to a second slice as well. The ice-cream cake was clearly a hit.

They all pitched in to clean up after dinner. As they walked out the door, Mars asked if he could take Daisy for a run in the morning. Naturally, I agreed.

WEDNESDAY

I was up early in the day, dressed and ready to go. Daisy already wore her harness and seemed to understand that we were waiting for Mars. I sipped my tea and ate a leftover slice of Bernie's Pumpkin Spice Ice-Cream Roll for breakfast.

When Mars arrived, he noticed my breakfast immediately. "Really, Sophie? Ice cream for breakfast?"

"It's eggs and dairy, so why not?"

He shook his head in dismay. "Maybe you should come running with us."

"And interrupt your special time with Daisy?" I teased. "I would only slow you down. Besides, I need to decorate my front door before Natasha puts up another skeleton."

After he left, I fed Mochie and promised to return soon. I had something in mind for the door, but I wasn't sure I would find what I wanted.

I thought about the Nofsingers as I walked. So much had happened, but I felt as though I couldn't trust or believe anything they said. My path took me by Helena's beautiful home. She was outside, watering bright orange mums.

"Hi, Sophie!" She walked over to me. "I usually see you walking your dog."

"Mars took her for a run this morning."

"Are you back together?"

"No. But he loves Daisy and I'm not much of a runner."

"Me either. I've never had a dog. Our father wouldn't allow it."

"You don't know what you're missing."

"Father was saddled with two little girls and no wife to help raise them. It made him bitter."

"I'm sorry. It must have been hard growing up without a mom."

"We had Annie. She was a mother to us. Her biological children often joke that she liked us better. Her children were a handful sometimes, but they all turned out well."

"You and Jacky were well behaved?"

"We had to be. We lived in terror. You know the saying 'children should be seen, not heard'? My father thought they should not be seen or heard. No singing, no music, no dancing through the house, no noise, no school projects, no messes. He didn't eat with us, either. He ate alone in the dining room every evening. Annie fed us in the kitchen. It was a different time then."

It wasn't that long ago! People ate evening meals at a table as a family. Maybe the rich did things differently. Who was I to judge? I wondered how I could bring up the whereabouts of her father. "I suppose he has passed on?"

Helena snipped a head off a mum. She nodded. "Won't you come in for a cup of coffee?"

"I would love that."

I followed her into the house. The last time I had been inside her house, people crowded around and there was quite a bit of commotion. Now, I took more time to appreciate the details. Her foyer was simple but elegant. A lantern style light fixture hung from a two-story ceiling. Stairs curved gently upward on the right. To my left, a beautiful mirror hung over an ornate console table that was probably an antique. A lamp in a brushed gold tone stood on it next to a framed photograph that had to be Robbie as a child, and a shallow crystal catch-all bowl, surely used for house and car keys.

"Is this Robbie?" I asked. In the photograph, he held a tennis racket.

"Yes! I always loved that picture. He must have been around fourteen then."

"Yesterday, he went with me to see Agnes Hampton."

Helena froze. She picked something out of the catch-all bowl and examined it.

"He was so kind to her. You would have been—"

A red flush spread up her neck and over her face. She still held something in her hand.

"Helena? Are you all right?"

The doorbell rang and Helena jumped, her chest heaving with each breath.

She opened the door. Gwen Adams hustled inside. "Hi, Helena, Sophie!"

"Good morning, Gwen." I had hired Gwen, one of the best housekeepers in Old Town, on occasion to help out with events. She was always reliable and very sensible. One was lucky to be on her list of regular cleaning clients.

Helena gazed at her. "Gwen," she murmured as if confused. After a moment she spoke softly and a bit slower than normal. "I'm sorry. I need to skip today. I'll pay you, of course. But something has come up. I'll mail you a check."

Gwen looked at me. "Is everything okay here?"

I shrugged.

"Yes. Of course. I'll see you next week."

Gwen sidled out, still watching the two of us. She whispered, "Should I call the police?"

"Oh!" Helena faked an unconvincing laugh. "No, no. Nothing like that. I am sorry for springing this on you at the last moment. Look at it as a paid day off. I'm sure you deserve one." Helena closed the door and leaned against it. She still held something in her shaking right hand.

I waited for her to speak. She wouldn't be able to get rid of me as easily as she had Gwen.

"Maybe we can have coffee another time?" she asked.

"What is that?" I pointed at her hand.

She lowered her gaze to her hand. "Nothing. It's nothing."

I held out my hand for it.

"It's just an old ring."

I kept my open palm outstretched and she finally placed it in my hand. It was a plain gold ring. A wedding band, I guessed. I spotted engraving inside. *18K Ollie & Jill 1951.* "Your parents?"

Helena nodded.

I guessed it had belonged to her father, given the size. "Maybe you should sit down."

"No. I'm fine."

"I don't think so."

"It's just that I don't know how his ring came to be in that bowl. That's all."

"So this is your father's wedding ring?"

"Yes. Don't worry about me. I must be losing my mind. I'm sure I put it there and forgot all about it."

I didn't believe her. If she lost the ring and just found it, wouldn't she be glad about that? "When did your father pass?"

She took in a sharp breath. Her eyes wide, she said, "Thurman. Could it be Thurman?"

She wasn't making any sense. "Could what be Thurman?"

She reached for the ring and examined it. "It must be a duplicate." Her chest heaved with every breath.

"Why would you say that?"

"Because he left us. He went to look for our mother. Our father was a bitter man. He had no interest in his children and was angry that his wife wasn't there to keep us

out of his way. In fact, sadly, he didn't care for most people. Children lean on their parents for emotional support.
There's a certain security that family offers. Just knowing
they're there, even when you don't need them. It provides
a sense of assurance that you're not alone in the world. Father ran the family business by himself and wallowed in
pity for himself after my mother left."

"I thought he brought you into the business."

"Only to do the parts he didn't like. But in the long run,
I must concede that was good for me. At a very young age,
I learned by doing. And then he left. That was the last we
ever saw or heard of him. We assume he must have died
simply by virtue of his age. He would be quite old today."
She examined the ring. "Don't you see? Someone is trying
to scare me."

"Your father left with his wedding ring?"

"Yes."

"And now his ring has suddenly reappeared. Do you
think someone is gaslighting you?" I asked Helena.

"What else can it be?"

"Who has been in your house?"

"Just the two of us. I'm at work most of the day, of
course. Would you excuse me, Sophie? I need to speak
with my sister."

"Of course. That's understandable."

She opened the door. "I'm sorry that I can't visit with
you longer. Maybe some other time." She closed the door,
and I could hear her running up the stairs.

"Well, that was weird," I said aloud to no one. I continued on my way in the direction of the flower business. I
had heard a lot of strange things before, including rumors
about a vampire, but Helena's father's ring suddenly appearing ranked up there with the most bizarre. Of course,
that explained the lack of a gravestone or obituary. How
awful for the family not to know what had become of him.

In the back of my mind, though, I still wondered if the skeleton could be Helena's father. Someone had moved those bones to keep them hidden. If it was her father and if he was wearing his wedding ring, that would explain how someone got it. Someone who also had access to Helena's home. But why? Why would anyone do that?

I decided it was high time I paid Annie a visit. Initially I thought she probably wouldn't know much about Denise and Rachel. At ninety-eight, she probably didn't get out a lot anymore. But she had been very alert when I met her. Maybe I was dead wrong about just how much she knew.

When I called, she sounded delighted that I wanted to visit. I asked her not to go to any trouble, but she just laughed and asked if one o'clock in the afternoon would suit me. I told her I would be there.

I walked on to the shop that sold outdoor décor and knew instantly where Natasha had obtained all those gourds. Fortunately, they had exactly what I was looking for. I bought a substantial dried willow leaf garland long enough to frame my door. The slightly faded green of the leaves looked like fall to me. To contrast yet complement that, I purchased small white pumpkins, as well as a few orange ones, and faux flowers in colors that matched the rust-red and pink and yellow daisy chrysanthemums that I bought. All of them could continue right into the Halloween season with a few added spooky effects. And best of all, the chrysanthemums could be planted and would return in the fall every year.

The store offered to deliver my purchases, which suited me. Pleased that they'd had what I sought, I dawdled and looked at storefronts as I left. Once again, I passed Nofsinger & Lawson and paused, wondering what had happened to Mitzi.

As I peered into the showroom window, a mouse flew through the air and dropped on the floor.

Chapter 24

Dear Sophie,
I'm trying to decorate my front door for fall. Every-
one has orange wreaths and pumpkins. I'd like to
do something different like a garland, but with
work and the kids, I don't have time to make one.
My mother-in-law says it's too tacky to use one
with plastic leaves! Unfortunately, she lives across
the street. Please save me?
Wish I Could Move in Garland, Utah

Dear Wish I Could Move,
Go ahead and buy a narrow plastic garland in the
colors you want. Faded green would work well.
Then collect fall leaves from your yard (they don't
have to be perfect) and attach them to the garland
in bunches with rustic twine or florist wire. Your
mother-in-law will never know the difference.
Sophie

I shrieked and jumped back.

Seconds later, a slender, young, orange tabby pounced
on the mouse and played hockey with it, which I now re-

alized was a gray toy. I suspected I had found Mitzi. She was right under our noses the whole time.

Just to be certain, I rounded the corner and entered the alley in search of Mitzi's car. I realized that was folly because I didn't know what she drove. But the rental car parked next to the rear door of Nofsinger & Lawson made me think that I was on the right track. I peered inside the car windows.

Part of me wanted to be like a private investigator and do a stakeout to watch the car and the back door. But that took hours. Instead, I rapped very softly on the back door of the office and whispered, "Mitzi?"

The door opened. An arm reached out from behind the door and pulled me inside. A newly blond Mitzi released me and planted her fists on her hips. "You're going to give me away!"

"Everyone is worried sick about you!" I had to admit, she looked terrible. Worn out and frazzled.

"I've been so afraid someone would find my location." She spoke sternly, "You cannot reveal my whereabouts to anyone. Do you understand?"

She was already stressed, so I didn't point out that her name was on the door.

"You saw Rachel." It was a guess, based on what Agnes had said.

Mitzi ran her fingers through her curls. "Of course I saw Rachel. Why do you think I'm hiding? I was supposed to meet her at the Inger House that day. I got out of there as fast as I could before I was next."

"Could we sit down for just a minute?" I looked around to see if there was any place to sit. She had one of those blow-up mattresses on the floor. A couple of chairs had probably been moved in from the showroom, and a good-sized computer screen sat on a desk. "It must be hard to live this way."

"It's cramped, but so far you're the only one who has looked inside, so that's good."

"How do you know that?"

"Oh, Sophie. This is a business. We have cameras mounted."

"I guess there's a bathroom?"

"And luckily whoever built this building put a shower in there!"

"Where do you cook?" I sat on one of the chairs.

"I order takeout to the address next door and tell them to leave it in the alley on the little table."

"You've thought it all through."

"Mars's rental was a lot more comfortable, but this way I'm getting work done and I have to pay rent here anyway."

"Did you hire Rachel?"

"Only on a temporary basis. I needed help because I couldn't handle everything without Denise. When Rachel came to me asking for a job I said yes immediately."

"Did Rachel say anything to you about Mike?"

Mitzi groaned. "She talked about him endlessly. It, um, it bothered me when she tried to pump me about Denise and her relationship with Mike."

"Eww. That would have upset me, too."

"She was definitely fixated on him. I hated that. But I owe it to Denise to make the changes that she planned for the Inger House."

"I saw the chairs in the dining room."

"That room came together beautifully, didn't it? I'm so sad that Denise isn't here to see it. Apparently, she took the chairs to be reupholstered before she died. I was surprised when they delivered them to the house. She ordered a lot of stuff."

I nodded. "It's all gathering in the foyer."

The orange tabby sprang onto my lap. I stroked him. "I was worried about you, little kitty. What's her name?"

"Poppy. Why were you worried about her?"

I told her about going into her house. "I saw the food bowls and wondered where the cat was."

"I missed her. She makes this cramped living more bearable for me. I wish you would catch the killer so I can go home."

"Me too. Tell me what you saw when you went to the Inger House and found Rachel."

Mitzi brushed curls off her forehead. "I went in through the backyard so fewer people would notice me. The kitchen door was open, which worried me. But then I saw her bag on the kitchen table, so I knew she was there. I called her but I didn't worry too much when she didn't answer. It's such a big place. I thought she was looking around. I admired the dining room and took some measurements in the kitchen. When she didn't come downstairs, I went back to the little bedroom because we were planning to move the armoire. It was part of Denise's plan to place it in the living room, which is so big and would have been a much better fit. She wanted to put shelves in it. The armoire had been moved forward, like maybe a foot on the left side. I thought Rachel had probably done that. All the clothes on the floor were in the way. I couldn't believe she would have been so unorganized and would dump them on the floor like that. When I started to pick them up, I saw the slats on the wall behind the armoire. I threw the clothes on the bed and tried to get a better look. I picked up more clothes because they were in the way, and I was stepping on them. That was when I saw Rachel. I couldn't find a pulse. She was dead. And I knew I was next. Especially since I had seen the slats on the wall behind the armoire."

"But you didn't know what was behind them."

"Sophie, I have helped people renovate a lot of old houses in town. I have seen strange things, including many makeshift patches that people covered up with paintings and furniture over the years. It's the first time I have ever seen anything like that."

"You think Rachel was murdered because she saw what was behind the armoire?"

"Well, yeah. Someone didn't want us to find the skeleton."

I gazed at her scared expression. "Did you push the armoire back into place?"

"No! I grabbed my bag and got out of there."

"Did you take Rachel's bag?"

"No. It was on the kitchen table, but I was so scared that I flew out of that house."

"What did her bag look like?"

"About the same size as mine." Mitzi pointed at a periwinkle blue canvas bag that sat on a bench.

Bag, as opposed to purse. We used the words interchangeably. But the pretty periwinkle bag was huge, more like a big tote. Of course! Interior designers carried tons of things with them. Samples, swatches, laser measuring devices, notepads, sketch pads, laptops. I wondered if Wolf realized that. I had been thinking of handbags.

"What did hers look like?"

"Her bag? It was trendy."

"Can you be more specific?"

Mitzi sighed. "Black-and-white striped with her monogram in pink."

I had seen a bag like that at Lillith's shop. But that didn't mean anything. Rachel worked there. She probably bought one because they were cute.

"Someone told me that Denise's bag was sort of a beige, I think?"

"Light camel with pockets on the outside."

"Why would someone take their bags?"

"I don't know. Maybe there were laptops or phones inside? They could sell those, I guess. And the laser measurer. They're not all expensive but some are pricy and they're very cool."

"So all this time, you've been working?"

"Hiding is exhausting. But I have to keep money coming in and I can't let all our clients down. I've contacted everyone and they've been very understanding. But I've had to visit a few of Denise's clients to actually see what they have in mind. So I sneak out in the rental car."

"And you died your hair blond."

"I had to! My curls are a dead giveaway that it's me. I thought the new hair color would be misleading if anyone caught a glimpse of me."

"Are you certain you wouldn't rather stay with me? Poppy is welcome and you could park in my garage."

"Thanks, Sophie. You're too close to the case. Everyone knows you found the skeleton." She shuddered.

"How do you know what everyone thinks?"

"I watch the local news. I guess I'm hoping I'll hear that the killer has been caught."

I stood up. "Take care of yourself, Mitzi. Call me if you need anything."

"Please, Sophie. Not a word to anyone about where I am. Not even to Wolf. If anyone knows, I'll end up dead."

I hugged her. "I promise."

I hurried home just in time to receive my delivery. Daisy was waiting for me inside the house. She accompanied me outside to look at the chrysanthemum daisies. They really stood out. I loved them!

We went back inside. I ate a quick lunch of yogurt and fed Daisy and Mochie, then changed into a forest-green belted dress for my afternoon visit to Annie.

She lived in a yellow two-story house located at a corner

where two streets crossed, which enabled me to see how huge it was. Green shutters hung at the windows and in Old Town tradition, the front door matched them.

I rapped the pineapple door knocker, known throughout the South as the symbol of hospitality.

A young woman answered the door. "Welcome. Annie is expecting you." She showed me to a living room with cream-colored walls and white trim on the windows. The sun streamed in. Annie sat in a club chair with her cane leaning against the arm.

"Thank you for coming. I wondered when you would get around to me."

"You must have a clear conscience. Most people dread my visits," I joked.

"Not me!" She looked up at the young woman, "Nala, would you please serve the tea?" When Nala had left, Annie leaned toward me and whispered, "She's my sister's great-great-granddaughter. Her parents are too self-centered to raise her right. She'll end up being like them if someone doesn't intervene. My sister is long gone, so I consider it my responsibility to bring her into the fold and put her on the right path for life."

"That's kind of you."

"It's what we do for family."

Nala brought tea and cups on a silver tray and set it on the table. "I'll be right back." When she returned, she brought cream, lemons, sugar, and miniature pastries.

Annie smiled at her. "You go ahead and help yourself to some in the kitchen. I know you don't want to sit out here with us." She pointed her forefinger at Nala. "But don't you call that boy. You know who."

Nala grimaced and went off somewhere.

Annie shook her head. "Relationships get us into so much trouble." She poured the tea and when we were settled, Annie sat back and started to reminisce. "When I met

Jill Inger, Helena and Jacky's mama, she was young. Probably the most vibrant person I have ever known. She was a free spirit. An artist!" Annie pointed to a lovely painting of Old Town that hung on the wall. "Jill painted that. Now mind you, it was a different time. Things were changing fast. But Jill and I had a lot in common. You know how it is. Women always have things in common. Babies, children, cooking, fashion, hair, makeup, and especially men. We can talk and talk. Men have to find something in common, like a hobby or a sport. But women are bound together. Jill had married Ollie, short for Oliver. She liked to call him Jolly Ollie. The poor girl didn't know the first thing about cooking or caring for a home." Annie laughed at the memory. "But it was a happy household. Helena was born, and I had a baby, too. Jill was wonderful. She didn't mind if I brought my Tommy to work with me. We set the two of them together and took turns changing diapers and taking care of our babies. But about a year later, the demon drink took over Ollie."

Annie sipped her tea and stared at nothing, as if she was remembering. "That was when everything changed. He became angry. The slightest thing would set him off. I started to see bruises on Jill. She would try to explain them away, but I knew where they came from. Oliver shouted at both of us constantly. And at the babies, too. Heaven forbid that one of them should cry. And he continued to drink. Personally, I've never had so much as a lick of alcohol except as a cooking ingredient like vanilla. I couldn't understand. He was a mess. And then when Helena was almost two, Jill became pregnant again. Back in the day, women didn't have rights like they do now. Jill knew she had to leave. She lived in fear that she would lose the baby when Oliver was abusive to her. I'm proud to say that I helped her pack."

I reached over for a mini cream puff.

"Jill knew she couldn't handle Helena and the new baby by herself. She didn't even know where she was going to live. I promised I would take good care of Helena until Jill came for her. When Oliver fell into an alcoholic stupor, Jill seized the moment and left."

"I can't believe she left Helena behind!"

"It tore her up. The plan was for Jill to come and get Helena after the baby was born when she was settled somewhere. We couldn't see any other way. Her parents would have sent her back to Oliver. That's what happened to women back then. She was striking out on her own. A couple of years went by, and we didn't hear a word. I thought something terrible must have happened to her. Then, one day, a couple showed up on the doorstep with a two-year-old."

"Jacky?"

"They said her mother had passed away from an illness. She gave them an address before she died. They didn't know what else to do with the baby, so they brought her home. Oliver never believed that Jill died. Never. Things were bad before, but after that they got much worse. He couldn't deal with it. He did a one hundred-eighty-degree turn from the sweet man he was when they married. The anger ate him up inside. I guess he thought Jill found some other man.

"I kept the babies safe, and often took them home with me at night if I was worried about him. But then he stopped leaving the house unless he had to. He stayed home most of the time, like a hermit, drank himself stupid, yet still managed to run the business. I guess rent checks came in and he was sufficiently capable of cashing them. He paid me and when I asked for more, he raised my pay. He grumbled but he knew he needed me. When Helena was ten, he started sending her out to collect rent checks. Age ten! That child should have been out playing with other children, but he had her working, entering data into the records and taking care of business. Can you imagine?" Annie sipped her tea before setting it down. "He refused to buy clothes for the girls. He'd go to church basement sales when they offered secondhand clothes for the needy. Those children looked like old ladies in frumpy house-dresses! And that was when your husband's aunt, Faye Winston, stepped into their lives. I'll never forget that day. She knocked the door knocker, and I opened the door to this elegant woman wearing one of those suits like Jackie Kennedy used to wear. She said, 'How do you do? I am Faye Winston. Is Mr. Inger in?' Well, I ushered her into the living room and went upstairs to get him. It was two in the afternoon, and he was just waking up! I told him, 'There's a fine lady here to see you. She's waiting in the living room.'" Annie slapped her thigh. "You never saw such a confused man. I made a pot of coffee while he got dressed and I brought it into the living room to serve to Faye. She asked me what my name was. I told her Annie Griggs. She held out her hand to shake mine. 'Thank you, Annie,' she said. Mr. Inger walked in like he had awakened in a house he'd never seen before."

Chapter 25

Dear Sophie,
My monster-in-law is scaling down and has offered
us a lot of furniture. It's not my style at all. I prefer
new, white furniture. I just can't afford everything
I would like yet. Monster-in-law's pieces are old,
maybe even antique, with scratches and nicks. My
husband loves it! How do I decline her offer?
Daughter-in-law with Good Taste in Chestnut Wood
Village, Pennsylvania

Dear Daughter-in-law with Good Taste,
A Japanese decorating trend is making its way to
the US. The concept is to appreciate the beauty of
imperfections and appreciate that things are beau-
tiful as they are. If you still really hate them, use
them in a man cave for your husband.

Sophie

"I left the room, but I hid just around the corner so I
could hear what was going on. Faye was smooth.
She said, 'Mr. Inger, it has come to my attention that you
have two beautiful daughters. You are a gentleman of stand-

ing in this town and I cannot for the life of me understand why a wealthy man with a lovely home would allow his daughters to run around dressed like old women in sacks. What will people think of you?' He stammered a bit, and I could hear the coffee cup clanking. 'I had no idea,' he said, which was a bunch of baloney. So Faye said, 'I have a proposition for you. I own a fine dress store. I will take your girls under my wing and dress them properly. And you, sir, will pay the bills that I send to you. Additionally, I will make arrangements with hairdressers, see that they get proper dental care, and will host parties on behalf of your daughters. You will be expected to pay the hairdressers and the dentist. I won't charge for the parties I arrange so they can meet other girls their age and learn how to be ladies. Are you agreeable to that?'"

Annie could hardly control her laughter. "Nobody ever spoke to him that way. I heard him say 'yes.' She thanked him, then walked out of there with her head high. She stopped and asked if I had daughters in the same age range. When I said I did, she told me to bring them by her store and that she wanted to invite them to the parties she would throw for Helena and Jacky. She never charged me one cent for clothes. Not even for mine. She'd say, 'You deserve it.' I tell you, it was as if a fairy godmother had knocked on the door and taken over. Helena and Jacky thrived in the hands of Faye, and my girls did, too. She was a wonderful woman who wasn't scared of anyone."

"I am so sorry that Mars missed hearing this. I don't believe he knows anything about it. What happened to Oliver Inger?"

"Oh my. One day he announced that he was going to find Jill. He had never believed that she died. He took off and never came back. Helena stepped into his shoes. She'd been doing most of the work anyway at that point."

"Poor Helena and Jacky. They went through so much.

No wonder they see you as a mother. You're the only mother they ever knew."

Annie beamed. "I'm proud of those girls. They are my children. And my biological children treat them as sisters. After their mother left, Oliver didn't want any holiday festivities. He was too drunk anyway. So on special holidays, I brought them to my house to celebrate with us. I couldn't have those sweet babies growing up without celebrations."

"You may give Faye a lot of credit, but I can't imagine what would have happened to Helena and Jacky without you. Did you ever find out what happened to Jill?"

"I always thought she died. If she had had one breath left in her body, she would have tried to come home to her babies. No one knows who that couple was that dropped off Jacky. If she hadn't been the spitting image of Helena, Oliver might have turned her away. Instead, he withdrew, and drank, and ruined his life."

"Did you ever hear from him again?"

"Nah. When he left, it was for good."

"Jill left when Helena was about two. Is that right?" I asked.

Annie nodded. "Poor little thing was just a baby."

I debated whether to mention his wedding ring and decided I might as well. "This morning, Helena found her father's wedding ring in her house."

Annie drew her head back as if she thought I was crazy. "That can't be."

"Not unless someone found him and kept the ring."

She laughed. "Not a chance! Somebody is pulling a fast one on Helena. Why would she think it's her father's wedding ring?"

"Because it's engraved *Ollie & Jill 1951*."

"Anyone could have that done to a ring."

"But *why* would someone do that?"

"I don't know. That girl is keeping too much from me."

"Do you think it could have something to do with Denise or Rachel?"

"Now, how could that be?"

"I was hoping you might have some ideas."

Annie gazed at the fireplace. "It doesn't make any sense at all."

"I'm certain you have thought about the murders of Denise and Rachel."

"I certainly have. Everybody is talking about them."

"And?"

"I don't understand it. Denise was as sweet as they come. I've heard a few stories about Rachel, but nothing that would have gotten her killed."

"You see, my problem is that I think it has to be someone in the family."

"Why would you say that? People break into homes and kill other people all the time."

"That's true. But no one broke into the Inger House. There isn't a broken window or door lock. So that leads me to believe it was someone who was familiar with the house."

"Well! A lot of people have been in that house."

"I would agree. But the only real tie between the two women is Mike."

Her eyes opened wide. "Now, don't you go blaming Mike for their murders."

"It's too late for that. The police are already looking into that possibility."

Annie gasped. "Oh, that Helena! She did not tell me that."

"And here's another little tidbit. Their killer took their bags."

"How do you know that they brought purses with them?"

"When is the last time you left your house without a purse?"

"Some women don't carry them. They just tuck some money into their phones and carry them in their pockets. You know, they make so many pretty phone jackets now."

"That's true. But the police didn't find phones, either. And interior designers carry big totes filled with the things they need."

"Someone must have stolen them to sell."

"How long did you work for the Nofsingers?"

She smiled. "A long time. Until Robbie went to high school. And then Helena hired me to help out with little Mikey when he came along. So you might say that I raised three generations of the Inger-Nofsinger family."

"That's very impressive."

"When people ask me the secret to living a long life, I tell them to keep working. You have to get up every day with something to do. No lying around in bed!"

"So you would have been working at the Inger House in 1969?"

"Yes, indeed."

"Did anyone tell you that we found a skeleton in the wall?"

Annie stopped smiling. "I heard about it on the TV."

"That person died in 1969 or thereabouts. When did you say Ollie left?"

"Right around 1970, I think. You're asking me to go way back, and my memory isn't as good as it used to be."

I didn't believe that for a second. She had a very vivid recollection of Faye and exactly what she said and did. "Do you have any recollection of a fight or disagreement? Maybe that's the real reason that Ollie left town?"

"There were plenty of fights going on. It wasn't a peaceful time. They protested about the Vietnam War, and I believe that was when we had the Watergate scandal, and probably more than that."

"I meant something personal involving one of the Ingers. Was anyone angry with them? Did a visitor arrive and leave abruptly? Was there a fight?"

For her age, Annie looked remarkable, but now it seemed to me that the wrinkles around her mouth deepened. "I don't recall anything like that. No. I'd have to think on it a bit."

"I wish you would. It's so strange to find a person in a wall. Something truly terrible must have happened. In the winter, I think."

She stared at me. "Why would you say that?"

"My friend, Nina, and I were talking. If she murdered someone, she would bury that person in the yard and make it look like a garden. The Inger House backyard is plenty big for that. So I think it must have been when it was cold out and hard to dig. After the frost sets in at night."

"I heard tell about you. You think these things through, don't you? I like that."

"Before I came here, I thought it might be Ollie himself who was hidden in the wall. But given what you told me about his drinking and temper, I wonder if Ollie didn't kill someone and hide him in the wall. That might also explain why he left town."

"That would make sense," she said. She pursed her mouth and gazed at me. "I know they can find biological moms and dads of adopted children through DNA. Do you think they'll be able to identify the man in the wall?"

"Yes. I think that's a real possibility. It might take some time, though."

Annie seemed tired and worn out. I feared I might have pressed her too hard. "This has been a delightful visit. Thank you for sharing so much information about Faye. I had no idea she was such a spitfire! Maybe you can come for tea one day to see little Marshall and the beautiful portrait of Faye that hangs in my kitchen."

I rose. "May I give you a hug?"

Tears welled in Annie's eyes. She nodded.

I embraced her and felt the warmth of her body. She smelled like lilacs.

"Sometimes, life doesn't work out the way we want," she whispered. "Sometimes you have to do what's right, you hear?"

"I will," I whispered.

I looked back as I walked away. Annie had closed her eyes. I peered through a doorway in search of the kitchen and found Nala scrolling on her phone.

"Hi, Nala. I'm afraid I wore her out. Do you need help getting Annie to a place where she can lie down?"

Nala flicked her hand. "No, thanks. I'll get her caregiver. She's watching her soap."

I waved at her and slipped out the front door as quietly as I could.

A cool breeze blew off the river as I walked home. I appreciated Annie's last words to me, but they made me think that she suspected a member of the family was involved as well. That wasn't anything terribly new, since I had thought so all along, but she might know something that I didn't.

I couldn't get over Faye's boldness in dealing with Ollie. I cherished her gorgeous china and crystal even more now. When Mars moved out, I made him take boxes of papers in our attic that belonged to her. I knew she had been a remarkable hostess and entertained politicians and dignitaries. Maybe she had kept diaries. I hoped Mars hadn't thrown everything out.

When I approached Lillith's shop, I paused and decided to go in for a closer look at the type of bag Rachel had used.

Her assistant greeted me with a big smile. "Did you come back for something you saw?"

"Sort of." I pointed at the display of bags. "I understand Rachel used one of those with the stripes and the mono-gram."

"They are so cute!" she gushed. "One of our popular sellers. The monogram makes it so special. It's a great gift."

"Were you friends with Rachel?"

She didn't respond immediately, but appeared to con-sider the question and followed me over to the bags. Glanc-ing at the door to Lillith's office, she whispered, "I wouldn't have said we were friends. We didn't socialize together. I don't think I was good enough for her."

"That's rude."

"I know! I think so, too. But some people are like that. They think they're better than other people."

The black-and-white striped bag sat in the rear of the display, about five feet off the floor with other bags clus-tered in front of it. Intending to remove it from the display, I took the handle and tried to lift it over the other bags, but it weighed much more than I had expected. "Have you got bricks in there?" I joked.

"No. Let me help you."

I moved some of the bags in front of it so we wouldn't knock them over.

"Wow! That's not an empty bag. Maybe it fell over and Lillith put something inside to stabilize it," said the assis-tant.

Together, we lifted it off the display and were about to lower it to the floor. In excruciatingly poor timing, Lillith emerged from her office. "Don't you dare set that on the floor unless one of you intends to buy it."

Her assistant promptly let go. Fortunately, it wasn't as heavy as I anticipated. I parted the handles to see what it contained. The inside pockets carried marble and quartz samples, a laptop computer, a laser measuring device, markers, sketch pads, and a small matching pouch that could double as a clutch. I placed the bag on the floor in defiance of Lillith, removed the clutch and opened it. Inside I found a phone as well as a wallet with Rachel's driver's license and credit cards in her name. I zipped the pouch and returned it to the bag. My eyes on Lillith, I phoned Wolf.

Lillith moved toward me in her graceful gazelle manner. "There shouldn't be anything inside that bag except for matching accessories." She reached into the bag.

"I wouldn't do that," I said as Wolf answered my call. "Wolf, I'm at Lillith Rollins's shop and I think I've found Rachel's bag."

He assured me he would be there as soon as he could.

"Rachel's bag?" Lillith asked. "That's impossible."

Her assistant stepped back and said, "It is her monogram. Rachel Anne Powers, RAP."

"I thought this was a floor sample," said Lillith. "Did you want to order one, Sophie?"

"It's very cute. And practical. But to be honest, I heard that Rachel carried a bag like this." I met her gaze directly. "And it vanished when she was murdered."

The assistant gasped and backed away.

"Then how did it get to my store?" asked Lillith.

I didn't respond. The only way I could imagine was that the killer had cleverly hidden it there among the other bags.

Wolf must have been nearby. He walked in calmly, as was his nature. If I had been a cop, I would have rushed in, causing more chaos. But Wolf kept his cool. "Hello, Lillith. What's up, Sophie?"

"I think I found Rachel's bag."

"I'm sorry to bother you," said Lillith. "This must be a mistake."

Wolf pulled on gloves. "Why do you think this belonged

to Rachel?" Wolf shot me a sideways glance, as if he thought I had dragged him into the shop for a bogus reason.

"There's a small clutch inside with her driver's license in it."

"She worked here," Lillith said. "She was one of my employees."

"This was her work bag," I explained. "I think we've been under the mistaken impression that she and Denise carried purses, which they may have done. But interior designers have to carry a lot of stuff. They need to make notes and measure and draw sketches and bring samples. So they usually carry a big tote like this."

"I pride myself on the best selection in town," said Lillith. "One can't walk into a meeting with a client carrying something that looks like it's full of screwdrivers and nails."

"There," I said, pointing to the clutch.

Wolf removed it and looked inside. His expression never wavered, even when he examined the contents of the wallet. "Where did you find this?" asked Wolf.

I had promised Mitzi to keep her name quiet. I didn't like to lie to Wolf, so I fudged a little bit. "I'd heard that Rachel carried a black-and-white striped bag. I saw this one when I was here the other day and figured this was where Rachel bought hers. After all, she worked here. I wanted to get a feel for just how big it is, and when we took it off the display, I found her wallet inside."

"What about the other things that are inside? Are they hers, too?"

"I didn't look at them. As soon as I saw her driver's license and credit cards, I put them back as I found them and phoned you."

"Lillith?" He gazed at her.

"I have no idea how it came to be here."

"How many employees do you have?"

"One and a half."

"Half?"

"She's part time."

Wolf smiled at the full-time assistant. "Is there somewhere we can talk?"

Lillith appeared pained. "My office."

We heard a door slam somewhere. "Lillith?" It was a man's voice.

Chapter 26

Dear Sophie,
I'm using a spare bedroom as a home office. I've painted the walls a fresh white. The windows look too tiny, even though they're a decent size. Can I fix that without replacing them?
Work at Home Mom in Window Rock, Arizona

Dear Work at Home Mom,
That's an easy fix. Install Roman shades at ceiling level. They will make your windows appear much taller.
Sophie

Thurman walked into the shop area from Lillith's office. He carried a beige tote bag and stopped dead at the sight of us.

"Great to see everyone! It's like a party." He dropped the tote bag and came over to hug me. "Sophie, it's always nice to see you." He patted Wolf on the shoulder. "You haven't been at the club much lately. Working overtime?" Thurman looked at Lillith and her assistant. "Is something wrong?"

"May I borrow gloves?" I asked Wolf.

He handed me two. Pulling them on, I walked over to the beige tote, which was actually more of a light tan color. I opened the handles at the top and perused the contents in search of a clutch style bag that might contain personal information. I didn't see one but found a phone case. It opened like a book. On the left side, credit cards and a driver's license had been placed in slots. Cash peeked out of a pocket. I slid the driver's license out knowing exactly whose it was before I saw the name on it. It belonged to Denise Nofsinger.

I handed it to Wolf and asked Thurman, "Where did you get this?"

"Lillith"—he glanced at her—"left it . . . at the house. What's going on?"

"It belongs to Denise," said Wolf.

Lillith's eyes widened. "Thurman!" She looked at Wolf and raised her palms. "I didn't leave that anywhere."

"It belongs to Denise?" asked Thurman, sounding convincingly surprised. "I thought it was Lillith's."

"I would *never* carry that bag." Lillith scowled at Thurman. "It has no panache. I'm surprised that Denise would have used it."

"Where exactly did you find it?" asked Wolf.

Truman paused a few seconds too long before answering. "In the Inger House."

"What were you doing over there?" Wolf kept his eyes on Thurman.

"I went over to check on things for Helena. She worries about it now that it's vacant. People might break in what with all the publicity," said Thurman.

I smiled at the assistant and sidled up to her. "Could I borrow a pen and a piece of paper?"

"Yes. Of course." She flicked a look at her boss before

leading me to the checkout counter and handing me a pen and paper.

"Thank you." I wrote a note to Wolf.

Seems odd that Thurman wouldn't know Robbie is living in the Inger House. Even stranger that Denise's bag would show up there when we've searched the house for it repeatedly. I think he's lying.

I handed the note to Wolf, who read it. His annoyingly impassive poker face didn't change.

"I think it's time you two came down to the station for a little chat," said Wolf, pulling out his radio.

"Not me!" cried Lillith. "I was standing here minding my own business. It was Thurman who brought Denise's bag in here. I had nothing to do with it."

Thurman glanced at me with an annoyed expression. "Could I speak to you privately?" Without waiting for a response, he edged up to Wolf.

I could still hear what he whispered.

"I was trying to preserve some dignity for Lillith and my wife. Lillith left it in the trunk of my car, if you catch my drift."

Wolf calmly asked Lillith, "Did you place the beige bag in Thurman's trunk?"

"I did not!" she said. "I had nothing to do with it."

"Then how did Rachel's bag end up on your display?" I asked her.

"I have no idea." She looked to her assistant again.

"You are not blaming this on me, Lillith. I didn't put it there." The assistant's face had flushed pink.

"Well," said Lillith in an annoyed tone, "it didn't jump up there by itself and I know I did not rearrange that display."

Mimicking her, the assistant said, "Well, I didn't re-arrange it, either. So there."

"Then you must have seen someone swap it for the empty bag that was on display," Lillith persisted.

"I did not!"

"Did you put Denise's bag in the trunk of Thurman's car?" Wolf asked Lillith.

"Of course not. How would I know what kind of car he drives?"

I murmured to Wolf, "They're having an affair."

"Are you sure?" he asked me.

I nodded. "Pretty much. You can ask Nina. She was with me."

"All right. I'm calling a squad car to take you down to the station." Wolf ignored their protests.

"Thurman!" Lillith shot him a look that could have fried eggs. Her lips pulled tight, she marched over to him. Even though she spoke in a low tone, I was fairly certain everyone could hear her.

"Why would you do this to me? I loved you! What happened to all our plans? Were you playing me for a fool? Using me as a minion whom you planned to cast aside? How dare you!" She slapped him squarely on the side of his face.

He caught her by the wrists. "Lillith, stop it. I don't know what's happening. I thought you left that bag in my car. I knew it wasn't Helena's. It had a laser measuring thing in it. What was I supposed to think when I opened the trunk and found it there? I came here to return it to you. I couldn't have Helena find it in my trunk."

"It's too late for kissing up to me, Thurman. You were never going to leave Helena, were you? All the things you promised, they were never going to happen. I feel like such an idiot. Young girls make this kind of mistake, not women my age. How could I let you con me this way?" She took a deep breath, wrested her arms away from him, and marched into her office. I could hear her calling a lawyer.

I watched Thurman, who smiled at the assistant. He walked over to Wolf. In a low voice, Thurman said, "Look, Wolf. You've known me for years. You know I'm a good guy. I don't understand how Denise's bag ended up in my trunk. I honestly don't. Can't you just let us go?"

"Sorry, Thurman. I think it's best if we straighten this out at the station."

A squad car pulled up outside and another behind it. Police officers escorted Lillith and Thurman out of the shop. Wolf followed them.

The shop assistant turned to me. "Do you think I should close up?"

"Probably. The police will want to collect the bags and might do a search. Lillith has keys if the police need to get in. I'll stay with you while you lock up."

It didn't take her long. She seemed eager to get out of there.

"I guess I should look for another job, huh?"

"I wouldn't be too hasty about that unless you're uncomfortable about working for Lillith now."

"Really? You think they'll let her go?"

"I honestly don't know what will happen."

At the corner, I turned one way, and she went the other.

Heading for home, I took a shortcut through an alley. A door swung open, and Jesse stepped out.

"Sophie! What a nice surprise. Sneaking through alleys, are you?"

For a split second I was taken aback. "Hi. I guess I could say the same thing about you!" I teased.

He wiped his brow. "I use the back door all the time. Everyone stops me to talk if I try to go out the front door."

"This is the back of Synergy?" A chill ran through me.

"Yup. The back door is a little-known secret." He smiled and placed his forefinger against his lips, letting me know to keep it under wraps.

"Can customers use the door?"

"In an emergency, of course. Fire regulations require an accessible back exit. But we slapped a big sign on it that says Management Only. Most of them probably think it's a utility closet."

"Can you re-enter that way?"

"Sure!" He pulled the door open to show me. "It's no big deal. Most stores have a back door for deliveries and emergencies."

That was true. And yet, I had overlooked that possibility entirely.

"What's wrong? You look like you saw a ghost. I'm not that scary, am I?"

"So Stu or Jacky could have left Synergy that way? And no one would have been the wiser. They could have walked out and back in without anyone noticing?"

Chapter 27

Dear Sophie,
I'm engaged! My parents and my soon-to-be in-laws are coming for brunch to discuss the wedding. I have my heart set on making Eggs Benedict because they are so classy. My sister says I'm insane. I've never cooked them before. What do you think? Is Eggs Benedict for six do-able?
                    I'm the Bride! in Benedict, Maryland

Dear I'm the Bride!
Do-able? Yes. Do-able if it's your first time making them? No. You will have a lot of stress on you that day. They aren't hard to make—once you know what you're doing. Buy the ingredients and practice poaching eggs and whipping up the Hollandaise sauce. Then do a test run and you'll be ready to serve that elegant dish.

                                        Sophie

"Oh. That's what you're after. I see," said Jesse. "Yes, they could have left and returned, but we steer everyone to the front. I'm probably the only person who uses the back door much."

"There's no bell or alarm that goes off?"

"There is at night. But not when we're open for business."

I looked around for cameras and spied two aimed at Synergy's back door. "You have cameras!"

Jesse nodded. "Can't have anyone sneaking in at night and wrecking the place."

"If I tell you the exact day and a time range, say morning from ten to eleven—"

He interrupted me. "Sorry. The cameras are off during the day. We only use them when we're closed." He moved closer to me and whispered, "Do you suspect them of murder?"

I was mentally kicking myself. I had written off Stu and Jacky without another thought.

Before I responded, Jesse said, "I don't think you have to worry about them. Jacky is very sweet, and I could learn a thing or two about how to treat women from Stu. The way he looks at Jacky, you can see how he adores her. Did you know that he busted lifting one hundred twenty-five pounds the other day? It's nothing for the young guys who come in, but he was so proud of himself that we gave him a round of applause and a challenge coin."

"Challenge coin?"

"Yeah, in addition to the pins, we give little coins when people work toward a goal and reach a milestone. He was so excited! Then he lost it somewhere. He didn't want to tell us, but Jacky mentioned it, so we gave her another one for him to find in their house." Jesse grinned. "Nice couple. I wish I could find someone who felt that way about me."

"What day did he win that?"

"It was last week. He lost it on Friday, I think. I remember Jacky saying she went to her book club meeting. She teased him about not being able to leave him alone for a minute."

I smiled at the muscular man. "Did I invite you to our brunch? Natasha will be there. And most of the Nofsinger-Inger crew."

"A brunch? Sounds great!"

I gave him the date and time along with my address.

"I know exactly which house it is."

"Have I stumbled upon a hot spot for secret meetings?"

I knew that voice with a British accent and turned to my right. "Hi, Bernie."

"Hope I didn't interrupt anything. There's usually no one back here."

"Not a thing. Looks like we're all taking shortcuts," I said.

Bernie and I waved goodbye to Jesse and began to walk to our street together.

"What was that about?" Bernie asked.

"You know how I confidently said we could mark Jacky and Stu off our list of suspects? Turns out there's a back door to Synergy. Either or both of them could have left and returned that way without anyone noticing."

"But I heard they arrested Thurman. Was that just gossip?"

"Wolf took Thurman and Lillith down to the station for questioning." I told him about their connection to Rachel's and Denise's work bags.

"Got a minute?" asked Bernie.

"Sure."

"Let's time it."

We returned to the back door of Synergy.

Bernie set the stopwatch on his phone and said, "Okay, go!"

I wasn't as long-legged and probably slowed Bernie down, but it only took us five minutes and twenty-two seconds to reach the front door of the Inger House.

Robbie must have heard us coming up the front porch steps because he swung the door open. "Are you here about Dad? Come on in."

Mike emerged from the living room. "Hi." He gazed at his father and appeared to defer to him.

Robbie kept talking. "I'm so glad you're here. Sophie, we're in a mess. Mom is a wreck. She's always the strong one. Our rock. She's at the police station with Dad and called me, very upset. You have to do something. Dad is a lot of things, but he's not a killer. I know him. There's no way he would kill anyone, let alone his granddaughter-in-law. I don't understand why he's there."

I sighed. I didn't feel I should be the one to tell Robbie and Mike about their dad and grandfather's affair. On the other hand, they would hear about it sooner or later anyway. Taking a deep breath, I said, "Thurman has been having an affair with Lillith Rollins."

Robbie's eyes opened wide.

"No way!" said Mike.

"Okay, okay." Robbie's breath was ragged. "It's totally unimaginable and I'm certain there must be a mistake. But the last I heard, that wasn't a crime that you get arrested for."

"I happened to be in her shop when Thurman turned up with Denise's work bag."

Mike staggered backward. "Grandpop? That can't be!"

"I agree with Mike. Dad must have found it somewhere."

"That's what he claimed. He said he found it in his trunk and thought it belonged to Lillith."

"You see?" Robbie looked over at Mike. "A perfectly reasonable explanation."

"It gets a little bit more complicated than that."

"Oh no." Robbie took a deep breath.

"Rachel's work bag was found in Lillith's shop as part of a display."

"I don't understand," said Mike. "It's bad enough that it's my own family, but why would either of them murder Denise?"

"I can't know for sure, but I think someone didn't want them to find the skeleton in the wall. Did Rachel mention to you that she wanted to move the armoire?"

Color drained from Mike's face. "Yeah! Several times. It was too big for that room. I agreed with her."

"That makes no sense," said Robbie. "None of us knew the skeleton was there."

I had a bad feeling that Helena had left them out of the loop about some things. "The initial findings indicate that it was a man, and he was murdered around 1969. Someone knew about it."

"The year I was born," said Robbie. "Dad?" He thought for a moment. "No. I'm not buying it. Dad loves everybody. Maybe one too many if what you're saying about Lillith is true. But I stand by my dad. He is not a murderer."

"Someone is," said Mike, his face flushed with anger.

"We better get over to the police station. No wonder Mom is freaking out." Robbie moved toward the door.

"One quick thing," I said. "Did one of you happen to find a coin? Not a real one. It's a challenge coin from Synergy."

"Yeah. Yeah, I did." Robbie frowned at me. "Is it yours?"

"Stu lost one."

"Oh yeah." Robbie nodded. "He's so into that place. I should have realized he dropped it when they were packing up. I think I tossed it in the trash."

We followed him into the kitchen where he pulled the trash bin from under the sink. Robbie extracted a small round disk and started to wash it off in the sink.

"No!" I leaped toward him. Seizing a paper towel to hold it, I grabbed it from him. "Fingerprints."

He looked at me oddly. "Fingerprints? I don't understand."

Holding it on the paper towel, I showed the coin to them. It resembled a barbell plate and said 125 LBS on it. "He lost it the day his wife was at her book club, giving him plenty of time to murder Rachel. If nothing else, it would prove that Stu had been in the house."

"He could have come back for something they forgot," said Robbie.

"Very true," I said. "And maybe he saw Rachel poking her nose behind the armoire."

I knew Robbie was eager to leave for the police station to comfort his mom, so Bernie and I made a hasty exit.

"You should have given the coin to them to take to Wolf," he said.

"Not a chance. This is staying securely with me until I can hand it over to Wolf personally. Even if I walked to the station myself, I'm sure I would not be able to see him right now. I'm not taking chances that someone will misplace it or toss it out. Hey, where were you going when you ran into Jesse and me?"

"Just home for a break. It does me good to get out of the restaurant once in a while."

"You probably need to hire more people so you can take entire days off."

"A guy can dream. Management turnover is wicked. But I will take your advice."

At home, I couldn't get my mind off the events of the day. Daisy and Mochie were happy to see me. I changed out of my dress to a mock turtleneck and jeans. After letting Daisy out, I made a strong mug of tea and sat down at the kitchen table with the notepad that Mars always used.

Right now, Wolf was trying to figure out whether Thurman had killed Denise and Rachel, and whether Lillith assisted him. There was no question in my mind that Thurman had lied about his whereabouts when Denise was murdered. He had also paid someone off to lie for him and give him an alibi. Both were serious indications of guilt.

It had become very clear that someone didn't want us to find the skeleton. Otherwise, why would that person have gone to the trouble of moving the bones and hiding them?

It had to be someone very familiar with the house. But nearly all of them had lived there for some period of time. All except Mary and Mike. What had begun with Mike being suspected had now made a major turn to Thurman.

But if it was Thurman at the root of the murders, then why was he so determined to hide the skeleton? As the patriarch of the family, he might want to protect Helena. Robbie had said it was the year he was born. Unless the family told stories about the man behind the wall, which I doubted, Robbie and Mike probably had no idea that the skeleton existed until now. And the lack of stories about him pointed to guilt. Something had happened there that left a man dead in 1969.

Helena, Jacky, and Stu remained as possible suspects. I could be wrong, but I didn't think Thurman felt the same allegiance to Jacky and Stu, which narrowed his motivation down to Helena. Had she killed the man in the wall? Had she and Thurman done it together? Why hadn't they done a better job of hiding the location of the skeleton?

On second thought, I could guess the answer to that. Thurman was a socialite. Not the type to get his hands dirty. They would have had to hire someone to do it and then the body would have been discovered.

It wasn't out of the realm of possibilities that Thurman had murdered Denise and Rachel to keep the skeleton hidden. Especially now that we knew he had the bag of at least one of them and seemed intent on planting it on Lillith. To get rid of her? How long had they been together? Had he taken her on as a mistress for this purpose? So he could point a finger at her?

But, if he murdered them to protect Helena, then why would he try to freak her out by placing her dead father's wedding band in the catch-all bowl where she would surely see it? Something did not jive.

I groaned aloud, startling Daisy and Mochie.

Stu was the more likely candidate. He was old enough to have been around in 1969. And now that I knew he and Jacky could have slipped out of Synergy, that changed everything. Had he murdered someone and placed him behind the wall all those years ago? Had they all done it together? Stu, and Jacky, and Helena, and Thurman?

The brunch we had planned wasn't that far off and I needed to spend some time preparing. I went up to my attic again and found a plain grapevine wreath and some cute faux berries and tiny blooms in rust-red, yellow, and pink. I carried them downstairs and attached the little white pumpkins first, then added the berries and flowers. Daisy and I went outside, where I hung it on the door. I fetched a ladder from the garage and was hanging the garland when Natasha showed up.

"You have to be kidding me," she said. "I never should have let you take over the exterior decorations."

I hung the last piece of garland and descended the ladder.

"It's exactly what I wanted. It doesn't scream anything. It's tastefully fall." I moved some of her gourds around the bottoms of the plants. "All done! Do we have a final head-count on the number of guests? I invited more people today."

"I certainly hope you uninvited all the Nofsingers. Can you imagine having a skeleton in your house? I bet Thurman gets kicked out of his swanky golf club. I heard he was arrested today in the arms of another woman! Who would want him after he killed those women? I wouldn't go near him!"

Rumors and gossip. They kept us living in a soap opera. I didn't correct her because she had the fundamentals right. "Nope. They are most certainly invited! I hope they come."

"What if they poison the food?"

"Yes, I'm sure that's what they have in mind, Natasha."

"I did like Thurman, though. Always so gentlemanly and friendly. And well dressed, too. Just goes to show that anyone can be a killer."

"Have you tested your brunch dish?"

She smiled at me as one might smile at a confused child. "Oh, Sophie. I don't need to do that. I know how to cook. I would like to examine your living room and dining room, though. They may need help."

"You don't need to do that. I know how to decorate." I had trouble hiding my grin.

Chapter 28

Dear Sophie,
Our dining room has white wainscoting and deep
gray walls. It's dramatic and eye-catching. We love
it, except it sometimes feels too dark. Any sugges-
tions that won't break the bank?
                    Loving My Gray in Gray, Maine

Dear Loving My Gray,
You probably have a sideboard in your dining
room. Hang a horizontal mirror over it and place a
lamp on each end. When it feels too dark, turn on
the lamps. They will reflect in the mirror and
brighten the room.

                                        Sophie

Nina saw us and ran across the street. "Anyone up for
dinner?"

Dusk was upon us and I was exhausted. It had been a
long day.

Natasha sounded energetic when she said, "I would love
that! Sophie, go get dressed."

"I *am* dressed." I was wearing jeans and an old sweater. They couldn't compare to Natasha's trendy dress.

"We'll go to Bernie's bar," said Nina. "No one will care."

I grabbed a blazer to wear over my sweater, surprised by how much it dressed up the comfortable outfit, and we were off. The bar was packed, but we found a table and were settling in when Stu and Jacky came over to our table to say hello.

Stu was all smiles and hugged each of us, reminiscent of Thurman. He wore a familiar scent that lingered in the air. "We are devastated by Thurman's actions," he said. "But relieved that this is finally over."

"How is Helena?" I asked.

Jacky wasn't as overjoyed as Stu. "We wanted her to come with us. Sitting in the police station was dreadful, but she declined. She just wanted to go home. Imagine how you would feel if you found out your husband was seeing another woman and had murdered two young women as well! That's an awful lot to take in. I loved Thurman like a brother. I still can't believe he did those things."

"They're certain it was him?" asked Nina.

"There's no doubt about it," said Stu. "I'm afraid Thurman will be going away for a very long time."

"So he's in jail right now?" I asked.

"No!" Stu shook his head in dismay. "Helena bonded him out! Can you believe that? The power of a good lawyer and money!"

They were called to their table in a dining room and hustled off.

We ordered sandwiches and fries. I thought about Thurman while Nina and Natasha argued about the brunch.

The shock of Thurman's affair alone would have been enough to devastate Helena. They had been married such a long time. But to even imagine that he had murdered someone? I didn't know if I could ever get over that. But maybe she didn't believe it. Would she stay by his side anyway?

After dinner, we strolled home in the dark, enjoying the lights on houses. All I wanted to do was fall into bed. After letting Daisy out, I did just that.

At two in the morning, I was awakened by a crash.

THURSDAY

I threw on a bathrobe and ran downstairs. "Mochie!" I called. Had my little rascal knocked over a piece of heavy furniture?

But I didn't see anything. I peered into the sunroom. Bright beams of light shone in through the floor-to-ceiling windows. I shielded my eyes with my arm, unlocked the door, and went outside.

A car in the alley had crashed through my fence and hit the corner of my garage. Steam rose from the hood. I ran to the car to help the driver or any passengers. It took me a few seconds to grasp the situation. No one was inside. The door on the driver's side hung open. I ran back to the house, called 911, and got dressed.

The police responded quickly. I walked around the car. In the rear, I saw the distinctive BMW badge on the white car. Thurman. It had to be Thurman's. But why would he run into my fence? Had it been an accident or intentional?

One of the officers questioned me, but I had been asleep. I didn't know anything helpful.

About forty-five minutes later, a very tired Wolf showed up.

"I guess this is Thurman's car?" I asked.

He nodded. "They found the registration in the glove compartment. Are you okay?"

"My fence and garage have seen better days, but I'm fine. Do you think he was drunk?"

"I wouldn't be surprised if that were the case."

"Wolf!" called one of the officers.

I followed him to the car.

The officer shone his flashlight inside on two syringes and a bottle of insulin.

Wolf walked away. I couldn't hear clearly what he was saying, but I caught *Thurman Nofsinger,* and *may be dangerous.*

I didn't know where Thurman had been going, but I also didn't think it was a coincidence that he hit my fence.

My neighbor, Francie, pulled her bathrobe belt tighter as she walked up to me. "What a commotion!"

"I'm sorry. I guess it woke you, too."

"Drunk driver?"

"Probably."

She groaned and went home.

I returned to my kitchen to reassure Mochie and Daisy, and put on coffee. It would take some time to get a police tow truck to take Thurman's car away.

Wolf found me in the kitchen.

I poured him a mug of coffee. "Any word on Thurman?"

"Not yet."

"Are you worried that he'll inject an officer with insulin?"

"Naturally. Sophie, there's something you should know. This will probably make the news tomorrow. The skeleton that you found is Helena and Jacky's father."

"I thought so! Do you know who killed him?"

"We're not certain yet, but it looks like Thurman and Helena ran off to North Carolina to get married when she was seventeen. Seems that was a common thing to do. A few of the counties there didn't check a girl's age under certain circumstances."

"You mean if she was pregnant?"

He nodded. "It's possible that her dad blew up when he found out."

"You think Thurman murdered him and hid him in the wall?"

"He hasn't confessed to it yet, but that's very likely."

I placed coffee mugs, sugar, and cream on a tray for the officers outside.

"I don't like this situation," said Wolf. "The insulin and syringes in the car suggest that he was planning to murder someone else. It could have been you. Sophie, you need to be very careful. I'm trying to get an officer to hang out here until we've caught him."

"Maybe he had Lillith in mind. She turned on him pretty fast."

"I've already sent someone to notify her and stand guard."

His phone rang.

While he answered it, I carried the tray outside to my deck and returned for the pot of coffee, which I carried out to them. Officers helped themselves.

Wolf joined us. "I don't think Thurman was drunk. Officers found him at home in his pajamas. They have him in custody now."

"Why don't you think he was drunk?"

"I doubt that he could have run home that fast. They'll test his blood alcohol level and we'll know for sure."

The police impound truck pulled up. We watched as the driver skillfully attached the BMW and drove it away. The other police cars left behind it. Suddenly, the neighborhood was dark and quiet again.

"I'll keep you posted," said Wolf. He pointed at the fence and the garage. "When it's daylight, get some photos of that for insurance." He walked across the fence that lay on the ground and disappeared into the darkness.

I was wide awake. I figured I would crash later in the day, but there wasn't any way I would get back to sleep at the moment.

I shared a snack of cheese and crackers with Daisy and offered Mochie some cheesy cat food. It was still dark outside and I was restless, so I took the opportunity to finalize interior decorating for the brunch. I took out a harvest-themed Provençal style tablecloth in mustard and white and threw it over the dining room table. I mixed rustic wood candleholders with crystal ones in various sizes for a relaxed elegance and fit them all with white candles. I used small white and orange pumpkins in between them and left three spots to be filled with fresh sunflowers from my garden the day before the brunch.

Done with that, I put Daisy's harness on her and took her for a walk. At that early hour, few people roamed the streets. Dedicated runners shot past us. We walked by the Inger House and I spotted a toy in the window of Robbie's childhood bedroom.

Daisy and I made our way down to the waterfront where my favorite walk-up latte window had already opened. I bought a pumpkin spice latte and a pup-cup. We strolled toward the almost empty benches. A lone woman sat in one. I aimed for a bench away from her, but as we drew closer, I recognized Helena.

Hoping she wouldn't mind, I sat down next to her.

She pulled to the side and looked at me with annoyance. Then she relaxed and said, "Oh, it's you." She focused on the Potomac River. "I'm sorry. Sophie. I'm so sorry. I have an excellent carpenter. I'll send him over to fix your garage and the fence."

"Thank you. That would be great!"

She turned her head to look at me. "You don't sound upset."

I shrugged. "It's nothing that can't be repaired."

She nodded. "I never imagined that the killer would be someone so close to me. I honestly thought it would be one of Mike's friends. I even wondered if some young man formed an obsession with Denise." She took out a tissue and wiped her eyes. "It's hard to imagine that it could have been Thurman. Well, not the affair with Lillith. That I could live with. I'm not happy about it, but compared to murder, it seems almost insignificant. I just . . . Thurman? I can't wrap my head around it. Do you think he could have a brain tumor or something? None of this is like him. It's so out of character. I don't understand it. He's in jail now. Yesterday, he was so relieved to be bonded out. Why would he continue to kill? They said he had insulin and syringes in the car. Why, why, why would he do it again when he'd been caught?"

I had no answer for that. I was as stunned as she was.

"Thurman isn't a genius. He hasn't a business sense at all. But he was always kind and solicitous of everyone. A wonderful dad to Robbie. Oh my. He took him to ball games, taught him every sport you can think of. Sat on the floor with him for hours constructing things out of Legos and Lincoln Logs. I thought he was a good man. Now I wonder who he really is and whether he has done this before. Will other unsolved cases pop up?"

I could sympathize. If Mars had been accused of the same things, I would be in shock. And the fear of learning about other cases might be legitimate.

"Did he murder your father after you were married?"

Helena gasped. "No! Definitely not."

"I heard you were underage and your dad had a fit when you married Thurman."

"Oh that. Isn't it odd? It's been so long that I'd forgotten about that." She looked at her watch. "Excuse me. I need to change and go to work."

"You're working today?"

She stood up and looked at me with a surprised expression. "Of course. Someone has to. Besides, there's not a thing I can do about Thurman's situation now. I don't think even *you* can get him out of this."

I watched as she walked away. Her back was ramrod straight. Her allegiance to the family company was unimpaired.

Daisy and I finished our treats and ambled home. I opened the kitchen door to a full house.

Mars was on his phone, Nina came running down the stairs into the kitchen, Bernie rushed toward me for a hug, and Natasha held a platter of muffins.

Mars hung up. "Where have you been?"

"Are you all right?" asked Nina.

"We heard a crash last night, but had no idea it was here," said Bernie.

Natasha offered me a muffin. Something black oozed across the tops of them. I shook my head. Black squid-ink muffins? I didn't think I could stomach that. But there was that smell again. I recoiled.

"And why aren't you answering your phone?" Mars demanded.

"I took Daisy for a walk." I pulled out my phone. "Oops, looks like the ringer was off."

"We thought you were in the hospital," said Bernie.

"And I took Daisy with me?"

"She could have been taken by Wolf. Or the police. She wouldn't be at all happy in the pound!"

Daisy was happy now. She leaned against Mars's legs for petting.

"Daisy and I appreciate your concern. Apparently, Thurman drove his car into my fence. The police found syringes and insulin."

"He was coming after you?" Nina's eyes widened.

"I doubt it. How would that help him? In any event,

he's in jail now, so no one needs to worry. And since you're all here, I guess we should make some breakfast."

Bernie strode to the fridge. He pulled out eggs and bacon. "Scrambled or fried?"

"Fried!" said Mars and Nina simultaneously.

While Bernie handled the eggs, I made the bacon and toasted bread, Nina set the table, and Mars made coffee and tea. Natasha placed her muffins in the middle of the table.

When we sat down to eat, I broke the news that the skeleton was Helena and Jacky's father. "Apparently, she was pregnant and underage when they got married. Her father was angry, and Wolf thinks Thurman murdered him and hid him in the wall."

"How would they ever be able to prove it?" asked Bernie.

"Fingerprints on the studs inside the wall, maybe?" suggested Nina. "They would be very old, though. I don't know if they deteriorate."

"If there weren't any witnesses, they might not be able to prove anything," said Natasha, picking at an egg white with her fork. "He was such a nice man. I can't get over that."

"This might be one of those situations where Thurman would be wise not to confess." Mars poured more coffee for everyone.

We were almost through eating, and I was trying to figure out how not to hurt Natasha's feelings. Maybe if I tore up a muffin, the way she usually treated her food, she might not realize I hadn't eaten it.

I boldly helped myself to one and picked a little piece of the bottom.

She beamed with pride and watched me.

Someone banged my door knocker. I flew out of my chair,

relieved by the reprieve. I opened the door with Daisy by my side.

Stu stood on my doorstep.

"Good morning," I said cheerfully.

"I heard about what Thurman did and wanted to apologize on behalf of the family."

"That's very kind of you. But no need. I've already spoken with Helena."

"Oh! I'm sorry. Do you have guests?"

"Won't you come in?"

He walked past me, and I smelled that scent again. It was licorice. Or anise. The same thing that I smelled in the staircase where someone had hidden the bones.

I followed him into the kitchen, wary. He couldn't harm all of us, though.

Natasha asked him to join us and offered him one of her muffins.

"What kind are they?" asked Stu. "Is that chocolate on top?"

"No, silly! That's licorice."

"I love licorice!" exclaimed Nina, promptly grabbing one.

"I do, too," said Stu. "My wife says I smell like licorice because my cologne has a lot of anise in it."

Nina sniffed in his direction. "Oh, you're right! How is Jacky doing? We heard the skeleton is her father. That must be difficult for her."

"Where did you hear that?" Stu frowned at Nina.

I stepped in quickly. "On the news." It was a lie, but according to Wolf, it would be there soon.

"We hadn't heard that. I'm sure she'll take it hard. We lived there for so long without the first clue. I'm relieved that we moved into a new building. At least we know there aren't any skeletons in our walls."

"You hope," said Bernie drolly.

"These are delicious, Natasha." Stu finished a licorice muffin and sipped coffee that Mars had poured for him.

Stu lingered for a short time longer, thanked us, and left.

I breathed easier when I closed the door behind him. I rushed to the kitchen window and watched him walk away.

Chapter 29

Dear Natasha,
Some wack job told my husband there should be
no more than five pillows on our bed! It's none of
her business and she clearly knows nothing about
decorating. He thinks you're beautiful (and you
are!), so I know he'll listen to you. What is the
maximum number of pillows for a bed?
        Keeping My Pillows in Pillow, Pennsylvania

Dear Keeping My Pillows,
There is no limit on the number of pillows for a
bed. Pile them on!
                                Natasha

"Are you spying on Stu?" asked Mars.

"Bernie," I said, "do you remember the scent of licorice in the stairs where we found the bones?"

"Yes. Did the muffins remind you of that?"

"Stu did."

They all looked at me like I had lost my mind.

Bernie asked, "Are you saying that Stu moved the bones?"

"That's exactly what I'm saying. He gave me a hug the

other night and I smelled it then, but couldn't quite place it. Bernie noticed it in the stairway, too, so I'm not imagining it. And Stu admitted that his cologne contains anise, which has a similar fragrance."

"But what about Thurman? If he wasn't the killer, why did he crash into your fence?" asked Nina.

"Maybe it wasn't Thurman," said Bernie.

"We have keys to one another's houses," I said. "I bet anything Jacky has keys to Helena's home."

Mars groaned. "That's impossible. Who wouldn't hear someone taking their car?"

"Helena was in the police station with Thurman for hours yesterday. It would have been easy for Stu. All he had to do was park it somewhere until he needed it."

"That's nonsense. What did he think he would accomplish by running into your fence?" asked Natasha.

"Making Thurman look guilty," I said.

Bernie and Mars offered to help with the dishes, but I shooed everyone out because I wanted to notify Wolf. Maybe I was dead wrong about Stu, but I didn't think so. The only part that bothered me was Jacky's claim that she didn't meet Stu until she was out of college. I wasn't sure of her exact age, but she was younger than Helena, who was seventeen in 1969, so it stood to reason that Jacky hadn't met Stu in that year. But she might have told her husband the truth about what happened to her father. And he doted on Jacky. If she was involved in her father's death, he might have been willing to kill to hide the discovery of the body.

I phoned Wolf, but as usual, he didn't answer the call. He was probably tied up with Thurman.

I was scrubbing a cast-iron frying pan when Mochie pawed at the bay window. He looked out as if he was watching a squirrel who was scampering close to the house. I looked out, too.

My heart skipped a beat when I saw the top of some-one's head move just beneath us. I hurried around to be sure all the doors were locked and called 911. "Someone is creeping along the front of my house!" I gave the dis-patcher my name and asked her to contact Wolf or Wong. I doubted that she would, but it didn't hurt to ask.

I looked around for a weapon in case the person, who I assumed was Stu, tried to break in. The frying pan I had washed was perfect. I dried it and set it on the stove over low heat.

Then I called Mars and Bernie. Mars's line rolled over to voice mail and Bernie was at The Laughing Hound. "Call nine-one-one," he said. "I'll be there as fast as I can run."

The glass in my kitchen door shattered as a fist wrapped in newspaper punched through. It pulled out and another hand tried the lock. Stu looked at me through the unbro-ken part of the glass with a fury in his eyes that I hadn't seen before.

Daisy barked at him. I pulled on a pot holder with a sil-icone grip and grabbed the hot cast-iron skillet.

I hoped Stu wouldn't move on to the sunroom door, be-cause it had a simpler lock that only needed to be twisted.

But then I lost sight of him.

I inched along the sliding glass doors. A concrete urn crashed through them and flew into the house, shattering the door into thousands of tiny bits.

Stu smiled as he stepped inside.

I swung the cast-iron skillet at his face with my right hand. "That's for Denise!"

He seemed to be in shock for a moment. "Gah!" A sy-ringe fell out of his hand to the floor.

I took that opportunity to repeat the procedure on the other side, with a two-fisted backhand. "And this is for Rachel!"

Stu screamed as the hot pan hit his face. He collapsed to the floor as Wong and Bernie ran up outside.

"He's a mess," said Wong, calling for an ambulance.

"He dropped the syringe. It's on the glass."

Bernie stepped over the broken glass and delicately shooed Daisy away. He wrapped an arm around me. "Are you hurt?"

"I'm fine. Just fine." And then I passed out in his arms.

When I came to, Wolf, Wong, Bernie, Mars, and Nina were all looking at me. "Daisy? Mochie?" I choked out.

"They're safely in your office. Both of them are fine," said Mars. "I checked their paws for slivers of glass."

Wolf teased, "Remind me to keep out of arm's reach if you've got a cast-iron pan in your hand."

I struggled to sit up. "Very funny."

They moved aside so an EMT could have a look at me. "I'm fine," I protested.

"What's your name?" he asked.

"Sophie Winston."

"You'll be all right. Just take it easy for the rest of the day. No more swinging that pan around."

"Ha ha."

Wolf followed the ambulance to the hospital and Wong went back to work. But Mars, Bernie, and Nina made tea and helped me find someone to secure the doors until the glass could be replaced.

I begged them to let me take Daisy for a walk. They finally agreed, probably pleased to get on with their own lives. I walked over to Nofsinger & Lawson, slipped down the alley, and knocked on the back door.

Mitzi opened it. "Is it true that Thurman was arrested?"

"It was true. But he wasn't the killer. It was Stu."

"Stu Finch?"

I nodded. "He's in the hospital under police guard. I'm

afraid I banged him up pretty badly. So you and Poppy can go home and back to your old life. Well, as much as possible."

Mitzi threw her arms around me. "Thank you! I can't believe it's over. Stu Finch. Who'd have thought it. Do you know why?"

"We think he was trying to prevent everyone from finding the skeleton."

"Ohh. So he had killed before?"

"Probably not. We suspect he was trying to protect his wife. She may have been involved."

"Jacky? But that can't be!"

"Why not?"

"Because she's so nice."

"It takes all kinds, I guess. Hey, you are coming to our brunch now, right?"

"I wouldn't miss it."

I walked home thinking that Mitzi had saved her own life. She might have been a victim, too, if she had continued working in the house.

That evening, Wolf stopped by. Bernie, Mars, Nina, and I had ordered Chinese takeout for dinner, and there was plenty for Wolf, who ate as if he was starved.

"Well?" I asked. "What happened?"

"Stu is in bad shape. Both sides of his face are burned. He has a broken jawbone and missing teeth. It's not pretty. But, on the bright side, he confessed to killing Denise and Rachel because they intended to move the armoire which would expose the skeleton."

"Did he kill Helena and Denise's father, too?" Mars picked up a piece of duck with his chopsticks.

"I don't think so. Jacky says they didn't meet until years later. So I brought in the three people most likely to know what happened to Ollie Inger. Helena, Jacky, and Annie Griggs." Wolf helped himself to more food.

"And?" asked Mars.

"Annie said, 'I killed Ollie. What are you going do, put a ninety-eight-year-old woman in prison?'"

"Annie murdered him?" I stopped eating. "I don't believe it!"

"And Helena said, 'I murdered Father.'"

"Maybe they did it together," said Mars.

"And Jacky said, 'I killed Dad. He was a beast.'"

"What are you going to do?" I asked.

"I don't know. This has never happened to me before." And then he ate more Peking duck.

I gazed up at the portrait of Aunt Faye, which hung over the mantel. "You must have lived here then. Helena and Jacky remember you. In fact, they were very fond of you." I sighed. "It's too bad you can't tell us what happened at the Inger House." I looked at Mars. "Or maybe you can."

Bernie's eyes narrowed. "Do you feel all right?"

"I feel fine. When Mars moved out, I insisted he take Faye's belongings with him. She was *his* aunt, after all. Whatever she left behind belonged to him and his family. There were loads of boxes with her papers in them. Things like letters and bank statements. What if she kept a diary? It's a long shot, but worth a try. Do you still have all those boxes of papers that belonged to Faye?"

"I think so," said Mars.

"I know so," Bernie chuckled. "There's a big pile of boxes in the attic."

Mars snorted. "It's a long shot. But I'll help you."

"You've never looked in those boxes, have you?" I asked.

"I'm busy! I have better things to do than look through Aunt Faye's old bank statements."

After dinner, Wolf went home to catch up on sleep. Nina picked up her husband at the airport, and Bernie returned to The Laughing Hound.

Mars, Daisy, and I walked over to their house. Mars led the way up the stairs. Daisy and I followed along behind him. The house in which he and Bernie lived had to be as old as the Inger House. Close anyway.

Mars opened a small door. A narrow staircase took us up to the attic. He showed us to a small mountain of boxes, neatly stacked.

"Maybe this wasn't such a good idea," I said, daunted by the number of boxes.

Mars glanced at his watch. "I can pitch in and help."

"Okay. At least we can get a feel for what's in them. If it's just financial stuff, then we can give up."

"That doesn't sound like the Sophie I know," Mars teased.

I glanced around. The attic was fairly tidy. Mostly just boxes and a few pieces of furniture. "Is it safe up here for Daisy?"

"Oh sure. Bernie's cats come up here all the time."

"Then let's get started." I opened a box and peeked inside. It looked like bank statements. I pulled some out to see if there was anything underneath. "You really could get rid of these." I glanced at the balance. "Goodness! How did your Aunt Faye get this much money? Did she secretly rob banks or something?"

"I'm guessing that bank robbers probably didn't keep their money *in* banks," he teased. "It was the sixties, you know. Beatles and astronauts walking on the moon. Gloria Steinem and bra burning. Aunt Faye believed in the women's movement. She wanted to open a clothing store and it infuriated her that her dad had to sign the lease for her."

"Maybe I should go into that business. She certainly did well. She never married?"

"She married a doctor who became a congressman. According to my dad, he invented some kind of surgical gadget that took off. He sold it to a big corporation for a lot of money."

"But she continued to use her maiden name, Winston?" I lowered another box to the floor and opened it.

"Like I said, she was into women's liberation. Besides, her store was called Winston's."

"Makes sense. I didn't know her husband was a congressman. That explains why she entertained a lot. Now I understand why she had so many dishes and sets of stemware." I placed the box aside. "Are you having any luck over there?"

"This box looks like it's full of her husband's things. Kind of interesting. I might take it downstairs and look through it."

I lost count of how many boxes I went through. On the verge of giving up, I had pulled out one more when Mars shouted, "I have a diary!"

Daisy and I ran over to him. I opened it at random and saw the year 1969.

I hugged Mars, who said, "Thank heaven. I thought I would be stuck up here for days looking through this stuff."

Daisy and I hurried home. It wasn't late yet, but I was pooped. I made myself a glass of warm milk and took Faye's diary up to bed with me.

Daisy and Mochie nestled on my bed, also exhausted from the chaos.

I was glad to be home and safe, relieved that Stu was in the hospital under the watchful eyes of the police.

The pages of Faye's diary had gone stiff with age. They were legible, though. She wrote in a fine script that was easy to read. I felt a bit guilty reading the first few entries. But I soon settled in and read about her parties with congressmen and their wives. Her descriptions of people made me laugh. I felt I could see them, and it was all the more special because I knew a lot of the parties had taken place downstairs in the dining and living rooms.

November 15, 1963
   I saw one of the Inger girls walking along the sidewalk today. The older one. Helena, I believe. I can't imagine what her father is thinking. Poor little thing. She's old enough to need a bra, and the dress she wore was little more than a worn-out housedress. And why wasn't she in school? I feel so sorry for those two girls. If only their mother had lived.

March 2, 1964
   I was visiting Stanley today when Helena Nofsinger came by to collect the rent. It appears he was late in paying! She's the sweetest thing and quite pretty, too. The nerve of her father sending her around to wheedle money out of tenants. She should be in school. And she deserves proper clothing. Can her father really be so stingy that he won't dress his girls properly? She appeared to be wearing a limp housedress that had seen better days. From a church donation center, maybe?

May 5, 1964
   I saw the poor Nofsinger girls again yesterday. They look neglected, so today I went over to see their father. From the smell of his breath, bloodshot eyes, and mumbling, I'd say he had a major hangover. Perhaps that's a persistent state with Ollie, as he introduced himself. I think I prefer to call him Mr. Nofsinger to his face. Maybe that will remind him that he has a family name to keep respectable.

I told him straight out that I was taking his daughters under my wing. I will dress them, and he will pay the bills. I'm also taking them to a dentist. Heaven knows what other kinds of basic needs he has overlooked. I enjoyed meeting the housekeeper or nanny or whatever she is. Annie Griggs is her name. She listened in the whole time I was there. Many would frown on that, but someone has to keep that household straight. I'm glad there's a sober adult to keep things going for the girls.

May 6, 1964

I met Helena and Jacky today. They are lovely young ladies and so eager to learn! I outfitted them with new clothes from top to bottom. If their father sobers up enough, he may get a shock from the bill, but I don't care. The man has a responsibility to those darling girls. Annie Griggs's girls, Sheila and Lisa, joined us and selected some clothes as well. I talked Annie into trying on some dresses, too. She has a terrific eye for style. I let them have everything they wanted and added it all to stingy Nofsinger's bill. I'm certain he doesn't pay Annie what she's worth.

June 6, 1964

I threw the first tea party for Helena, Jacky, Sheila, and Lisa, and invited the daughters of other fine families in town. Twelve girls in all. They had so much fun. The party dresses and hairdos and precious purses. Oh my! The sweets and sandwiches were all delicious, but the miniature cupcakes with tiny sugar roses on top were a runaway hit. I must remember that.

August 29, 1964
   *Gossip flew around the table at today's tea
party. The girls were delightful as always. I can't
believe the difference in the Nofsinger girls. They
appear to have overcome their shyness and I believe they're quite popular!*

I fell asleep, but woke restless and paged forward to
1969 to see if Faye mentioned Ollie.

April 2, 1969
   *Jacky has put on some weight. I'm worried that
she might be feeling stressed.*

May 1, 1969
   *Annie called me today and begged me to come
to the Inger House immediately. She sounded frantic and hung up the phone without saying goodbye, which is not at all like her. I rushed over. I
could hear screaming all the way out to the street!
No one opened the door when I knocked. I tried
the door handle, and it swung open.*
   *Ollie Nofsinger pointed his finger at me and
shouted, "This is all your fault! I never should
have allowed you near my children."*
   *I told him to calm down and closed the door
behind me. "People can hear you on the street.
What on earth is going on?"*
   *Ollie's face was so red I feared he might have a
heart attack.*
   *And then I saw Jacky. She wasn't just putting
on weight. She can't hide it anymore. She's
definitely pregnant.*
   *I had heard of parents who turned away their
pregnant unwed daughters and told them never to*

come back. I can't imagine anyone doing that. It's a common practice these days to ship a girl to a home for unwed mothers. The babies are placed for adoption and the girl returns home claiming she had been to visit relatives.

But never in my life did I imagine that any sane person would attempt to murder his daughter and his grandchild by throwing them down a flight of stairs. But that is exactly what Ollie attempted to do.

There was a tussle at the top landing. A terrible fight with Helena, Annie, and I trying to protect Jacky. We clung to her, and as Ollie wrested her from us in a vile fit of temper, we pushed him away, and it was Ollie who tumbled down the stairs. I will never forget the crack we heard as his head hit the floor.

I write this now for several reasons. One, to clear my head. Two, because my brother, the judge, told me once to make contemporaneous notes of things that happen so I can refer to them should I be called upon to testify. Three, because later in life, I will wonder about that night and think it couldn't possibly have happened the way it did. It's unthinkable that any man could act that way. And four, because I was the one who pushed Ollie to his death. None of us should ever be blamed for what happened that day. We were protecting Jacky from a drunk and terrible man. Defense of a minor for sure. But should it ever come up, and should I ever be called to testify, I want it clear that only I am to blame.

We hoped to bury Ollie in the backyard, but their neighbor, Mrs. Collins, is a dreadful

*busybody and gossip. We don't dare take that
chance. If anyone finds out, the girls will be separated and placed in foster homes, if not jail. The
baby will be taken away at birth. The house will
be sold, as well as the business. Helena will be
eighteen in one year. They have to muddle through
until then. Sometimes in life, one has to do what is
necessary. I think God will forgive us for Ollie's
unusual "burial."*

May 26, 1969
    *I went with Helena to enroll her in a bookkeep-
ing class. She knows a lot already, but it's best if
she learns how to do it correctly. She's still very
jittery. She and Thurman Nofsinger are driving to
North Carolina tomorrow to get married because
the minimum age in Virginia is eighteen. He's a
fine boy from a good family. I think his parents
will be very pleased that he's marrying an Inger,
even if they do elope. I'm throwing a private little
party for them. Very low-key so Jacky can attend.*

May 29, 1969
    *Annie called a midwife she knows. Everything
looks fine. She'll come as soon as she's needed.*

July 4, 1969
    *It seems somehow fitting that little Robert
Michael Nofsinger was born on Independence
Day! He's darling and weighed in at nine pounds,
three ounces. The midwife listed Helena and
Thurman Nofsinger as the parents on the birth
certificate.*

September 9, 1969

Jacky returned to school today. She looks great and is very happy. Annie takes care of Robbie during the day. I sat down with Annie and Helena to work out budgets for the household and the business. They're in good shape.

October 10, 1969

It's a lucky thing Ollie hired Annie. She's discreet and adores the girls and little Robbie. There's no one to ask questions about their dad's absence. We're telling anyone who asks that he went in search of his wife because he received information that she wasn't dead.

November 15, 1969

Annie is a gem. The girls are thriving because of her. She's so kind and motherly with them. Hugs and laughter now fill the household. Helena bought a record player, so there's now the occasional impromptu twist with everyone joining in! I never expected to see such a big change.

December 1, 1969

Helena is running the business like she was born to it. I guess she was. Ollie probably didn't realize that he was training her by having her do much of his work for him. The real estate office looks much better already. I've been helping her update it a little bit with fresh paint and new furniture. The old stuff reminded me of bus station seating. It's much more appealing now. Jacky is class president in high school!

Little Robbie is the center of attention. It's like

*he has three mothers. No baby could ask for a
more loving home.*

*I'm breathing a little easier now that Helena is
eighteen. It would have been terrible if their
father's death had been discovered. Helena can
sign contracts and enter into business
arrangements now, although some annoying people insist that Thurman sign, too. Fortunately, she
married well. He's charismatic and congenial, and
sweet as pie with Robbie. I've heard people talking about how successfully he has taken over
Ollie's real estate business. Little do they realize
that it's Helena who is the brains. She saved
enough money to put down a hefty deposit on an
apartment building, but was miffed that Thurman
had to sign the loan documents. I can't blame her
for that! She also opened an investment account
for Annie, but Annie doesn't know yet. Every pay-
day, Helena makes a deposit on her behalf.*

June 4, 1970

*I am so proud of Helena and Jacky. Helena re-
ceived a GED certificate even though she was
working full time. Jacky is doing well in school.
Her grades have actually improved and she's up to
her ears in social activities. Helena insists that
Jacky look into colleges. She confided to me that
she's going to take some night classes herself.
Helena is determined to get her college degree. I'm
only sorry that she didn't have the opportunity to
spend some fun, carefree years in college. Life
threw a lot at her, but she overcame it all. She's
my hero.*

The diary ended there. I hoped there might be more, but I was glad to know what had actually transpired. Maybe all four women were partially responsible for Ollie's death. There was probably a great deal of confusion with all of them trying to protect Jacky. Or maybe none of them pushed Ollie, and in his rage, he simply slipped and fell. In any event, the women were acting in defense of a pregnant minor. Annie's words came back to me: "Sometimes you have to do what's right."

Chapter 30

Dear Sophie,
Do I have to serve alcohol at brunch? My friends
are so into mimosas, but all I want is coffee.
                    Coffeeholic in Two Egg, Florida

Dear Coffeeholic,
When you are the hostess, that's entirely up to you.
But, if your friends love mimosas, it would proba-
bly be a good idea to serve them. You can drink
coffee and orange juice.
                                    Sophie

The day of the big brunch finally rolled around. I had done as much as possible in advance. Mochie had been sequestered in the attic level bedroom where it would be quieter, and he couldn't sneak out if someone left a door open.

I had planned to have Daisy join him, but the television crew loved Daisy, so she got to stay. We did a lot of shooting in advance. A good thing because when the guests began to arrive, it was harder to pose for the cameras.

It came as no surprise that Natasha wanted to be in the limelight all the time. Nina and I were more than happy for her to do that.

Thurman and Helena Nofsinger showed up first. Curiously, Helena had called and asked if she and Thurman could bring a friend. Naturally, I agreed. It turned out to be Matt Stewart, the local event planner who had made a lot of money off his mother's etiquette advice business. I was delighted to see him and he had been on the guest list anyway.

Thurman and Helena hugged me like I was their long-lost best friend.

Thurman couldn't stop thanking me. "For a couple of days, I honestly thought my life was over and I would spend the rest of my days in prison. That awful Stu did such a great job framing me that I couldn't explain my way out of anything."

Helena whispered to me later that the affair was still an issue, but given what they had been through, they were closer than ever, and she hoped Lillith would not be in attendance at the brunch.

"Did you ever find out where your father's wedding ring came from?"

Helena scowled. "Stu was trying to frame Thurman and did a pretty good job of it. He's the one who put Denise's bag in Thurman's trunk and hid Rachel's bag in Lillith's shop. Dad's ring fell off when Stu moved the bones. He and Jacky had a key to our home, so Stu planted it where he thought it would be noticed and blame would fall on Thurman. Of course, it was Stu who drove Thurman's car into your fence. I have to see how it looks! Did my guys do a great job on it?"

"They did. Thank you for taking care of that."

Jacky came by herself. She apologized to Mitzi and me

over and over again. I told her it wasn't her fault. I honestly think she had no idea what Stu was doing.

Her eyes lighted up when she saw Matt. "We went to high school together!" she said.

Naturally, Mars and Bernie showed up, as well as my neighbor Francie, and my old friend Humphrey, whom I hadn't seen in a long time. Wolf came without his wife, who was away. "Which dishes are Natasha's?" he whispered.

"The ones with the red-handled serving utensils."

"That was clever. She doesn't realize it, does she?"

"I don't think so!"

We stepped outside, away from the crowd for a few minutes. Bernie, Mars, and Nina followed us.

Away from the guests, Wolf told us what had transpired. "Early on in their marriage, Jacky told Stu that she got pregnant when she was in high school. When her father found out, he tried to push her down the stairs in the hope she would miscarry. But it didn't work out that way. Her father fell down the stairs and died. Because she and Helena were minors, they were terrified that they would be separated and sent away, so they hid their father's body in the wall. Stu didn't give a thought to the skeleton because the house was staying in the family. But when he went to the house to pick up something, he found Denise and Mitzi there, discussing big changes. When Denise mentioned moving the armoire, Stu panicked. He thought he bought some time by telling them it was too heavy to move. He was in the habit of carrying an AirTag in his wallet and another on his keys. He slipped them into their bags so he could keep an eye on them and know when they were in the house."

"Wicked but very clever," said Mars.

"When the AirTag notified him that Denise was in the

house, he returned to see what she was doing. Denise had begun to take clothes out of the armoire and had moved the armoire about an inch. She asked him to help her move it. Stu panicked. He frantically looked for a weapon. The kitchen knives were gone. He saw her bag and dug through it in search of something like a knife, or a measuring tape that could be wrapped around her neck. But he found two emergency insulin injectors. He took off the caps and readied them for use. He thought it would be easy. She wouldn't even notice what he had done. And if she lived, he could deny it and claim she simply collapsed and that he injected her to revive her."

"He is truly a horrible person." Nina scowled.

"He stuck her with one in the back of her arm. She ran to her phone in the dining room, but he seized it from her and gave her the second shot. She went to the kitchen, but it was quick acting. When she fell to the ground, he returned to the armoire, intending to put the clothes back, but he saw Sophie arriving through the backyard and hurried to grab Denise's bag because there was no time to paw through it and remove the AirTag. He ran out the conservatory door and through the backyard. The insulin had worked better than he could have expected."

"That's so scary!" I thought of the syringe he had dropped when he came to my house.

"When he found out about insulin being used for muscle mass, he bought a couple extras in case he needed them again because Mitzi kept returning to the house. But Mitzi's tracker put her at a hotel."

Mars hooted with pride.

"She went to the house one evening, but when Stu arrived, the police were crawling around the property and took Natasha away. He never entered the house that night. Watching the house was turning into a big job for him. Fortunately, Mitzi was skittish and concentrated on the dining room changes that he approved of. But then he caught Rachel in the house. She had no business there at all and had actually moved the armoire and ripped off the patch on the wall."

"Oh no," I said. "Poor Rachel. And it was all to protect Jacky?"

"Yup," said Wolf.

"What do you think will happen to him?" asked Bernie.

"I don't think he will ever walk the streets as a free man again."

Nina and I hurried back inside the house to make sure everything was going smoothly. Robbie was just arriving with Agnes, Mitzi, and Mike.

"We want to thank you," said Mike. "I never would have believed that a member of my family could have done anything so heinous."

Agnes smiled and patted Robbie's shoulder. "I hate that Robbie will be moving out. I feel like they're *my* boys. I liked having them around."

Robbie smiled at her. "Aww, Agnes. You know I was only living there on a temporary basis to keep an eye on things. Now that Mike is moving in, I need to go home to my wife and help her take care of her parents."

"I promise to check on you every day," said Mike. "And I'll put a sign in the window for you, just like Dad has been doing."

Robbie and Agnes went in search of coffee.

But Mike stayed behind. "I've asked Mitzi to go ahead and make the changes that Denise wanted. It needs to be updated anyway and Denise always had great ideas. I would be clueless. They're going to rip out the whole kitchen and that back bedroom, so I won't have to be reminded of what happened there. It's going to be one big, fantastic space overlooking a new garden in the backyard."

Annie arrived with her two daughters, who were excited to see Faye's house again. I led them into the kitchen.

"Now, this is different! It's lovely," said Sheila.

"Do you remember the orange countertops and mod daisy wallpaper?" Lisa laughed. "We thought it was the coolest thing ever!"

"It was still here when we moved into the house. You can imagine that I was in a hurry to update the kitchen."

"But you kept the fireplace," murmured Annie. "Faye and I spent many hours together here. I like the portrait, but I'm not sure it does her justice. She looks so calm when she was really a force to be reckoned with!"

I dashed upstairs to get Faye's diary and brought it down to Annie. "I thought this might interest you."

At that moment, Mars wandered into the kitchen.

"Annie," I said, "this is little Mars."

She nearly bolted out of her chair. "Why, you turned into a handsome devil!"

He grinned. "You must be Annie Griggs."

"I am. Your aunt Faye was one of my dearest friends. I wish she were here to see this!"

At that moment, the portrait shifted ever so slightly.

"Oh! Look at that. She is here!" said Annie.

Her daughters rolled their eyes.

Our guests began to serve themselves and I excused myself to bring in more frittatas.

When I spied Robbie standing beside Matt across the table from me, I couldn't believe the resemblance. Jacky must have seen me watching them, because she came up and whispered, "I'm Robbie's birth mother."

I said, "I know. I've been reading Faye's diary. Does Robbie know that Matt is his father yet?"

"I told them last night." She blinked hard. "Robbie took it surprisingly well. And Matt is over the moon! He plays the violin and Robbie plays the piano. They're already talking about getting the family together for a little concert."

I wrapped an arm around her. "How are you doing? Stu's behavior must have shocked you."

She pursed her lips and I thought she might cry. "He did it for me. I didn't know he had that kind of wickedness in him. But he did it to protect *me*!"

I hugged her. "I wish you all the happiness possible. You deserve it."

As I had thought all along, Nina's Pumpkin Spice Coffees were a big hit. Some licorice lovers adored Natasha's muffins, even though the melted black licorice on the top of them wasn't exactly appetizing. My butternut squash sheet pan breakfast got rave reviews and the cakes disappeared.

I snuck Wolf, Nina, Mars, and Bernie into the kitchen for a minute so they could see Faye's entry about the night Ollie died.

"What will happen to Helena, Jacky, and Annie?" I asked Wolf.

Wolf reread the passage. "Well, as far as I'm concerned, even though the other three also confessed, this is evidence that the woman who killed him is now deceased. We can't charge anyone for that." He snapped the diary shut and handed it to me.

"Why do you think Faye confessed in her diary like that?" asked Nina.

"Because she knew she was in the best position to hire an expensive lawyer and be found not guilty. Faye had friends in high places," said Mars. "She was protecting Helena, Jacky, and Annie."

When the guests and TV crew had left, and the house was a mess, I let Mochie out of the upstairs bedroom.

So many things would change for the Nofsingers. I couldn't imagine how Robbie could cope with the news that Helena and Thurman weren't his parents. But I knew one thing: they loved him like a son.

Bernie, Mars, Nina, Natasha, and I took drinks into the living room and relaxed before the big cleanup.

"I think that was quite successful," said Natasha. "The producer's wife adored me, so I'm hoping he might want to do this kind of thing again. Halloween is coming up. How about throwing a Halloween party here? This house must be haunted!"

The rest of us groaned at the thought.

Later that evening, I walked around my quiet house, collecting the odd napkin and glass that had escaped us earlier. In the kitchen, I reached up and straightened Faye's portrait, grateful for women like her who had shaped our world.

Daisy wagged her tail and Mochie purred. I looked up at Faye's portrait again and thought I saw her wink at me.

No, that couldn't be. . . .

Recipes

Eggs Benedict

Makes 4 servings.

Please note that this recipe uses poached eggs with runny yolks and a sauce made with egg yolks, which carry the risk of salmonella.

This is one of my personal favorites for brunch when I eat out. I don't make it often because I always fear it will be difficult. In all honesty, anyone can toast muffins and warm Canadian bacon. Poaching eggs is actually easy, too. After you have done it a couple of times, it won't be intimidating. The Hollandaise sauce is what always threw me off. But it's super easy to make with an immersion blender. You can still make it with a regular blender, but it just seems like so much less fuss with an immersion blender.

If poaching eggs makes you nervous, try poaching eggs for your breakfast a few times. You'll quickly see there's not a lot to it. Bring the water to a simmer, crack the egg, and lower it as close to the water as you can without burning your hands. Allow the white and the yolk to slowly slide into the water. It will go straight to the bottom! That's okay. The egg takes 3 to 5 minutes to cook. Set a timer. Bits of egg white will float to the top. I scoop those out so I can see what the eggs are doing underneath. As they cook, the eggs will float to the top. Take them out with a slotted spoon so the water will drain into the pot. If the egg looks ugly to you, flip it! The bottom side is always prettier.

If you still fear poaching, or you have more than two or three people to serve, you can use the alternate poaching method by doing it in a muffin pan in your oven!

The key is to remain organized. Do these things before you begin to cook.

1. Set the table. I'm not joking. This should be done in advance so you're ready to serve the eggs immediately.
2. Bring the plates to a place where you can easily prepare them and won't have to run around the kitchen.
3. Get all the ingredients out. Have the toaster, a frying pan, a small pot for melting butter, a large pot for poaching the eggs, and an immersion blender or a blender nearby and ready to use.

Makes 8 Eggs Benedict.
Serve two per person.
Halve the recipe if you only need two servings.

4 English muffins
2 sticks (8 tablespoons each) unsalted butter
Water
1 tablespoon vinegar
6 egg yolks
2 teaspoons Dijon mustard (or plain mustard)
Salt
8 slices Canadian bacon
8 additional eggs
Black pepper
Cayenne pepper (optional)

1. Slice the English muffins in half and set aside.
2. Set the frying pan on the stove. If nonstick or stainless steel, do not grease. Set it on the lowest temperature. Place the slices of Canadian bacon on it. When they are warm on one side, flip the slices to the other side.
3. Start melting the butter in a small pot over low heat.
4. Fill a large pot with water at least 3 inches deep and add the 1 tablespoon vinegar. Bring to a boil. When the water boils, turn it down to a nice simmer. Crack

one of the 8 eggs and gently let it flow into the simmering water. Repeat with the other eggs. They will sink to the bottom but should rise. It's okay if white foam develops on the top of the water. You may remove it if you like. Cook the eggs 3 to 5 minutes. Set a timer. *See alternate oven method below.

5. Meanwhile, toast the English muffins and place two halves on each plate.

6. Place a slice of warm Canadian bacon on each muffin half.

7. Put the 6 egg yolks, the mustard, and 1 teaspoon salt in the immersion blender cup (tall and slender) or the blender.

8. With the immersion blender or blender running, add the **hot** melted butter in a stream and blend! Add salt to taste if needed.

9. Using a pierced spoon or ladle, remove each egg from the water and place on top of the Canadian bacon. Spoon the Hollandaise sauce over the egg and sprinkle with cayenne pepper if using. Serve!

*Alternate Oven Poaching Method

Preheat the oven to 350. Place 1 tablespoon of water into each well of a muffin pan. Crack each egg and gently pour it into a muffin well. When the oven is at 350, slide the muffin pan in and set the timer for 8–9 minutes. They should take 8–10 minutes to poach.

Meanwhile, follow instructions above-steps 5 through 8. When the eggs are poached, use a soup spoon to slide each egg out of the well and place on the Canadian bacon. Pour the Hollandaise sauce over top and sprinkle with cayenne pepper, if using.

Sophie's Butternut Squash Sheet Pan Breakfast

I love this recipe and think it would make a good breakfast for dinner recipe as well. If you plan to serve it for breakfast or brunch, cut up the butternut squash, shallots, red pepper, and zucchinis the night before. It will speed up the dish in the morning!

Serves 6 to 8.

1–2 large, lipped baking trays
1 large butternut squash
3 shallots
1 red bell pepper
2 zucchinis
12 ounces kielbasa, sliced
Olive oil, 3–4 tablespoons + extra
drizzle of maple syrup
1 tablespoon thyme
2 teaspoons salt
½ teaspoon black pepper
6–8 large eggs

Preheat the oven to 425.

Peel the butternut squash with a vegetable peeler until the orange portions show. Cut the large part off. Cut the tubular portion in half, lengthwise, and cut it into ¾–1 inch squares. Scoop out the seeds and do the same with the bottom portion, discarding the hard part at the end. Scatter all the pieces on the baking sheet.

Peel the shallots and cut them into quarters. Add to the baking sheet. Cut the red pepper into small bite-size pieces and add to the baking sheet. Do the same with the zucchinis. Cut the kielbasa into slices and add it to the baking sheet. Drizzle the olive oil over the squash mixture, then the maple syrup. Using your hands, toss until everything is covered with the oil and syrup. Sprinkle the thyme, salt, and black pepper over the baking sheet and toss again to spread. If you have too much for a single layer on one baking sheet, then place part of it on another baking sheet and roast them at the same time. Roast 20 minutes.

Remove the baking sheets from the oven. Make 6 to 8 wells for the eggs. Crack the eggs individually in the wells. Roast for another 7 to 9 minutes. Serve by placing the veggie and kielbasa mixture on a plate and top it with one of the eggs.

Sheet Pan Pork Tenderloin

Makes four servings.

I am in love with sheet pan dinners. They're so easy! No big muss or fuss. This one got rave reviews from my testers!

2 sheet pans
Aluminum foil
⅓ cup balsamic vinegar
⅓ cup + ¼ cup olive oil, plus more
2 tablespoons minced garlic
1 + 1 tablespoons oregano
1 + 1 teaspoons thyme
1 + 1 teaspoons salt
2 pork tenderloins around 1 pound each
1 medium sweet potato
1½ pounds mixed small white and red potatoes
1½ cups shallots, peeled
¼ teaspoon black pepper

Whisk together the balsamic vinegar, ⅓ cup olive oil, garlic, oregano, thyme, and salt. Place pork tenderloins in a shallow flat dish and pour the balsamic mixture over them. Cover and refrigerate for 1 to 2 hours.

Preheat the oven to 450°F. Line the sheet pan with aluminum foil. Cut the sweet potato in bite-sized pieces. Wash and cut the potatoes in half, removing any blemishes. Mix together the sweet potato, potatoes, and peeled shallots in a large bowl. Mix together the ¼ cup olive oil, 1 tablespoon oregano, 1 teaspoon thyme, 1 teaspoon salt, and ¼ teaspoon black pepper. Pour over the potato mixture and toss to coat. Place the pork on the sheet pans and surround each with half of the potato mixture. Pour the remaining seasoned oil from the vegetables over them on the pan.

Roast about 20 minutes and check the internal temperature of the pork. Cook until a thermometer registers 140 to 145 degrees.

Slice the meat and serve with the vegetables.

Hazel's Doughnut Holes

Mini-muffin pan
Nonstick baking spray
1¾ cups flour
2 teaspoons baking powder
½ teaspoon salt
¾ teaspoon cinnamon
½ teaspoon nutmeg
⅛ teaspoon cloves
¾ cup pumpkin puree (not pumpkin pie filling)
½ cup milk
½ cup light brown sugar
⅓ cup canola oil
1 large egg
1 teaspoon vanilla
4-6 tablespoons unsalted butter, melted
⅔ cup sugar
2 tablespoons cinnamon

Preheat oven to 350°F. Spray or grease the mini-muffin pan.

In a large bowl, mix together flour, baking powder, salt, cinnamon, nutmeg, and cloves. Set aside. In a mixing bowl, combine pumpkin puree, milk, light brown sugar, canola oil, egg, and vanilla. Mix. Slowly add the flour mixture, a bit at a time.

Use a soup spoon or an oval tablespoon measurer to scoop out the dough. Use your finger to scoot it into the wells. Bake 12 minutes or until a cake tester comes out clean. Allow to rest on a rack a few minutes.

Pour the melted butter in a smallish shallow bowl. Mix the sugar and the cinnamon well and place in a larger, shallow bowl. Dip each doughnut hole into the butter and roll it in the cinnamon sugar. Place on the rack to cool.

These freeze very well. While best when fresh, you can make them ahead of time and freeze them. Allow them to thaw to room temperature to serve.

Frittata for a Crowd

1 pan serves 8 good-sized pieces.

If you're planning to serve this for breakfast or brunch, slice the ham, onion, red pepper and cheese the night before to speed things up in the morning. Shredded cheese melts the best, but you can also cut sliced cheese into tiny bits and use that instead. Have fun with it and make it yours. Instead of smoked paprika, use thyme or sage. Instead of sharp cheddar cheese, use your personal favorite cheese.

1 lipped sheet pan
2 tablespoons extra virgin olive oil
18 eggs
½ teaspoon smoked paprika (or thyme if you prefer)
1 teaspoon salt
¼ teaspoon black pepper
½ pound sliced ham, cut into ½-inch x ½-inch bits
½ chopped onion
1 red pepper, chopped
¾ cup shredded sharp cheddar cheese

Preheat oven to 450°F. Grease pan with olive oil.

In a large bowl, whisk together the eggs, smoked paprika, salt, and pepper. Pour into prepared pan. Sprinkle the ham, onion, red pepper, and cheese all over the eggs. Bake 20 to 25 minutes, until the middle is completely set.

Leave in the pan for warmth but cut into squares and provide a spatula for serving.

Applesauce Spice Sheet Cake with Caramel Frosting

13 × 9 cake pan
2¼ cups flour
1½ teaspoons baking powder
1½ teaspoons baking soda
1 teaspoon salt
1½ teaspoons cinnamon
¾ teaspoon nutmeg
⅛ teaspoon cloves
1½ sticks unsalted butter (12 tablespoons) at room temperature +1 tablespoon for greasing
1 cup lightly packed dark brown sugar
½ cup white sugar
3 large eggs at room temperature
1 cup unsweetened applesauce
1 tablespoon vanilla

Preheat oven to 375°F. Grease the pan with 1 tablespoon butter.

In a bowl, mix together the flour, baking powder, baking soda, salt, cinnamon, nutmeg, and cloves. Stir well with a fork to combine. Set aside.

Cream the butter with the sugars. Beat in the eggs, one at a time. Add the flour mixture and the applesauce in thirds, alternating between them. Beat in the vanilla. Pour into the cake pan. Bake 40 minutes or until a cake tester comes out clean.

Old Fashioned Caramel Frosting

One of my tasters tells me this is just like her grand-mother's caramel frosting!

6 tablespoons butter
1½ cups dark brown sugar
⅔ cup heavy cream
3 cups confectioner's sugar
2 teaspoons vanilla

Melt the butter over medium heat. Add the brown sugar and the cream. Stir. Bring to a boil and allow to boil for 2 minutes.

Remove from heat. Stir in ½ cup confectioner's sugar and the vanilla. Allow to cool slightly. Pour into a mixing bowl and add the remaining 2½ cups confectioner's sugar. Beat slowly until combined, then faster. This frosting will be very soft and will not hold a shape initially. Allow to cool until it's spreadable, then pour over the cooled cake and spread. It will continue to firm up when refrigerated and will cut nicely into squares.

Pumpkin Spice Ice-Cream Roll

This is such a fun change to a typical pumpkin roll. While vanilla ice cream is okay, Bourbon Pecan Praline ice cream is definitely the preference of my taste testers!

11 × 16 jelly roll pan
Parchment paper
¾ cup flour
1 teaspoon baking soda
1½ teaspoons cinnamon
¾ teaspoon nutmeg
Pinch of cloves
3 large eggs
¾ cup granulated sugar + 2 tablespoons
⅔ cup canned pumpkin puree
2-3 pints Bourbon Pecan Praline ice cream, softened
Confectioner's sugar

Preheat oven to 375°F. Line the jelly roll pan with parchment paper.

In a medium bowl, combine the flour, baking soda, cinnamon, nutmeg, and cloves. Stir with a fork to mix thoroughly. Using an electric mixer, beat the eggs with ¾ cup sugar and the pumpkin. On a slower speed, beat in the flour mixture. Pour into the prepared pan. Bake 13 to 15 minutes.

While it is baking, spread a clean kitchen towel on your counter. Spread a second very thin kitchen towel over the first one and sprinkle with the remaining 2 tablespoons of sugar.

When removing the cake from the oven, turn it upside down onto the kitchen towels. Remove the parchment paper immediately. Use the thin kitchen towel to roll the cake. Let it cool in the rolled position on a wire rack.

When cool, take out the ice cream and place in a big bowl. Allow to soften, but not too much! Working fast, spread the ice cream over the cake. Roll it up again. Wrap in plastic wrap and freeze.

To serve, unwrap and allow to stand at room temperature for only a few minutes. Dust with confectioner's sugar. Slice and serve.

Easy Baked Apple Parfaits

Four servings

You don't have to use parfait glasses. Use whatever you have, like martini glasses, old-fashioned glasses, even mugs!

Baking pan
Aluminum foil
4 large apples
Oatmeal cookies (make your own or buy some)
1 cup heavy cream or vanilla ice cream
If using cream:
¼ cup powdered sugar
1 teaspoon vanilla

Preheat the oven to 400°F.

Line a baking pan with aluminum foil against leakage. Wash the apples and place them on the aluminum foil, stem side up. Bake the apples for 40 minutes. (This is easy to do in a hot oven while you eat dinner.) Break up the cookies into crumbles and set aside. If using cream, beat the cream. When it begins to take shape, add the powdered sugar and vanilla. Beat until the cream holds a shape.

When the apples are soft, remove them from the oven and peel. Cut the apples in half and remove the core and stalk. Cut into small, bite-size pieces. Layer in a glass with the cream or ice cream and cookie crumbles and serve!

Quick and Easy Baked Pears

Serves 4

This is one of my new favorites. It's similar to a Pear He-
lene, but without the alcohol and so much easier! If you're
using your oven to make dinner, you can slide the pears in
on another level of the oven while dinner cooks or place
them in the hot oven to bake while you eat. I leave the
peels on. Wait until you take them out of the oven to core
them. It's so much easier when they're soft. This recipe is
so simple. If you're dieting, skip the ice cream and whipped
cream. The pears are delicious on their own.

Oven-safe pan large enough for 8 pear halves
Aluminum foil
4 pears
Vanilla ice cream
Whipped cream (optional)
Chocolate sauce

1. Preheat the oven to 400°F. Line the baking pan with
   aluminum foil. Cut the pears in half. Lay them on the
   aluminum foil cut side down. Bake for 30 to 45 minutes, until a fork can pierce the pear easily.
2. Use a paring knife to cut out the core and the bits
   above and below it, including the little end at the bottom.
3. Place two pears in each bowl. Top with a scoop of ice
   cream and a spoonful of whipped cream, if using.
   Drizzle with chocolate sauce.

Apple Sharlotka

This recipe has quite a history. It has been around for a long time so there are loads of variations on the recipe, many of them passed down for generations. I found Ukrainian, Polish, Russian, Jewish, and British versions. Most call for 3–4 apples and either bread slices or a sponge cake. Allegedly, it was invented by a famous French chef named Marie Antoine Carême. Some claim she created this cake in honor of Queen Charlotte of England and others claim it was named after Princess Charlotte of Prussia who became Empress of Russia. Over the years, people have used alternate fruits, like peaches, and some add nuts or dried fruit.

10-inch springform pan
Tray to catch juices
1⅓ cup flour
½ teaspoon baking powder
½ teaspoon cinnamon
6 large eggs at room temperature
1 cup sugar
3 apples, approximately 1.5 pounds
1 teaspoon vanilla
Powdered sugar (optional)

Preheat oven to 350°F.
Line the springform pan with parchment paper on the bottom and around the sides. Place an empty lipped baking sheet on the lowest rack to catch any juices that may leak during baking.

In a bowl, mix together the flour, baking powder, and cinnamon. Stir with a fork to mix well.

Place the eggs in a mixing bowl with the sugar. Beat 8-

10 minutes until it is thick and forms a ribbon on the mixture as it falls back on it.

Meanwhile, wash, peel and core the apples. Fold in the flour. Slice them very thin and place in a large bowl.

Add the vanilla to the thick egg and sugar mixture. Beat on high once or twice to combine. Pour the mixture over the sliced apples and mix well. Pour into the prepared springform pan.

Bake 1 hour and 10 minutes or until a tester in the middle comes out clean. Remove from the oven and let stand for fifteen minutes before undoing the springform.

Serve with ice cream or lightly sweetened whipped cream.

Sweetened Whipped Cream

1 cup heavy cream
⅓ cup powdered confectioner's sugar
1 teaspoon vanilla

Beat the cream until it begins to hold a shape. Add the powdered confectioner's sugar and the vanilla and beat until it holds a peak.

Apple Cider Mimosas

I particularly like this super-easy drink for a busy hostess because it's only three ingredients.

Sugar for rim of the glass
Sparkling apple cider
Champagne or sparkling wine

Pour sugar into a small, shallow bowl. Pour a small amount of cider into another small, shallow bowl. Dip the rim of a champagne glass in the cider and then the sugar. Fill the glass half full with apple cider and top it off with champagne or sparkling wine.

Pumpkin Spice Brunch Coffee

Makes one serving.

When I initially made this recipe, I used Captain Morgan Jack-o' Blast Pumpkin Spiced Rum, which is delicious and strong. Since then, it appears that it is not being made anymore but you still may be able to find it in some stores. I had to try newer pumpkin spice offerings and can recommend Fulton's Harvest Pumpkin Pie Cream Liqueur. It's not quite as strong, but it's deliciously indulgent.

12 ounces brewed coffee
3 ounces (6 tablespoons) Fulton's Harvest Pumpkin Pie
    Cream Liqueur (or your choice of fall liquors)
Sweetened whipped cream

Pour the coffee into a mug and add the liqueur. Top with a dollop of sweetened whipped cream.